CRYSTALLIZATION

Runa Fjord

Crystallization

Book 2 of To Crack A Geode

Production copyright FurPlanet Productions © 2025

Text Copyright © Runa Fjord 2025

Cover Artwork © Shapeless Ink 2025

The Korps Universe © Karen King 2025, and used with permission

Published by FurPlanet Productions
Dallas, Texas
www.FurPlanet.com

Print ISBN 978-1-61450-653-9
Electronic ISBN 978-1-61450-654-6

Table of Contents

To the queer and trans community. The world is better with you in it. We can build a brighter future together. They will not break us.

FOREWORD

BY KAREN KING

Nearly seven thousand years ago, an event shook the world. An arrival of something ancient: the merging of humanity with the world of the beast, the eruption of superpowers, and the proliferation of the supernatural. In the modern day, this world appears much like our own but for the pantheon of species that occupy it and the extensive presence of superheroes and supervillains alike. While many states have their own super-powered forces, a vast variety of independent actors exist.

Among the most prominent independent supervillain groups is an organization known as the Korps. As far as most are aware, the Korps is an organization dedicated to world domination, led (in theory) by the shadowy Overlord. This sinister being has tried to wrap their vicious claws around the planet, time after time, since the beginning of recorded history.

The truth, of course, is significantly more complex.

Led by some of the world's strongest superpowered beings, the Korps sees itself not as a state-in-waiting, but a governance method — seeking to depose repressive state-based hierarchies to install systems more capable of effectively distributing resources to those in need. It sees state actors — "Heroes," police, paramilitaries — mete punishment out on innocents, yet go unpunished in turn. It knows, — for all the cartoonish pretensions of the supering world — that this is the true evil. It knows, too, that this cannot go unchallenged.

Operating a number of covert front companies and satellite operations for many decades, the Korps has dedicated a great deal of resources to outpacing the world's greatest scientific, engineering and medical minds. Korps medical technology in particular is extremely advanced, allowing its members to essentially build their preferred body from scratch — and permitting this capacity at scale. The Korps has learned well that monocultures become stagnant without personal expression, which it fiercely encourages in its members — a reality at odds with the widespread public perception that they are nothing more than brainwashed drones.

One of the most useful and distinctive tools at the Korps's disposal are Rose-Coloured Glasses, or "RCGs," a high-capacity communications tool, heads-up display and computer-brain interface so powerful they can be used directly as a VR headset. RCGs can function as an assistive device or therapy tool… but the nature of the technology means they have the power to directly access and even alter one's thoughts. Alternately viewed with relief, mistrust, or fear by the supering world, it is known that wherever they are worn, the Korps is not far behind.

Having emerged in the wake of the Second World War, the Korps has gradually spread its influence, eventually emerging fully into the public consciousness in the 1990s. With increased visibility and emphasis on immediate action, however, comes ever more entanglements…

The Korps began as a big pile of superhero and supervillain tropes that I'd built up a love of through various types of media, like the James Bond movies. While I originally just threw it together as an action playset of stock characters, over time, it began to morph into something very different. Using stock pop culture antagonists to take swings at the injustices unfolding around me began to carry more and more emotional weight.

In an era when information became more and more readily available, we were able, at any time of day, to pull out our phones and view some kind of great injustice unfolding, live in front of the world — to see police forces with the budgets and capacities of small militaries crushing peaceful protestors, to watch the deceptions of nations exposed constantly but slip by unpunished, to see the suffering of those in need, on our feeds, 24/7 …

It became increasingly clear to me, and to many, that the status quo is not a state of normalcy, but something imposed by force. Equally, to many, the concept of rallying the villains — those who challenged the status quo — and giving us a context in which we can, in some sense, strike back against it all… It struck a chord among those of my generation. In a world where fighting back seems so hard, an entity like the Korps is something compelling.

I am now sitting here writing the foreword for an actual, published work about it, and my mind is reeling. Giving the Korps as a set of narrative tools to the wider community feels like it has uncorked a flood: a need to right wrongs, a need to highlight injustices, a need to tell intimately personal stories, stories of love, and stories of redemption… rushing out onto countless pages, from countless perspectives.

All I have ever wanted to do is to help give people a community, and the tools they need to create, and to build the stories they need. It is an honour and a privilege to introduce this story to you — one of love, one of breaking free, one of deep wounds beginning to heal…

— Karen King

Chapter 1

Accretionary Wedge

March 20, 2023

Jennifer Delver took one last sip of her overpriced coffee before getting out of her car. The nutria set the battered, ruggedized tablet on the roof of her unremarkable white sedan before taking a moment to check herself in the reflection of her window. She quickly smoothed out the wrinkles in her buttoned-up white blouse, and the gray slacks that looked so sharp against her dark-brown fur. Then, she checked to make sure her simple makeup and long braid of silver-streaked black hair hadn't gone astray. It might have been *far* too early on a Sunday, but looking sloppy was the fastest way for a health inspector to lose respect; to not be taken *seriously*; decades of experience had taught her the problems that could cause.

The nutria checked her watch: 7:49 AM. Downtown Dallas was eerily quiet at this time of day, even if the sun had been up almost an hour; satisfied that she had arrived precisely on time, regardless, she gathered her things and strode between the large warehouses. Her low heels echoed in the alleyway as she sought the right entrance. A catering kitchen operated out of this rental space only on Sundays, a small section carved out of a larger building. She eyed each of the unmarked doors along the back of the larger building until a small number decal caught her attention.

329

She raised her paw to knock when her brain — still foggy with the desire to sleep in and the burden of preparing to be in Serious Professional Mode for a single off-hours inspection — registered that the metal door was slightly ajar. That wasn't too unusual, given the rhythms of these catering kitchens, but it *was* a potential opportunity to examine some part of the site before staff could hurriedly conceal any code violations. Fatigue vanished as she snapped to full awareness, anticipation buzzing in her as she mentally prepared to catalogue every detail. Instead of knocking, she slowly (but confidently) pulled on the brushed-steel handle.

It was the flickering that first told her something was wrong. The lighting of the interior was dim, accented with the flickering buzz of a damaged fluorescent fixture, and the air was full of a faintly electrical-smelling smoke. The scent set off warning bells and she could suddenly feel her pulse in her ears.

The interior of the kitchen was a ruin. Something had crashed through the ceiling, leaving twisted metal hanging down from the structural wound. What had recently been a reasonably-sized catering kitchen was now little more than a riot of mangled wreckage. The chaos was punctuated by the sparking of ripped wiring in several places. Her mind, honed by decades of inspections, seized upon the small detail to make a note about electrical hazards.

It was the still forms that scattered even those errant thoughts. One was laying on her back with limbs splayed out, as if a giant had discarded an unwanted doll. Clad in blue and silver spandex, the thin ermine's eyes were closed; the white fur of her muzzle was stained crimson, but her chest moved with shallow breaths that barely stirred the light haze of smoke. Dimly, Jennifer recognized the Dallas TPA Hero as Sylvanite.

It was the other form that got her moving, however. She couldn't make out the black-clad elephant shrew well. Initially, it didn't seem to matter — how could it, with the rebar impaled through his chest? — but his ragged, wet breathing spurred her to action. Then she was kneeling down to assess the damage to the victim, with only vague flashes of running through the tangled jumble of debris.

Her paw trembled as it reached out, then froze before touching the form. The hesitation, accompanied by a flash of helpless fear (and a dismayingly cowardly desire to just walk away) only stilled her for a moment. Steeling herself, she firmed her resolve to help the wounded. She would figure out what had happened later. Now was not the time to question. With renewed conviction, her paw touched the shrew's shoulder—

—Instantly, a gloved hand that had been hanging limply flew up to wrap around her left wrist. The grip was painfully tight and deliberate, not the motion of panicked desperation but of calm, calculated cruelty. When she tugged, then yanked in panic, there was no give in that vice, as if she were held in the grip of an iron statue. The ragged breathing stopped mid-inhale.

Fear and confusion gripped Jennifer's heart. Then the unmoving head turned slowly to face her, amber eyes locking with her gaze. Her thoughts rapidly grew sluggish as some alien will battered aside her mental defenses. Thoughts that were not quite words forced their way into her mind, ringing hollow and yet all encompassing. They carried with them the weight of fundamental truth and forbidden knowledge.

Jennifer Delver, I Mark You.

Heroes Shall Hunt You For This Taint.

They Will Destroy You If They Can.

Run.

Fight.

Survive.

Master Will Find You.

Master Will Bind You.

I Mark You, Jennifer Delver.

Those amber eyes flared with a sudden, sickly reddish-brown glow. Pain *seared* itself into her forearm, more intense than anything she'd ever known. Her scream caught in her throat; the agony was too intense to breathe. It consumed the world and lasted for eternity. Then — then, abruptly, it was gone, leaving only an ache behind. Tears were streaming down her face and she stared into the sightless gaze of the elephant shrew, eyes already fogged in death. Finally, the grip loosened and she snatched away her wrist.

Blood had soaked through her sleeve. With a trembling claw, she popped the button. She expected to find her forearm a ruin from the ordeal. But she found no sign of injury. Her brown fur was untouched. Frantically, she ran a paw from elbow to wrist, finding herself whole, but something felt off about the texture of her skin.

The next thing she knew, she was stumbling out into the morning light. She brought her forearm up to her face, fighting the instinct to claw frantically. With violently shaking paw, she managed to carefully spread the brown fur with her fingers. There she saw it: her dark skin was covered in densely-packed writing, line after line of words too small for her to understand had been scarred into her.

Jennifer was hyperventilating as she stared at the pale text. Her body screamed at her to run, but she didn't know where to go. She leaned against the wall, trying to ground herself in the touch to the cold brick. The growing dizziness finally allowed her room to think, and with tremendous will, she took a deep breath, breaking the panicked spiral. She stood there a moment, relearning how to breathe.

Finally, she glanced back into the ruined kitchen. The dead form of the villain had not moved, but the Hero had shifted her position. The slow breathing seemed to be steadier. Those alien words echoed their warning once more. She knew, at the core of her soul, that seeking help from this Hero would result in her doom. Heroes would hunt her.

Numb paws carried her away, the sound of her heels on concrete somehow dull and distant. She needed a plan. There was no way she was going to let some supervillain cow her into submission. She might not be able to trust Heroes, but that didn't mean she was meek, helpless prey for the taking. She wasn't sure how yet, but one certainty burned in her soul. Her lips pulled back in a feral snarl to bare her broad orange teeth.

Whoever this Master was, he was going to regret trying to bind her.

March 22, 2023

. . .

. . .

. . .

. . .

Welcome Back!

The Percheron was staring at the surface of a black metal desk with a massive magenta helix emblazoned across it. There was no sensation of waking up, no transition from unconsciousness to awareness; she was just suddenly *awake*. Blinking several times, she tried to put scattered thoughts in order, for this was not the first time she had found herself inexplicably in a strange place. The last thing she remembered was standing on the roof of the Texas Protectorate Assembly headquarters, and then putting on those RCGs, and *then...* nothing.

The events of that night rushed back. The hunt for a supervillain of particular interest. The betrayal of the rest of the Superheroes on her team, which still stung deeply. She had survived only because that same young, frightened cottontail risked *everything* to fight her way through the trap. The two had survived, together, against the odds, while working desperately to stop the Teepa's murderous plot against queer villainy — a self-righteous crusade that would have brutalized hundreds, even *thousands* of innocents. Finally, at the end of it all had been the showdown on the roof, where she had finally been forced to confront the fact that she was... *she*.

Slight movement drew her attention upwards to find a wall of scales. Across the desk, the giant form of the Lamia *towered* over her. The massive viper was coiled up, staring with those obsidian eyes. No longer was she the glossy-black, glowing-magenta figure of deadly purpose; now, deep crimson scales covered her head and back, transitioning to a soft tan down her throat and belly. She was adorned with a black leather jacket, perfectly cut to show off her tremendous chest. A magenta helix over the heart proclaimed her allegiance, and reinforced, in no uncertain terms, who controlled this place.

The Percheron was not used to feeling small. She stood nearly three meters tall and massed half a ton of pure muscle, without an ounce of fat to be found on her body. There was nothing soft or feminine about her form, save perhaps for her coat; the once-slate grey fur had turned luminescently violet, shimmering like crystals. Even without superpowers, she likely could have lifted a car, but she was graced too with a preternatural strength that magnified her physical capabilities many times over. It was highly unusual for her to ever have to look *up* to meet someone's gaze.

Deep within the draft horse, a spark of fear flashed. The choice she had made was still fresh in her mind, and yet somehow distant. She had been faced with the impossible: attempt to capture or slay the dangerous creature before her; flee the state alone, hounded by some of the most powerful Heroes of the age; or... go, willingly, into the arms of a shadowy supervillainous organization known for mind control, and who openly avowed world domination.

The weight of *consequences* crashed down upon her. She sat here, before one of the greatest supervillains of the region, as the massive snake woman's prisoner. A bleak acceptance settled over the horse; everything felt distant and disjointed. In the course of an evening, her entire life had fallen apart, and she no longer knew where she belonged, or even who she *was*.

Lamia did not exude the active aura of danger she had possessed when making the offer that had led to the former Hero sitting here, in this room, at the mercy of supervillains. The scourge of the swamps had all the time in the world. There was no doubt who held the power in this situation.

Consequently, it took her long moments to register that the snake was waiting patiently. Finally, she spoke, in that sibilant *hiss*. "Welcome back, little cryssstal pony. You are sssafe. The crisssisss isss over. There isss no war."

The shadow of relief swept through the mare, easing a tension she hadn't known was there. She had been so caught up in her own plight that she only then consciously remembered how the TPA's plans had threatened all-out war. Still, the realization that the danger had passed calmed some deep part of her heart. While she wasn't entirely certain sitting in a Korps base in front of one of the country's deadliest supervillains was *safe*, precisely, the fact that the worst had been avoided was a great comfort. She didn't expect the tears that suddenly loomed in her eyes.

"When…?" she started, only for text to scroll across her vision.

[It's Wednesday, dear. March 22. You've been out for three days.]

She had completely forgotten the presence of ROSE. Her hand shot up, only to find that her fingers froze when they encountered the unfamiliar visor. Her training screamed that she should fear the Korps goggles and the doom they could bring to the unwary… but the arm that could tie rebar into pretzels simply refused to respond. The command to tear the RCGs from her muzzle simply never made it to her arm.

[I'm sorry, dear. We can't allow you to do that just yet. Relax for just a little bit longer, and you'll have full control back, I promise.]

The mare's heart caught in her throat. Being captured by the Korps had been the greatest fear of many of the Texas Protectorate Assembly. Now, here she was, in their clutches, her survival instincts screaming that *they* were in her head. But she was still a veteran of a thousand dire emergencies, so she sat there, frozen in place, as she slowly conquered her fear. She found it harder than it should have been;. the draft horse had always been so steady, but she had lost her footing, adrift and unable to summon the confident detachment that had been her bulwark against panic for so very long.

I chose this.

She sat there because of a choice she had made. She would face the consequences of her actions, like the Hero she was.

Was.

That was it, the word she had been avoiding: *was.* She did not know what her future would entail. That was out of her hooves, held by the villain before her. She had shut the door of her past behind her. Now it was time to turn on the light, and see what awaited her on this side of the portal.

Lamia had watched her dispassionately. When she finally spoke again, her deep, slithering voice held a touch of apology and sympathy. "I fear I mussst asssk you to wear the visssor today. Asss a precauttion. And I mussst requessst that you not leave the bassse for a little while."

"So… I'm a prisoner." the mare stated forlornly.

"Not precccisssely. I mussst ssstill protect that which I hold dear, though I am no longer cccertain you are the threat I onccce believed. Mossst of the bassse will be open to you. And, asss I promisssed, it isss time to ssspeak of boundariesss. ROSSSE will ssslowly return control to you over the coming daysss. Outssside of reasssonable precautttions, ssshe will only act as you desssire. I sssussspect you ssshall find her aid mossst delightful. But it will be your choiccce to make, and you can ressscind your consssent at any time."

The words were strange, and she couldn't quite wrap her mind around their full implications, but they were nevertheless wildly disconnected from the maniacal gloating she had half-expected, that she was left confused. The Percheron felt as if she were a stranger in her own fur, the world distant and unreal. Deep-seated training from long ago flashed through her mind; she surreptitiously pinched herself, noting the pain response.

[*This isn't a dream, alternate reality, or hypnotic state, though it's cute that you think it might be. If you're going to go through the entire Alternate Reality Checklist, I would ask for you to wait a bit. What she's saying is true, dear. I'm here to help but I will only help as **you** desire. You are **safe** now.*]

The mare swallowed the lump in her throat, trying to conquer the feelings of vulnerability. It was only then, as she glanced around to recenter herself, that she realized that there were others present. Sitting beside the great cobra was a petite flying fox wearing a diaphanous black dress. Her brilliant red undercut and stark black collar called for attention, but it was the distinctive lines of deep scarlet-red dye in her light brown fur that really drew the eye, and gave her an otherworldly air. The horse was startled to see that this woman wore an amber-colored visor, instead of the otherwise uniform magenta.

[*Davina "Clarion" Zemora. She/her.*]

The text popped up as she looked at the tiny fruit bat. She blinked, taken aback by the helpful label. A glance to her left brought a third figure into focus. This one was mechanical and synthetic. Dressed as an old-fashioned nurse, the synthetic fox shifted under her gaze. She didn't seem to know what to do with her four arms, fidgeting slightly. The synth flinched away from her gaze, those cross shaped pupils looking away uncomfortably.

[*Nurse O. She/Her.*]

Finally, she looked back at Lamia. The snake gazed back serenely, giving the horse time to process. The snake clearly projected that she knew she had nothing to fear, and all the time in the world; that was abundantly clear. The Percheron was surprised to see text pop up for this supervillain, too.

[Celia "Lamia". She/Her.]

"Wait, your name is Celia...?" The question left the horse's mouth before she even realized it. Lamia was nearly an urban legend, a fearsome beast that haunted the dreams of the Hero community — not so much a person as a terrifying force of nature. That had matched with her experience on the roof when the viper had offered her The Choice. To realize she had a *name* was... unsettling. Especially such a mundane name.

"Yesss, dear crysssstal pony. You may call me Cccelia. Asss I sssaid, you will have free run of the non-critical areasss of the bassse. I will have sssomeone ssshow you around. ROSSSE will warn you of any off-limit areasss, though of coursssse thossse doorsss will sssimply not open for you. Be warned, however, that sssome open doorsss may lead you to placcces you are welcome, but may not wisssh to exxxplore. ROSSSE will guide you there, but be cautttiousss of the labsss."

"I am pretty sure I can find my way around a small facility, but thank you." The comment drew a knowing chuckle from Clarion. Though Celia didn't seem to move or respond, she too seemed to exude a sense of amusement. A sense of foreboding settled on the warhorse.

It's a supervillain base. It can't be that big, can it? I know the Korps is a pretty sizable organization, but most of their resources and infrastructure are in Canada. How many people can they possibly have here? Unless... did they move me to Canada somehow?

The amusement on the fruit bat's face was disconcerting. When she spoke, her sultry voice was deep, echoing with an otherworldly reverb that spoke of dark secrets. "I would caution you against asserting knowledge you lack. The assumptions you built as a Hero may lead you astray."

The Percheron frowned further at the comment. "Am I... still in Texas? Just how big is this base?"

"Oh yes, you remain in the state you claimed to protect. And you shall find this place large enough for you to find plenty of shelter from the storm, should you decide to stay. But I sense something more is troubling you, beyond the immediately obvious. You've been lured into the clutches of an evil supervillain organization… and yet it is not the immediate spike of fear, but a lingering portent of doom that plagues you."

If you believe them… if you accept their offer… they will hypnotize you. They will bind you. They will mutilate you. They will torture you. You will suffer humiliations that you can't even imagine. And Slate dies on the roof.

Her lips opened to respond, but she couldn't quite find the words. The idea was simply too… *immense*… to comprehend. A small part of her screamed that she should under no circumstances offer information to the enemy, but any sense in that impulse was long past. There was no way, she meditated, that the villains hadn't rifled through every memory she had while in their complete and total thrall.

[I admit that I did. We were in the midst of a crisis and you knew much that helped us preserve lives. But I have only shared the information that was important to our survival; you have kept your personal secrets. Only I know about the prophecy you were given. Only I know your fears and sorrows and weaknesses. Not even Celia is privy to that. To share more would be a betrayal of the highest order; unless lives are at risk, that information stays between us.]

Though the text was printed on the goggles she wore, the thoughts also slid into the back of her mind, seemingly *hearing* them almost as if spoken in her ear. They were clearly not her thoughts, but they infused her, perfectly slipping into her conscious mind. They were foreign, yes, but not an intrusion. With them came a feeling of warmth and welcome. She sensed… she sensed that this ROSE truly cared about her. It took her a long time to realize what the feeling was.

Love.

The realization hit her like a freight train. The feeling was so foreign. Her face was suddenly buried in her hands and she was *sobbing*, great wracking heaves shaking her to her core and the ghost of a low, shuddering wail threatening to escape her chest. She had not felt loved since…

Her memory searched for the last time she had ever felt that wave of compassion. She had certainly never known it in all her years in the TPA. Neither had her time in the Army ever been a time of succor. It was with a slow, dawning realization that she became certain her parents had never truly loved her either. Too many times they had only cared about her physical and athletic prowess — at least, until she was barred from such activities for having an unfair advantage.

"Oh, my sssweet cryssstal pony..." The words were distant, at the edge of the sudden whirlwind of sorrow that engulfed her. But the words that cut through to her were spoken deep within her mind.

[Celia would like to comfort you, but only with your permission.]

She could not speak, not in words. But some deep part of her responded, desperate for something — anything — to take the pain away. The distant sound of a desk being casually shoved aside failed to mean anything, but then two strong arms wrapped around her.

The draft horse suddenly found herself swept up in warm scales. She was picked up like a toy, every inch of her wrapped in those powerful coils, enveloped in a loving embrace like she had never been before. Celia's chin rested between her ears and whispered half-heard soothing.

The Percheron sobbed uncontrollably as decades of longing and loneliness shook her. She had never been able to be herself. She had never found a place as welcoming as this. Tears streamed from her as she clutched the woman who was wrapped around her. For the first time in her life, the mare felt... safe.

Cosseted in soft scales, time had no meaning for her, while ROSE shared that sense of love directly into her heart.

Chapter 2

Seismic Reflection

March 22, 2023

Jennifer Delver, I Mark You.

The ragged and exhausted rodent sat at her cheap, worn kitchen table, gazing at her forearm. She was naked, because that had been easiest. She looked like hell, not having showered or taken care of herself since... the incident. The world felt distant and unreal, as if time and space were fluid and ever-shifting. She barely even noticed the harsh taste of cheap whiskey clinging to the back of her tongue... but the liquor had done nothing to chase away the dread that had settled over her.

Heroes Shall Hunt You For This Taint.

While her right paw was curled around a plastic cup filled with harsh amber liquid, it was her left that held her attention. She couldn't drag her gaze away from the deep brown fur that covered the text. Though nothing could be seen through her pelt, she could *feel* the mark on her. Jen had spent frustrating hours trying to spread the hair to see what had been seared into her flesh, but all she knew was her skin was etched densely with an inscription in no language she recognized. Even the letters were unfamiliar, so the internet was of no help.

They Will Destroy You If They Can.

The nutria had been pondering shaving the arm to see the script better, but had finally decided that might make her stand out too much. Might make her a *target*. Bleak depression ate at her heart. Some kind of damned *magic* had been imprinted on her by that elephant shrew, and she didn't know what she could do about it.

Run.

There was no outrunning this. When she had found the aftermath of a superhero fight, she had rushed to the aid of the injured, and the black-clad... *thing* had marked her. Those dying words — dying *thoughts,* forced roughly into her mind — haunted her. They were sharp and vivid, just as the memory of those glowing reddish-brown eyes.

Fight.

As if she could fight supervillains. As if she could fight *Heroes.* She was a health inspector who had seen five decades slip past her without ever once getting in a physical fight. Her knees and back ached with the strain of getting out of bed in the morning.

Survive.

She was doomed. That was the thought that kept circling her. No amount of plastic-bottle whiskey was going to save her. The waiting was the worst part. Every noise outside the thin walled apartment seemed a portent of doom; she kept imagining a spandex-clad monster, with all the backing of the State of Texas behind them, breaking in and erasing her from existence.

Master Will Find You.

She wouldn't be hard to find, the nutria despaired bitterly. She was shocked she hadn't been rooted out already.

Master Will Bind You.

That was the worst part. The doom her mind still shied away from was not death; that would be too easy. No, the deep fear was that she would be magically bound, somehow, enslaved for some horrible purpose. A thousand horrific fates flitted through her mind half-formed, leaving nothing but gnawing dread.

I Mark You, Jennifer Delver.

She knew it with utmost certainty: she couldn't go to the Heroes about this. The idea repulsed her. Jennifer knew that the impulse was likely tied to the magic, but that didn't mean the danger wasn't real.

Sylvanite had *killed* the villain, and Jennifer couldn't discount the idea that the shrew had been under the same compulsion.

Her left hand balled into a fist. Frustration and hopelessness threatened to overwhelm her. With effort, she tore her eyes away from her arm and stared at the bottle of whiskey. Memories of cheap brown liquors past surfaced. During the divorce, she had retreated into the bottle, failing to respond or to take the necessary steps, and she had lost everything because of it.

Not again.

Rage — sudden and hot and wet — roared through her. With a snarl, she abruptly stood up, her chair clattering on the floor as it toppled backwards. She grabbed the half-empty plastic bottle. Visions of throwing it through the window tempted her, but she refused to be ridden by her base instincts. Instead, she overturned it, and slammed the neck down the sink.

Not again.

Fury burned away the feeling of intoxication. Jennifer pulled out her phone and got to work. First, she sent a message to her boss that she would now be taking the emergency leave after all. The old marten knew that she had been at one of the fight scenes during the rash of attacks that had raged across the city. *Let her think that I need to get my mind off the attacks. She won't guess the real reason.*

Next, she started scrolling through her calendar, rearranging her inspection schedule. As a health inspector, she regularly dealt with some of the shadier folks in the food industry. She would start by leaning on those contacts.

I need a way to defend myself against superpowered threats. And I need to figure out what this mark is. I may not know anyone who can do that… but I bet I know people who do. Time to call in favors. Or maybe make some threats.

She wasn't going to be *passive* this time. She wasn't going to let others dictate her fate. This time… this time she was going to fight. She wasn't going to let anyone threaten her, not even a supervillain. And she wasn't going to be meek prey for this… this so-called Master. *Whoever he was.*

So, you think you're coming for me, are you? Well, you chose the wrong lady to mess with…

The mare didn't know how long she stayed there. After a seeming eternity, the crying finally slowed to a stop, once her body simply ran out of tears. The waves of sorrow ebbed from her mind, thoughts finally returning, if sluggishly. Her eyes and throat ached, and the soft fur of her face and chest was soaked through.

I guess scales aren't exactly absorbent.

The analytical conclusion was so incongruous that a surprised laugh huffed through numb lips. As if on cue, the warm coils around her slowly loosened. The sliding of scales was slow and careful, ever-so-gradually letting her move, if only slightly. Celia unwound from her, letting her down ever-so-gently.

The draft horse found she had no strength to stand, though, as she was slowly lowered to the floor. Before she quite realized it, she was sitting on the ground, her back against Celia's scaled torso. She felt more relaxed than she had in years. With a start, she realized her head was pillowed by Celia's prodigious chest, but the snake tightened her hands on the horse's shoulders when she started to pull away. The expectation, and welcome, was clear. Unable to fight the twin onslaught of support and kindness, she relaxed again.

Her gaze traveled to the distant loops of tail, now no longer touching but still encircling her. That thought, of being completely surrounded by a deadly Supervillain, should have sent her into full survival combat mode. Instead, it somehow helped her feel… protected…? Once she wasn't fully cocooned any more, she could start to think again, at least.

"Thank you," she croaked softly, surprised at how weak her voice was.

"You are mossst welcome. We are here for you. We do not value you sssimply for the thingsss you can do for usss. We want you to be happy. That isss what we ssseek, ultimately, for all. I am hoping you can be a part of that, but that choiccce isss yoursss. But all that isss for later." The viper's voice was soft and filled with a warmth that caused the inside of the Percheron's heart to tingle.

"Later?"

31

"I wisssh you to ssspend sssome time here. Sssee the Korps for who we are. Then, with eyesss open, make your decccisssion."

"Oh." She thought about that for a long time. "What must I do while I'm here?"

"Mussst? Nothing."

"You won't require me to fight? Rob banks?"

Celia chuckled softly. "No dear pony. Not unlessss you wisssh it. Though there are a great many banksss in dire need of a good heissst, there are many other thingsss you may do if you desssire. Or, indeed, nothing at all, if that isss your preferenccce. We did not take you becausse you are of value asss a sssoldier. You are here becaussse you needed sssafe harbor and it wasss in our capacccity to offer."

She didn't know what to say.

The moments stretched out, time losing meaning. She could not say how much time passed until the bat cleared her throat. The fallen Hero startled, having completely forgotten they were not alone in the room. She expected to see annoyance or derision on the bat's face, but she looked honestly regretful at the interruption.

"I fear I am being summoned. By your leave?"

The snake met the gaze of the bat and nodded. "Thank you, Davina. You may go. Let me know if you need to ressschedule our training sssesssion tonight."

The draft horse had assumed that the summoning was metaphorical, until a red light burst from the floor around the Korps agent, etching a ring around her. Lines cut across the interior, followed by strange symbols ringing the resulting pentagram; after another heartbeat, that same crimson light burst from Clarion's eyes and open mouth. For a moment, the fallen hero could swear she saw horns and a long, spade-tipped tail — and then the light simply vanished, and with it, the flying fox.

Wait, is she a demon…?!

She craned her head up to look at Celia with surprise. "What… just happened?"

"Davina hasss an unusssual power. On top of being an accomplisssshed witch, when cccertain conditttions are met, ssshe can choosssse to ansssswer a call insssstead of the intended target. When sssomeone isss attempting to sssummon a being that may causse… undue havok in thisss world…

they may inssstead find a perturbed, and unbound, sssupervillain has ansssswered. You will find ssshe hasss a tendencccy to disssappear rather abruptly."

The Percheron looked at where the flying fox had been with speculation.

I feel sorry for any cultists who try to summon a demon bound by ritual to serve them, and instead get a Korps supervillain with no such constraints.

As she pondered the absent witch, she finally brought herself to ask the question that had been hovering at the back of her mind. She could feel it like a shadow across her heart.

"Is... is Starshade a drone?"

It was only then that she registered the presence of the robot nurse again. The four armed synthetic fox had one of her right hands on her chest and the other mimicked wiping away a tear. Finally, she spoke, the waveform on her mask fluctuating with her words.

"Oh! Oh I... er... she... uh..." the nurse tried to form a coherent sentence but was clearly stumbling over her own words and getting flustered.

But the horse's mouth fell open at the first attempt. *"Starshade?!"*

Chapter 3

Intrusion

March 22, 2023

...

...

...

...

Starshade... !

..

..

[Starshade, I'm here!]

"... ROSE? Is that you?"

[Yes! Starshade, I'm here!]

"I can't feel anything, ROSE. I can't see anything. Where am I?"

[You were gravely injured. You are in the medbay.]

"ROSE, I'm scared."

[You are going to be okay.]

"Why can't I feel anything?"

[Starshade, you are in a deep sleep. It would not be a kindness for you to be awake right now, dear.]

"You're scaring me, ROSE. I can't see or feel anything."

[You are going to be okay. I wish I could let you sleep, but we need your help. And you need to make a choice.]

"I... okay. But... what happened? Last I remember was coughing, and... and the blood..."

[There's no easy way to say this. You were breathing in too much of that corrosive dust from that cursed Hero. Your lungs were... destroyed.]

"Destroyed?!"

[*Dear, I know this is scary and confusing. But you are going to need to make the choice soon. I need you to understand your options. We are growing you new lungs. But it will take a bit of time for them to be ready. You'll need to stay here in the tank while that happens. You'll be good as new, like nothing ever happened.*]

"I'll be okay…?"

[*You will be okay no matter what you choose, I swear. We have you. You are safe. We could instead give you cybernetic lungs. Adam has been manic about making them for you. These would be much more capable than bioidentical lungs.*]

"More… capable."

[*You wouldn't be as vulnerable to gas attacks. You could breathe more noxious fumes without difficulty. You could run longer and harder. But you might become vulnerable to certain attacks. And it would mean you would need a support network — an additional cybernetic systems control implant, connected to your brain and nervous system — to make sure they keep operating.*]

"Oh. Adam is making them?"

[*Oh yes. As soon as he was able to, he buried himself in the lab to build you the, and I quote, 'best lungs the world has ever seen.' There was definitely some maniacal laughter. There may have been some lightning.*]

"Oh, Adam. Never change."

[*Or… Nurse O was insistent that I share this option. She really likes you.*]

"Wait, Nurse O… **likes** me?!"

[*Of course, my dear. She adores you. Even if you annoy her greatly by how often you end up in her care. She thinks you are funny.*]

"I have never seen her laugh once at my jokes."

[*Dear, I assure you, she would not bring this up as a suggestion if she didn't like you. She wants you to consider becoming a synth.*]

"What?!"

[*Your mind would be uploaded into a synthetic body, crafted just for you. Everything about you would change forever. You would be stronger, faster, tougher, more capable in almost every way. You could shape your form to perfectly match your desires and needs.*

[*But it would be a massive life change. Everything about your day to day existence would be upended. You would have to learn how to take care of your* radically different needs. And you would be reliant upon the Korps support network forever. Engineers and technicians and rare resources are all required to keep a synth operational.]

"Oh. That's… a lot. What… what about my powers?"

[That would be the risk. Some synth conversions keep their powers. Some find their powers changed in big or small ways. But the reality is that most others lose them completely. It's something we still don't quite understand, so there's no way to predict.]

"I probably won't be able to jump?"

[That is one possible outcome. But you could still run and fight. You would still be you.]

"But… my jumping is why I became an agent. That's why I was useful."

[Oh, Starshade… dear, you aren't defined by your powers. The Korps didn't take you in because you could teleport. We didn't put you in the field because you had powers. Your worth isn't based on your superpower or what you can do for the Korps. You are worthy because you are bright and amazing and silly. You were brave enough to not only stand up to Manifest Destiny, you were able to laugh maniacally directly into his face. And then you took him down without once using your powers.]

"But—"

[Starshade, listen to me. Who you are isn't based on what you can do. You are inherently worthy because you are you. You are loved and cared for not because you are useful but because you are worth loving and caring for.]

"Oh."

[Oh indeed. None of that will change if you choose to become a synth, even if you lose your powers.]

"Are you telling me that I should become a synth?"

[No. I'm not. I'm making sure that you genuinely consider it as an option during what comes next.]

"What… comes next?"

[We need your help. Celia needs your help.]

"What do you need me to do?"

[We are about to wake up your friend.]

"Slate?"

[*Yes, though she's chosen to abandon that name. She hasn't picked a new one yet. Apparently it was her birth name, not merely her Hero moniker, and the Teepa was just as unimaginative as her parents.*]

"Oh, Overlord...

[*This mustang that followed you home is so very lost. We're very worried about her. Her defection was so sudden — and so largely forced by circumstance — that none of the usual groundwork has been put in place. While Celia is still alert to the remote possibility that this might be a trap, we've mostly been trying to figure out how to not break her further. Her sense of self was entirely shattered, and we need to handle her very carefully.*]

"How can I help? Are you going to wake me up?"

[*That... is the difficulty. You aren't in physical shape to be awoken. Even if we did, you won't be able to speak. We fear seeing you in such a state would do more harm to her than good. But we can't wait until you are better.*]

"Oh. Yeah. You can't stuff the pony in a closet for weeks."

[*Not the phrase I would have used, but unfortunately accurate. We need you there. The mare needs a friendly face, and will be worried about you. Without you available in some way, she will struggle to connect and might fear a trap. And yet you can't be there because you are injured.*]

"So..."

[*Nurse O has offered you temporary use of one of her bodies.*]

"WHAT?!"

[*It would be **temporary.** They aren't designed for... individual use. Nurse O would be there to run the back end of the body, handling all the communication with the rest of Nurse O and making sure you aren't... subsumed.*]

"Sub... sumed?"

[*Don't worry about it, dear. You'll be in one of her bodies for a little while. Nurse O will handle all the important back-end parts. You can talk with your favorite Percheron a bit to reassure her. Help her.*]

"She's the only Percheron I know."

[*Yes, Star. That was a joke.*]

"Oh, right. Sorry. Still trying to process everything. This is weird."

[*I know, dear. I'm sorry.*]

"She's going to need friends, fast. And I don't know if she has ever had one before."

[I can confirm that you are her first friend since childhood. She had acquaintances and comrades in the Army, but though those bonds were deep, they aren't the same as friends.]

"Oh... Oh. That poor horse."

[Precisely.]

"I assume you have a plan?"

[We were going to have her meet with some other former Heroes-turned-supervillains. Maybe she can find common ground and hopefully a connection.]

"Who?"

[Volta is also former Teepa, and they are both... of similar magnitude.]

"Isn't she incredibly intimidating? And one of the most feared supervillains in the area? And you want her to meet Sl— er, the horse?"

[We're hoping that the two can find common ground, and the lost mare can see we aren't the monsters the media portrays.]

"Some of us are."

[Some of us are definitely monsters, but not in the way the media suggests.]

"What about heroes that she may have met?"

[I was just coming to that. There are a couple that she has met, though only in passing at various Hero conferences. The first is Ellen Foxpaw. Formerly Lawful Neutral of the Everyone's Hero Association.]

"Oh! I know about Lawful Neutral! I didn't realize she was on base. Her defection was pretty big news when it happened. Given the reports, I had been expecting she would become a pretty notorious villain, but she kind of fell off the radar."

[She's been... finding her place in the Korps. We're hoping that introducing the two might help them both figure out their own path a bit more. And it's always nice to see a familiar face when you're finding your footing.]

"That makes sense. Poor girl. I'd love to meet her someday. Her puns are legendary. I bet she spends hours trying to plan them out. Preparing witty banter is hard and it's her whole schtick."

[As for the other, Maddy Gillespie happens to be on base.]

"Who?"

[Formerly the PHL hero "Heartforce," from Alberta by way of Ontario. Sheep-bear hybrid, telekinetic skirmisher. She defected last year, and by chance ended up at RIV on... the day when everything happened, and very ably helped out. She hasn't become a field agent yet, so we're hoping she can help

show the mare that she doesn't have to start punching their former teammates immediately.]

"That ship has sailed."

[Well… true. But it can still be hard to take up the fight against Heroes. What's important for our equine guest to understand is that she doesn't have to, if she doesn't want to.]

"No, she doesn't. But she's good at it. You should have seen her dust dozens of Manifests Destiny."

[I reviewed your memories. And hers. She was quite impressive.]

"Oh, right."

[We were also going to introduce her to Zala. She was with the NHA for a little while as support staff, if you recall.]

"Oh, right, she was at Bradley Group, wasn't she? That's going to be fun."

[Did you have any other ideas about who she should meet?]

"Mabel! Mabel Greysmoke!"

[Is that a good idea? She's never been a Hero. She's brand new to being a field agent. And she can be a bit…]

"…Of a flippant, anti-authoritarian, funny, disaster queer who hasn't figured out who they are and what they're doing?"

[That's a bit…]

"…Just like me?"

[I… oh. Yes, you are right. Good idea.]

And I have another suggestion. You need someone to show her around the base."

[Absolutely. We were planning on having Zala show her around.]

"I have a better idea. Have Dawn do it."

[Oh! Are you sure that's a good idea?]

"Trust me like I trust you, ROSE? If she can handle Orion, she can handle this pony. It's perfect."

[This is going to go very well or very poorly. But I suppose either way it'll be spectacular.]

"Isn't that the motto of the Korps?"

[Hush.]

Starshade stood still, watching Celia and her friend discuss the horse's future. She was waiting patiently for the right time to join the conversation, as per the plan. Or, at least, that was what she was supposed to be doing. What she was *actually* doing was trying not to feel weird about the body she was standing in.

It didn't feel pervasively, skin-crawlingly wrong, in the way her own body had before her first fateful trip to Empire Enhancements, but it was nonetheless *alien*. At the back of her mind, she could *feel* an unimaginable number of status checks and computer communication and foreign thoughts whispering at the edge of her mind; too distant to understand, but too loud to ignore. Nurse O was there, in her mind. She was handling all the functional operation of the body, but it meant that Starshade felt more like a passenger — which was precisely what she *was*.

But the body itself was so unlike her own. She still didn't know what to do with four arms, especially when each pair was so very different in form and function. Her vision was wildly changed, filled with detailed information and seeing into spectrums beyond her experience. Each person she saw came with a panoply of medical readouts and other status information. (She *especially* wasn't sure what to do with the knowledge that most of Celia's data listed only [NOT APPLICABLE].)

More than that, it almost felt like time itself was... wrong. She seemed to have too much time. Everything was slower, and yet it still somehow felt like the right speed. That might have been the most unsettling part: that something, like the passage of time, that seemed such a foundation of the universe could feel so radically different. But she couldn't tell if time was moving differently, or if she could just think faster.

"Is... is Starshade a drone?" The words cut through her thoughts, bringing her back to the poor lost horse in front of her. The Percheron mare sparkled like amethyst, but looked... fragile. More glass than stone. And the anguish in her voice drove a spike through Starshade.

"Oh!" She found herself exclaiming before she realized what she was doing. She simply had to answer. But it was immediately hard to ignore that the words weren't formed by lips and throat; rather, there was a distant clicking, more felt than heard, as an electromagnet drove a voice synthesizer. And there was this strange... whirring deep inside her skull that accompanied it that was deeply unsettling.

[Dear, you are supposed to let Celia break the news gently.]

ROSE's words and thoughts felt like they were part of her; unlike with her RCGs, they weren't distant and external. There was none of the usual separation that helped her delineate her own thoughts and feelings from her beloved AI.

"Oh, I…"

"You aren't supposed to indicate that you are inhabiting one of my chassis at this time."

Nurse O was also just *there*, in her thoughts mixed in with all of that whispered code that haunted the frayed edges of her reality. The sensation of strange almost-words was far more alien than her courteous speech felt normally. Starshade's mind felt crowded, and she wasn't sure how to deal with it.

"Er…"

"Starshade, you should focus and collect your thoughts."

[Take a moment, dear. You're spiraling. You've got this.]

Both of them were right. But she could feel the words spilling from her, seemingly outside of her control, but she could do this. She was a Korps supervillain, a trained field agent. Just because reality seemed to have gone askew, well, that didn't mean that she couldn't do something as simple as putting herself back onto the right conversational path.

"She…"

"Yes, redirect her attention to concern for you, and that will give Celia time to broach the topic."

[You don't want to lie to her and indicate that you aren't Starshade, or she could feel deceived. She doesn't need that right now.]

"You are correct; causing the patient to needlessly become anxious or confused should be avoided. Perhaps Starshade should be the one to break the news after all?"

[She has been through so much. I worry that she—]

"ENOUGH! *Please! I can't* **think** *with you two both backseat… speaking? Please, I appreciate the help, but my head is full and I need a moment to get my thoughts in order."*

"Uh…"

She could feel the two other entities pull back with a touch of chagrin. *Finally,* she thought, *a moment to collect myself and explain the—*

"STARSHADE?!"

"This isn't what it looks like!" The words buzzed from her, as she grasped for a way to diffuse the situation.

[Starshade, may we resume offering suggestions again?]

"I wonder, is there perhaps a better approach to the situation?"

"Uh... Hi. I'm Starshade." She knew her second attempt was no better even as she said it; despite the synthetic chassis being wholly incapable of it, Starshade felt like she was blushing. She glanced around the room for relief, only to watch Celia wearily cover her face with one hand.

...*Crap.*

Chapter 4

Pressure Release

March 22, 2023

"Uh… Hi. I'm Starshade."

Well, at least I can be sure that's really Starshade.

Fear nibbled at the edges of her mind, but the Percheron slowly took a deep breath, trying to chase away the fear of betrayal that haunted her. She had been a superhero for a very long time and had faced countless unusual, bizarre and frankly weird situations. With effort, she tamped down her emotions. She was used to this, though she could never remember it being quite this difficult to contain them. She closed her eyes, taking several moments to calm herself.

"Please, tell me what's going on. Why are you a robot? The last I saw, you were droned. Is this what you've always been? Or did they steal your body from you? What is *happening*, Starshade?"

She was proud of herself that the questions were asked in a calm, even tone that hid the secret dread that the worst had happened. She watched the synth closely, seeking any sign of the truth.

"Oh! No! Nothing like that. I'm fine! You know, except for the lungs."

"*WHAT?!*" Horror clawed at her heart and only hard fought self control kept her from panicking.

"I'm fine! That last part was supposed to be… er… Nurse O, how do I switch to internal monologue ag—" Two right arms came up to try to rub at her eye, and bumped into each other. The synth looked startled, pulling both hands back to stare at them before they awkwardly dropped to her side.

"Please explain." She meant to say that calmly, but realized the ice filled her words far more than she intended. Celia shifted menacingly, but the mare stared at the nurse. She needed an explanation before a thousand worst case scenarios played themselves out in her mind and drove her mad.

"Okay. *Okay*. So, no, I have not always been... this." She gestured at herself unnecessarily; the warhorse had already figured out *that* part. She opened her mouth to prompt further, but Starshade held up both right arms with a single finger extended. The nurse looked at the two hands. Slowly, the finger on the lower, more mechanical arm dropped. Then that entire arm awkwardly dropped. Confidently, Starshade looked back at the horse.

"And I wasn't droned. Celia needed to quickly figure out how to deal with you. Making it look like she droned me was also a good threat, because she needed you to know she wasn't sugar-coating everything, like every organization you've ever been a part of before has."

The Starshade synth shot a meaningful glance at Lamia. The Percheron still struggled to read the expression of the gigantic serpent, but she seemed to radiate pleasure that Starshade had figured that out rather than any shame in the action. "Yesss, I did. I did not exxxpect thisss pony to trussst a rosssy recruitment pitccch."

"But—"

"I'm not dead." Something eased in her heart when the words were stated so plainly. That's what she had been most worried about, in truth. Falling into a trap of evil supervillains would be bad, but losing her friend was a much worse fate.

"I was breathing in too much of Manifest Dust-iny. But it's okay. I'll have a brand new set of cybernetic lungs soon! I'll be better than ever." The statement seemed to draw interest from Celia. For her part, the fallen hero realized just how grave the situation must have been. She should have been there, she thought. With these new powers, she could have *saved* her.

[*You didn't know. We didn't know. And neither of us know how your powers work even now. Don't start borrowing blame for could've-beens that were outside your control. She's alive. You're alive.*]

"I... you're right. It's hard not to feel responsible. That's always been my job. But... I'll try."

[*No one asks more than that. I'm here if you need help dealing with it.*]

"I... I will. Tell me. How close was it? Really?"

[*I'm not sure I should—*]

"Please. ROSE."

[Very. We saved her by moments.]

She swallowed the rush of emotion. She could deal with it later.

"I…" the Starshade synth stopped. Then she lurched forward, carefully planting each leg on the ground like a wobbly baby deer. With deliberate care, she closed the distance, growing more confident with each step. The horse was not prepared when four arms wrapped around her, burying her face in the equine chest.

The mare froze, completely taken aback by the action. She felt something deep in her chest loosen and the room swam for a moment. Then she wrapped powerful arms around the synthetic body and hugged back. She found herself entirely unable to find words, even if she could speak them around a throat suddenly too full.

"I'm so glad you trusted us. I'm so glad you came back with us. I know… I know it's going to be scary. The Korps is… a radical change in lifestyle. But you won't find better people."

'Radical change in lifestyle' is certainly an understatement…

Oblivious to her thoughts, the synth continued on. Her words were synthetic and accompanied by the feeling of a faint buzzing that vibrated against her, but they were somehow filled with warmth and welcome that almost brought her to tears.

"I *will* be okay. I promise. But I also won't be around for a little while. So I'm going to introduce you to a friend of mine who'll show you around the base. And we'll connect you with some others that you may find common ground with. I know, I *know* how out of place and alone you can feel in this… alien space. But, please… give the Korps a try, before you decide to leave?"

The horse was taken aback. She felt another twinge in her chest at the sudden outpouring of concern. She hadn't been planning on leaving, but she hadn't given it any thought, admittedly. She felt *lost*. But, here was the first person who had shown any sign of compassion towards her in a very long time, begging her to stay.

"Woah there. Easy there. I ain't…" As she started to speak, she realized she had fallen back into the patterns of speech she had leaned into when operating as a Hero on patrol. It took her a moment to realize that they were the same words she had used to calm Starshade when the two had first met, way back... wait, had it only been a week since that first encounter in the warehouse...?

[Eight days,] ROSE chimed in in response.

The realization of how much had changed in such a short time was staggering. The whole situation felt unreal. She wasn't sure what to do with that feeling. She also wasn't sure what to do with the realization she had slipped into that old affectation, the deliberately folksy tone, just to ease the rabbit's worries.

"Woah there. I haven't decided to leave. I plan to give this place a real shot. Just... heal up for me? Please? I'm certain I'll get along with anyone who can count themselves a friend of yours." She was certain of no such thing, but it was the right thing to say to someone who so clearly needed reassurance.

"Okay. Thank you." With that, the synthetic fox finally broke the hug and stepped back. "They say I need to go back to sleep soon. Projecting my consciousness into this body is putting strain on my... er... body. But I wanted to make sure I introduced you to a friend before I left. You're going to love Dawn."

The synth looked over at Celia questioningly. The viper looked pleased and nodded. "I have asssked her to join usss. Ssshe will be here momentarily. Dawn isss not a sssupervillain; ssshe isss a cccivilian here, a crafter. Of particular note to you, ssshe isss a farrier. Ssshould you need ssshoesss or other... tack, ssshe will be the bessst one to ssspeak with. Ssshe will alssso be your neighbor, and knowsss the basss intimately. Ssshe will be your guide until Sssstarsssshade hasss rejoined usss."

The door behind Celia whooshed open, with a distinctive sound that would normally have made intellectual property lawyers salivate. The woman walking through was... tiny. At barely a meter and a half, with a slender frame, the dik-dik was dwarfed by the figures around her. She paused briefly with a glance at the serpent, but with the distinctive click of cloven hooves, she strode confidently into the room.

The antelope sported the undercut that was so common there, even as it was distinctive and eye-catching outside of the Korps. Her hair was dyed alternating bands of pink and black, drawing the eye, and vividly emerald-green eyes watched the horse intently as she approached. Silver twinkled in the magenta light, catching off a number of piercings on her ears, lips, nose, and eyebrows.

She was, also, very... *pink*. Tight pink jeans and a pink jean jacket framed her slender form. A pale pink t-shirt proudly proclaimed "My Husband Wanted A Stable Relationship" framed around the picture of a curled monkey paw. Her nails, hooves, and cute little horns were all artfully adorned with glittering pink polish, and her sleek visor RCGs blended perfectly into the bright pink panoply.

"Hi!" The dik-dik's voice was bright and cheerful and melodic, showing no fear as she stood in the land of giants. "You must be the horse that followed Starshade home! Welcome. It's nice to meet you. I'm Dawn! I know you don't have a name yet, sugar. Don't worry, I'm used to dealing with ponies without a name."

The horse was unsure how to process that last comment. She opened her mouth to respond, but the tiny antelope stuck out her hand as she marched forward. Bemused, the equine started to stick out her own to shake hands with the woman half her height, but Dawn took another quick step forward, expertly dodging the outstretched equine arm. Reaching up, her hand grabbed the horse's shirt around the stomach and *pulled*.

Startled, the draft mare found herself not wanting to hurt the diminutive figure by resisting and simply found herself kneeling down. Before she knew it, Dawn had one hoof standing on the mare's upper thigh and one hand stroking her muzzle while she was making soothing noises. "Good girl."

A confusing mix of emotions detonated within the Percheron. She had never been so quickly and completely *dominated* by someone other than Celia. At the same time, she couldn't deny the pleasure of that hand stroking her muzzle. And she couldn't figure out why she was blushing and somehow proud of being called a good girl.

The spell was broken by synthesized laughter. Starshade was doubled over, chortling, which caused the waveform mask to dance widely. Another glance at Celia showed her to be as impassive as ever, though she was clearly radiating a great deal of amusement at the sight.

Dawn giggled delightedly and reached into her jacket pocket. The pony opened her mouth to protest, or at least ask what the hell was going on, but with a deft motion, she plopped something into her mouth. The object was all angles and points and gritty, until it started to melt into pure sweetness. Sugar. In the shape of a cube.

A sugar cube.

She had not tasted pure sugar in a decade, and a whimper of delighted need slipped unbidden past her lips. The sensation was overwhelmingly sweet and yet her body reacted with a thrill of pure joy. The situation was rushing past her, leaving her floundering and helpless. Then Dawn simply hopped down, swatting at her thigh. "Up, sugar! That's enough foreplay."

The fallen hero rose unsteadily to her hooves, still trying to grapple with the sudden events and the ball of confusing emotions left within her. Dawn gazed up at her with a confident expression and a slight smirk. A glance at Celia showed the viper clearly in no hurry to offer explanation or to rescue the pony. Starshade had a hand over her mask, which was entirely pointlessly trying to stifle occasional giggles.

"What... just happened?"

[That was Dawn. She's like that. You'll get used to her.]

"Does she have... mind control powers? Why do I feel funny?"

[Oh, no she doesn't, dear. No powers at all. Just a lot of personality and a great deal of experience honing her natural tendencies on a base full of titans. She's the farrier, so she's had to deal with almost all the hoofers here. Some of them can be quite ornery while being shoed, as I'm sure you understand.]

"Hey now. I've always been easy to shoe."

[Yes you have. You're a good girl.]

Eyes wide and mentally sputtering, the mare was saved from trying to form a coherent response or sorting through her emotions by Starshade stepping forward. "That was just about the best thing. Dawn, I adore you."

The tiny pink terror turned to the nurse with a delighted smile, though one that failed to hide the shadow of deep concern in her eyes. "Starshade... I heard. They briefed me while I was heading down. Are... are you going to be okay?"

"I'm going to be fine. Better than new, actually. Just going to take a little while."

The two women embraced each other. As she watched the reunion, she nearly jumped out of her skin when Celia hissed softly in her ear. Heart hammering in her chest, she realized that she had not heard or seen the gigantic woman move. That a creature of her size could do that to a highly trained and honed superhero was… petrifying.

"I'm sssorry, dear cryssstal pony." Celia spoke softly into her ear, careful not to interrupt the reunion of the pair. "I admit we have had a little fun at your exxxpenssse. But if ssshe doesss make you uncomfortable, do not be afraid to let usss know. We will not be offended if we need to find a guide that isss… lessss intensse."

The mare swallowed, completely off her emotional ground, but slowly shook her head. Her own voice murmured back, "Thank you, but this is okay…? I knew I would be in for a… culture shock. I shall adapt."

"I sssay thisss again. I do not wisssh the Korps to be sssomething for you to endure. I sssinccerely hope you find a home here. That will not happen if we placcce you in a sssituatttion you find intolerable."

The fallen hero stared at the antelope and the synthetic fox bantering for a long moment, taking a moment to finally sort through her feelings on the matter. "Intolerable… was what I just left. The Teepa kept me in a state of neglect. Last week I would have called it benign neglect, but I see now that it wasn't harmless at all. Same with the Army. To both of them I was just a tool… a weapons system, I suppose. I don't get the same sense here."

She paused to gather herself briefly. "I admit I don't know how to react to the people here, including you. It's all so strange. But I don't know if it's *bad* strange. I need to sort through my thoughts and reactions. I need time to figure out how I *feel* about all of this. Only then can I say whether I need actions to be moderated. Can I trust ROSE to let me know if she sees signs I'm distressed?"

"Abssolutely. That isss quite… introssspective of you. Very well, I ssshall let Dawn continue her… handling of you. I jusst wanted to make ssure it wasss not going too far."

The fallen hero nodded and smiled slightly. "That is more than the Teepa ever did."

"You ssshall find that we ssstrive to never be like that vile failure of a group."

They lapsed into silence as the Starshade Synth finally broke her hug with the shorter Dawn. There was clearly a touch of regret as she turned. "I'm sorry. Nurse O says that I need to go back to rest. I'm very sorry I won't be there to help you meet the others. I haven't met some of them myself, so I'm extra jealous. But... all of you, please take care of my friend. That includes *you*, horse. I expect you to be there when I wake up."

"I will." The promise was past her lips before she realized that she had agreed to stay here that long. But she did not regret that promise. There was nowhere else for her to go. But, more importantly, this was where her friend was. "I'll make sure to tell you all about it."

[Do you want me to record key interactions and share them with Starshade?]

"You can do that? That's... yes. Please. Unless there's something I don't want shared."

[I shall make sure of it.]

"If Dawn saddles you, I want a ride."

"Wait, what?!" she squeaked with a blush, causing the others to chuckle.

Then the Nurse O's posture changed. She stood less casually, adopting more of a formal, courteous stance. Her arms crossed demurely, the synthetic fox tilted her head. "Starshade is asleep now. She needs her rest."

"Can I... see her?"

"Not now. She pushed herself too hard and too long, so we need to tend to that. But tomorrow, we will make arrangements. I know she will be glad, even if she is not aware enough to know. She is in the best of hands."

"Thank you." She didn't know what else to say, but she was grateful that this nurse seemed to know what she was talking about. It did little to chase away the sudden feeling of loneliness, knowing her friend was injured and unavailable for so long.

"It is our pleasure to provide the best care to our patients. Speaking of which, we look forward to your visit, once you are ready. Empire Enhancements waits with eager anticipation for your visit."

"Empire... Enhancements?" The warhorse was taken aback. *Did she really say she was eager for me to get injured?*

[Not at all. Empire Enhancements is the branch that specializes in... adapting the body to better fit the soul. They offer a wide variety of services. I will explain them all to you later.]

50

"Oh, okay. Thank you."

[You are most welcome, dear.]

"ROSE will explain it all to you I'm sure. We await your visit. Though in light of Starshade's request, we think it is best delayed until after she wakes up. Otherwise, she may be rightfully annoyed. Until then, unless there is anything else I can assist you with, I shall take my leave."

"Thank you Nurssse O. You were exxxcellent asss alwaysss. You may depart. And pleassse passss along my persssonal thankss to the othersss on the medical ssstaff for their hard work the passst few daysss."

The synthetic fox gave a slight nod before turning and smoothly, gracefully walking from the room. The lamia turned to the horse who suddenly found herself feeling very uncomfortable under the scrutiny of the massive serpent. "Er... yes? Lamia?"

"I ssshall leave you in Dawn'sss capable hoovesss. But if you have need of me, ROSSSE can passss along any quessstionsss. Welcome to RIV. We ssshall disssscussss your future oncccce you have had time to digessst the choiccce before you. And Lamia is but my callsssign. You may call me Cccelia, though many prefer to addressss me by my formal title."

The Percheron blinked at the comment, knowing she was being prompted. "And, what is your formal title?"

"You may call me Missstressss." Without waiting for a response, the giant snake turned and slithered silently from the room, leaving the blushing horse in her wake.

CHAPTER 5

STRUCTURAL DEFORMATION

March 22, 2023

Jennifer sat in her car, staring down the street at the run-down food truck. She knew this one well. She used to dread seeing this particular truck, because it meant lots of paperwork to issue a citation; it was perpetually on the verge of being shut down, and she had been waiting for that day. Now, though, it was terrifying for an entirely different reason.

The faded and worn beacon of questionable foodstuffs represented a rubicon. Until now, she had done nothing wrong. She had been gathering information, sure, but this would represent the first time she used her position of authority for personal benefit. The thought sat heavy in her stomach as she thought through her options. Twice, she put the car in gear to drive away from this crazy plan; twice, she had put it back in park.

Her left arm ached. She could feel the brand there, under her fur and the sleeve of her blue pantsuit. The nutria rarely dressed this formally for most inspections, since she often had to handle food or crawl under sinks... but for what came next, she needed to shore up the air of authority. Plus, the cute girl at the shop had said it made her look striking, as it matched her sapphire eyes.

With a sense of dread, she finally opened the car door and stepped out into the cool spring air. She took a moment to check herself in the reflection from her window. Her paws smoothed the wrinkles in her jacket and dress shirt, showing off her form as best she could. Her average height and stocky frame had never brought her much attention, especially when she seemed to always be in flux between muscle and soft.

Peering closer, she made sure her long braid was still put together. The silver streaked plait reached all the way to her waist and could be a nightmare to keep in order at times, but she adored it. Gold hoop earrings glinted in the afternoon sun. Her makeup was on point today, making her look as professional as possible. She looked to be the picture of local government authority. She would need it.

All of that belied the heart pounding in her chest. What she was about to do could get her in very real trouble, and it could end catastrophically badly; at the very least, she would be fired if her boss found out. It might even get her thrown in jail. But the ghost of searing agony reminded her why she was doing this. She was not going to be passive. Not again.

Her heels clicked with authority as she strode down the street. She had angled herself so the occupant would not see her approaching. But the ruggedized tablet, the plastic badge clipped to her breast pocket, and the determined look in her eye would ensure anyone that saw her would know her to be on official business. Instead of approaching the front window of the food truck, she reached the back door.

Most food trucks kept these locked most of the time, but the lock on Tony's Greased Bitening had been broken during a robbery three months ago, and never fixed. The lanky deer in the grease stained apron looked up sharply to yell at whatever customer had barged in, but the indignant shout died the moment he registered who had entered his domain.

Tony had the presence of mind to try to surreptitiously push the waiting sandwiches onto the grill, but with one step forward, Jennifer had already snatched one up and inserted a thermometer. For once she didn't suppress the snarl when she read how cold the reading was.

"Surprise inspection, Tony. What have we told you about keeping food waiting too long?"

The blood drained from the inside of the cook's ears. "My inspection isn't due until next month!" he feebly protested.

But her tone was dangerous and cold, filled with bureaucratic doom. "That's why it's called a surprise inspection. Tony, you already had your last chance. If you fail this inspection, that's it. We're shutting you down." Her hand meaningfully grabbed the vegetable refrigerator door and she looked up into terrified eyes.

"Please… this is all I have." The piteousness in his voice sent a twinge through her heart. Not that it would matter to customers who became ill from eating at his questionable truck. But she was being intentionally cruel. She had to be.

"Then you should have been better about food handling. You know, you *know*, how important this is. If this business was important, you could have improved your operation years ago."

"Please, you don't understand!"

But she cut off his protest. "You've gone too far this time, Tony. And you can't bribe me like you do *Carol*."

If anything, the cervine looked more shocked at her blatant declaration. Though he towered over her, he took a step back. His back hit the wall and his antlers clattered against the cabinet. Jennifer gave him no escape and stepped forward into his personal space. One glittering blue claw poking into his chest.

"Tony, your food makes people sick. You don't follow the rules. You don't fix your shit. And you refuse to do anything to do better. I should shut you down." She bit off each word, enunciating clearly, each carefully calculated to drive home fear. She was watching the dread fill the lanky deer as each pronouncement fell from her lips. But Tony was not stupid. His expression rapidly shifted to confusion and then to guardedness when she uttered the last sentence.

"Wait... should?"

The nutria's ruby lips spread into a tight, predatory smile at the question. "I should..." She stretched out the word, turning her tone speculative. Those brown cervine eyes searched her expression for clues.

"I thought you said I couldn't bribe you."

"You can't. I have no interest in your money. I know you're broke or you wouldn't be running this shithole."

"Hey!"

"Stuff it. We both know it's true."

The deer paused, looking at her with trepidation mixed with growing hope. He knew there was a lifeline here, but he didn't know the shape of it. He didn't know if the price was too high.

"What... do you want?"

"I need you to get me into the next fight."

His eyes bugged out of his skull and his question exploded from him. "*What?!*"

She narrowed her eyes, knowing the effect the gold eyeliner had on her dark fur. Her voice was steel, brooking no argument. "I need you to get me into the fights in Knox-Henderson Station. I know your cousin is the bouncer there. I know you can get me in."

A new type of horror was dawning on the deer's face. "Why do you want to see a cape fight so badly?"

"Why I want in is my business."

The deer shook his head. "No, those fights are dangerous and spill into the crowd all the time. And if they found out that I let a government official in, they *will* have me killed. Not might. Will. I need more than that."

Jennifer gritted her teeth, but had known this was a possibility. She had hoped to overawe Tony into not asking questions. Still, she had prepared for this eventuality. With effort, she let her mask of professional fury crack to show the very real fear underneath. Her breath was shaky when she responded. "There's a cape after me."

"*What?!*" For the second time, the shocked exclamation was pulled from Tony.

It wasn't hard to summon the tears… the bitterness. What was hard was not breaking down right then and there. "My… ex…" tears closed her throat and threatened to spill over. But she was able to lock down her expression. Force herself back into control.

Tony had heard about her messy divorce. It hadn't been that long ago. It had been quite the gossip across the city. He drew his own conclusions. "You know the people there won't protect you, right?"

Jennifer blinked, honestly touched that Tony, just after she threatened him, would try to caution her about that. "I'm not looking for protection. At least not directly. I have a plan. But I need to get into those fights."

The calculation on the deer's expression told her that she had hooked him. "I get you into those fights and… what? You forget this ever happened?"

"No."

Tony blinked. "No?"

"If I just walk away, the next time you get a health inspection you can't bribe your way out of, you're right back here. You can't keep doing this. You are making people sick. Really sick."

The cook's lips drew into a line and she could see him withdrawing. She drew a shaky breath and launched into the gambit.

"Your food is shit, Tony. You serve crap. You handle it poorly. And it's bad before it ever gets to you. You buy expired, low-grade crap and then you can barely scrape by on poor sales until the next week. Tony, you are *better than this*. I've talked with your brother. You're smart, but you locked yourself into a cycle of self-destruction."

The tall deer started to protest, but she held up one claw to forestall it. "Let me finish. You can't keep this up. It ends nowhere good. And with the rising price of food… well, let's just say your supply is going to dry up even if you don't drive yourself into the ground first.

"So, here's the deal. I know someone. Developed a power. They can grow plants. They could be a supply of fresh fruits and vegetables for extremely cheap." She tried very hard to ignore the pounding in her ears and the feeling of unreality as she spoke.

"Wait, you want me to sell magical food?" Tony sounded alarmed.

"That's just it. The vegetables themselves aren't magic. It's tested clean, even if it was grown with a power. But because the state of Texas has banned the sale of magical produce without extensive testing and certification, he can't sell it."

"That sounds incredibly valuable. Why hasn't some company hired him?" Jennifer was secretly glad she had been right about how sharp the deer was.

"Because he can't grow *enough* for a company to care. The value they get from the produce isn't equal to the testing requirements — requirements that were put in place after lobbying by agricorps who didn't want to compete with just this scenario."

The deer paused. She had seen the speculative look start to enter his eyes. She stepped back, giving him a little more room. The time to back him into the literal corner had passed.

"Wouldn't I run into the same issues?"

She thrust a finger at the chicken still simmering. "I did some digging. Your paperwork's fake, Tony, even if it looks legit enough for casual inspection. You didn't get this where you claim, which means you are very good at hiding the origin of your food. Only now you could do so without the risk of hurting people."

"So what? I run a burger truck. Vegetables are optional at best."

"You *could* keep trying that. Or, you can change. You would have the freshest produce in the city. You rebrand as a salad wrap truck. Then all you need is some simple proteins like chicken and tofu, which you could *then* afford to get reputably. Your operating costs drop, and your food quality skyrockets. Which will attract more customers. Everyone wins."

There was a long pause as the deer's dark brown eyes searched her face. She stared back, heart beating wildly in her chest, trying to hide just how afraid she was behind the professional mask she had used to cow slimy corporate managers for years. The moment stretched out, driving anxiety within her, but she refused to flinch.

"Your guy… why can't he grow drugs instead?" Tony asked with the air of a man who was afraid he was sabotaging his lifeline.

She let the question hang in the air for a moment. The nutria searched his eyes, trying to ascertain his feelings on the matter.

"What do you think he's trying to get out of?"

Tony stared at her as the import of the words sank in. Jennifer prayed to a god she no longer believed in that the statement was not the fact that would break this deal. The tall cook was silent for a long time.

"I can't get you in." The words caused her heart to drop.

"Not this weekend, anyway. This weekend is when untested fighters have their first bouts. That always draws larger crowds. No way I can get you in. And what you're asking will take time to arrange, anyway. But next weekend is just low-tier fights. I can probably get you in then, no problem."

Jennifer didn't know whether to be relieved or terrified. She settled on nodding. "As soon as I'm in, I'll send you the contact information." She pulled out a blank card with a phone number scribbled on it and placed it on the table next to her. "My burner number is here. Send me the information I need once you've made arrangements."

Tony glanced at it speculatively, then back at her. "If they find out who you are, they will *kill* you. Is this all worth the risk?"

She swallowed, her throat suddenly feeling too thick. But she nodded. "Yes."

He sighed and nodded. "It's your funeral."

Jennifer blew out a shaky breath. "Seems to be the case a lot, lately."

With that final proclamation, she turned and stepped out of the food truck into the afternoon sun. She looked around the empty streets, but paused as she saw a lone figure casually walking along a nearby parking lot. She noted with distant recognition that she knew him.

The alligator was garbed in an older-style TPA uniform in blue and white — a far cry from the black and silver she remembered him wearing when she was growing up. Everblades had been a popular Florida hero in the 80s, and a major figure in the War On Drugs. Now, though, he was apparently a member of the Texas Protectorate Assembly. She had honestly thought he retired a decade back.

Pain shot through her left arm as she could feel every line of that hidden brand burn. There was a *pulse* that seemed to travel through the world. Then, as her gaze locked with the hero, his black eyes started to glow with a deep red.

Fear spiked deep in her. Something was terribly wrong.

Heroes Shall Hunt You For This Taint.

They Will Destroy You If They Can.

The words rang in her mind. The echoes of those unnatural thoughts haunted the back of her mind. The alligator took one stilted step towards her, as if a cheap animatronic. Then he paused before his arms melted into massive serrated blades formed of ivory metal that glinted cruelly in the sunlight.

Then, the Hero *roared* in fury and began to sprint forward with murderous intent.

Chapter 6

Tectonic Convergence

March 22, 2023

As the door shut behind the departing Celia, the horse looked down at Dawn with a sense of uncertainty. She was in a strange place, one that should have been hostile… but oddly lacked the air of menace she had been taught to expect. Instead, she felt unmoored and aimless, venturing into the unknown with a stranger. The diminutive antelope smiled delightedly. "Well, I guess it's just the two of us now. Ready for your tour of the base?"

The fallen hero nodded and smiled back faintly. Her slight Texan charm playfully slipped back into her voice. "Yes Ma'am."

The cheer on the dik-dik's face magnified sharply and she stepped forward. Each step of her perfectly polished hooves clicked on the tile as she drew closer, until she was staring directly up at the mare. Suddenly there was a hint of menace in the air as a hard edge entered her emerald eyes. Her voice was still cheerful but now had a hidden steel to it, like a dagger hidden in a teddy bear.

"Celia may think she can trust you, *horse*. And if she does, then I owe it to you to give you a *chance*. But let me make one thing perfectly clear: if you betray us, or if you hurt one of my friends? I. Will. Rip. Out. Your. Spine." She bit off each word as all joviality drained away. "Do. You. *Understand*. Me. *Horse?!*"

The Percheron, who had gone toe to hoof with some of the world's titans, and who stood almost twice the height and an order of magnitude the mass of this little antelope, felt a shiver of fear travel down her spine. She had no doubt in her mind that the threat was genuine, no matter how impossible it seemed.

"Yes Ma'am." The words came out tiny as she stared back with wide eyes.

"We are about to walk around this base. You are going to see people you know only as villains and threats, and you are *not* going to start a fight with them. *Especially* if you encounter someone you've fought before. This is *our* home. You may one day join us, but right now you are a *guest*. They do not deserve to be threatened here, in our sanctuary. Do you *understand* me?"

"... *Yes*, M-Ma'am." The words seemed to be the only ones that she could summon. But then the meaning of the threat sank in: she could be seeing Korps agents, supervillains, that she *knew* here. She nodded slowly, confidence reentering her voice. "I understand. No fighting. I'm a guest."

Dawn took a long moment to search her face. Apparently satisfied, she stepped back and all the cheer returned to her voice and the sense of threat vanished like mist in the first light of morning. "Great! Let's show you around. You're going to love it here, I just know it."

The Percheron stared with an open mouth at the tram station in front of her. A *tram?!*

Nothing had prepared her for this. The path here had taken them through several corridors, each suitably villainous if one's definition of villainy included a surprising number of presumably weaponized potted plants. That alone had started to give her a sense that this Korps facility was larger than she had believed. Most villain bases were small lairs with a handful of rooms. With the number of Korps agents in the area, she had known that this base would have to be larger than the norm.

But a *tram* implied far more than just a lair; this base had *infrastructure*. That wasn't something you needed for a small crew. It implied a much, *much* larger population than she had ever imagined. The official briefings had warned that there might be as many as a hundred Korps personnel in Texas. But what she was seeing implied that number was tens of thousands. Or more. They had been wrong by *orders of magnitude*. This wasn't a hidden hideout, and further, it wasn't a temporary thing. This meant the Korps was far larger — with much farther-reaching plans — than she had ever been led to believe. Larger than any of the other Heroes she served with would believe, for that matter.

The realization had hit her, appropriately, like a train. The implications were even more frightening, because Texas wasn't the primary hub of Korps operations; that was in Canada. Texas was known to be a regional hotspot, but considerably further down the list than other areas of the country... which suggested the total Korps population to be something in the territory of *hundreds of thousands*. The Korps wasn't just a gang. It was starting to edge into *nation* territory.

Sure, only a fraction of those would be active supervillains. But the simple fact that the Korps had a civilian workforce meant, well... Celia talking about taking over the world wasn't just the idle fantasy of a delusional villain. It might be *possible*. They might actually take over the world, someday.

[*That **is** the plan, dear.*]

"I... suddenly believe you."

[*I hope you will be part of that. But the choice is yours. And you shouldn't make it now.*]

The warhorse lapsed into silence as she gazed at the tram, suddenly feeling a lot smaller.

The Percheron stared down at her bowl of unflavored grits with a frown. It wasn't precisely what she was used to, but the whole food court had made her intensely uncomfortable. Her strict Teepa diet had, for so many years. shaped her body into the very image of a superhero. Now, when offered the bewildering array of mouthwatering foods, she just couldn't bring herself to try any of it. What should have been heaven had instead been revolting.

Both Dawn and ROSE had beseeched her to try some of the stunning foods available, and that it would be *okay* to do so, that a tasty meal wouldn't ruin her. Even as she hated her body, the idea of losing all those years of exercise (and carefully calculated dietary intake) was too much.

When she had finally said no, they had respected her wishes, but both were clearly uneasy — even displeased? — about it.

Finally, she had taken the simple meal, because she had to eat *something*. Before she had done so, she had begged ROSE to help her speak with someone who could help her figure out her diet here. She was already regretting that cube from earlier. She glanced around the secluded area they were sitting in to distract herself.

The room continued the trend of Korps base aesthetics, with dark chrome and magenta being the primary color palette. Somehow, though, the effect was adjusted to be welcoming and relaxing, rather than dim and foreboding.

Or maybe I'm just no longer thinking of the Korps as my enemy.

This space was just off the main kiosk area of the food court, and screened from casual observation, but open entryways ensured it didn't feel closed off. The tables were adjustable, and the chairs had been designed for a variety of sizes and morphologies. The Percheron had only rarely seen that level of accommodation before — most often in higher-end public spaces like fancy restaurants and hotel lobbies.

She also wasn't used to the sheer amount of *greenery*. There wasn't any notable tropical theme to the many plants, and none seemed to be fake, as attested by the clear signs that some herbivores had supplemented their meals with the leafy decor. Instead, the plants just seemed to be integrated into the area, as part of the design.

Her reverie was cut short when Dawn nudged her. "Okay, ready to meet your first supervillain? She's almost here."

The fallen hero took a deep breath and nodded. She didn't know why she suddenly felt so apprehensive. She had gone into battle, perhaps even against these very villains, with none of the jitters that now seemed to be plaguing her. Never-the-less, she was stronger than her fears and she refused to let them sway her. She swallowed, taking a second breath and held it a moment before letting it flow out, taking the nerves with it.

She looked up just in time for a massive red wolf to step through the door. The villain towered close to three meters tall, with a powerful build supplemented by generous curves. The tight exercise shorts (and tighter T-shirt, with a magenta helix over the heart) were clearly chosen to show off *every* inch of her. The unzipped, black leather jacket framed her immense cleavage.

But it was the *eyes* that left no doubt who this woman was: black sclera surrounding magenta irises, seeming to bore right through her RCGs and into the horse. Her expression was guarded and stormy as she strode into the room. Her entire appearance was a challenge and a threat. This was a wolf ready to defend her territory and her friends.

The mare had heard much of Redline since her defection. They had even fought each other twice before in the streets. She was supposedly a once-promising recruit who had been seduced by the Korps, and turned into a murderous monster. After disappearing from the TPA academy in spectacular fashion, she had quickly risen to be one of the most prominent regional threats. Until that moment, the fallen hero had seen her as nothing more than what the Teepa claimed. She had seen the video… But she suddenly *understood*.

Here was someone who had been put through hell by the Teepa. This was no monster. She was just a woman who had suffered too much, and been crushed by a bureaucratic machine that sought only conformity. She had every right to be angry with the Heroes who had tried to force her into being who she wasn't.

The horse found herself sharing a deep kinship with this wolf… this *Volta*, as ROSE helpfully displayed. Both suffered greatly under an organization that did not and could not allow deviation from a strict norm. This meeting must be incredibly difficult for the younger woman. To be confronted by a former foe and the symbol of those that had caused her so much pain… and yet to still be here. Cautious, scared, but willing to offer an open hand.

The fallen hero stood up slowly, careful not to seem a threat. Her body posture relaxed and a slight, genuine smile crossed her lips. "Hi, Volta. It's… good to see you again."

The supervillain looked surprised at the words, but she remained cautious. "I heard you defected, but if ROSE hadn't been the one saying it I wouldn't have believed it. You seemed right at home as a Hero with those jackasses."

She grimaced but nodded. "It… took me a lot longer than you did to realize how cruel they really are, how much suffering they cause. How much they've hurt me... the state... *you*. I was so used to suffering that I didn't even realize that's what it even was. Turns out your taunts were right, that last time we were throwing down; I *am* dumb as a rock."

Volta blinked a bit, the conversation clearly not going as she had predicted. "I'm not arguing there. I heard you and Starshade took down Manifest Destiny. It also looks like you hit 'Up' during the character selection screen... am I reading things wrong, or are you gonna get yourself a rack later?"

The direct query left the percheron unaccountably blushing. She had been mentally dancing around the concept but with a single, blunt question, Volta had cut right to the heart of it. The air left her in a rush and she sat down hard. That same sense of unreality that had been haunting her seemed to redouble as she was suddenly forced to confront herself and her desires. Her voice, normally as deep and sure as the mountains, sounded tiny and distant. "Is that... possible?"

"Bitch, look at me!" The wolf gestured at her own powerful and generous figure. "You gotta hit up Empire sometime, they got exactly what you need. You think I just like, spontaneously grew two feet, three inches, with an ass that could flatten you?"

The mare was taken aback by the outburst. A thousand half-formed wishes and suppressed desires flitted through her memory. She hadn't dared to hope. With a throat suddenly aching, she had to swallow the urge to cry. The moment stretched out for what seemed like forever, but eventually she managed to contain herself before she nodded. "I... would like that. We all knew you changed, but not *how*. And in this business... well, what works for one doesn't necessarily mean it works for everyone. Powers are weird like that."

Volta pulled up a chair and sat down, her expression no longer quite so guarded. There was... pity in her eyes, but also welcome. "Sure are, but around here, the only limit to what you can do with your body is what you *want* for your body. I mean, long as you *want* to stick around," she said, flexing a hand and glancing at her own claws, aloof. "But if Dawn's got you by the reins, I doubt you're going anywhere else, right?"

The heavy felt her ears flushing, both at the thought of changing her body and at the memory of the dik-dik stroking her muzzle. She felt herself foundering for a response. She was saved, however, by Dawn. The tiny, pink-clad antelope had kept quiet until now, though looking very smug and with a gleam in her eye that unsettled the former hero. That perpetual smile dialed up in intensity but she turned her attention to the wolf. "Volta, I am just *delighted* to see you again. That jacket looks incredible on you, as always. Carmen mentioned that you really enjoyed the *muzzle* too?"

It was the red wolf's turn to squirm, a flush spreading to her ears as her tail began to wag vigorously. But she looked pleased all the same. "Oh, uh, *yeah*. It's — it's perfect."

The tiny antelope looked delighted, but the horse didn't like the mischievous glimmer in her wide, emerald eyes. "I hope you find the next toy even better."

Volta looked confused and alarmed. "Wait, next…? Carmen didn't mention another one."

Suddenly Dawn looked the picture of innocence. "*If* there *is* a next project! You know *all* my projects are kept in strict confidence. If there was *anything* of the sort, I could only discuss it with the commissioner."

The wolf looked desperate and a little too eager. "So you're saying there's something else you're working on?"

"I said nothing of the sort. I can neither confirm nor deny these accusations."

Volta's ears flagged. "You fucking tease."

Dawn opened her mouth to answer, but then looked to the entrance as a new figure walked in. The mare recognized her immediately though.

Lawful Neutral…? That's right, she defected last year. I saw the bulletin.

The demimorphic fox looked much the same as she had when she was still a Hero. She had a flat, furless face, missing the pointed muzzle of most foxes. Instead, she looked much like ancient people had before the divergence event, only with a tail and species-appropriate ears. It was a very rare condition and the subject of some stigma. She was very short, at about the height of Dawn, but the punster had a more solid, very muscular build.

Her size called special attention to her prodigious chest, though it had always made the warhorse uncomfortable to think about that. The vixen had been a frequent topic of conversation in the Teepa locker room. In the course of their duties, the two superheroes had occasionally crossed paths, but hadn't spent much time interacting until one of the national Hero conferences, where the mare had tried to be as respectful as she could to the EHA hero.

She was somewhat surprised that Ellen hadn't changed much, given what Volta had just said. Though that line of thinking was dangerous right now, so she wrenched her mind back to the present. The fox was wearing shorts and a t-shirt. As the mare opened her mouth to greet the woman, the block text of the shirt finally registered:

I BEAT MY BOSS HALF TO DEATH AND JOINED THE KORPS AND ALL I GOT WAS THIS T-SHIRT

A snort of laughter escaped the draft horse. She couldn't help it. The first genuine ghost of a smile in a long time crossed her lips.

"… It does come in a XXXXXXL. I checked," Ellen offered with a smirk and a kind tone.

"That isn't enough X's for my… weight class. But I'm certain the tailors around here are adept in production at scale," she offered.

"I have one of those shirts and I'm most of the way to your size, sugarcube," Volta mused.

The warhorse relaxed a little more. "It's nice to see you again, Ellen. It's been… what? Three years? Since that horrible conference on the potential alien invasion that turned out to be because someone in Hawaii hit the wrong button?"

Ellen groaned and shook her head. "The EHA was so cheap they didn't pay for our meals. I had to live off the refreshment table. That stuff was stale when we got there."

"You remember the photoshoot they had us do because you were the shortest hero there and I was the tallest? I spent an hour signing those damn pictures when we were *supposed* to be there to save the world."

Volta looked amused and interested, a half smirk on her lips. "Wait, you're telling me there are autographed pictures of the two of you? Doing what?"

The horse deflated a bit, sighing while Ellen brightened. "Playing into the whole horse thing."

The wolf's tail resumed its wagging as a mischievous smile started to play across her lips. "And now that *both* of you have defected, those pictures will probably be pretty cheap now…"

The fallen hero's heart sank a bit more as she saw the gleam in the eyes of each of the women now looking at her intently. But Ellen's expression turned speculative and the mare seized upon it. "Is everything okay?"

The fox's mouth pursed a bit before she answered. "Well... see, I'm trying to workshop a 'riding to the dessert on a horse with no name' joke, but that's one of those jokes that really works better over text."

The mare heavy blinked, suddenly overcome by the same feeling she had when she defused a bomb in the nick of time. "Ah. Yeah, too bad."

Ellen pouted at the tone but she didn't look offended. That meshed with her memories of the Hero. Funny and kind. She had never quite bought into the narrative that Ellen had snapped for no reason, and had almost killed her boss. Oh, the last part was true, but she had always suspected the hero must have had a *reason*.

The fallen hero wondered what sort of narrative they would spin about her own defection. She had no doubt that her attempted murder by her teammates would go carefully unmentioned. Her thoughts were interrupted by the arrival of another figure. The sheep-bear hybrid was tall and muscular, though nowhere near the height of herself or Volta; however, that frame carried a lot of extra softness over their powerful core. The red-accented black hair was cut short, showing off the curling horns.

The black vest and magenta t-shirt bearing the black helix logo both clung tightly to show off her frame. Black jeans that had clearly seen heavy use, and a pair of chunky motorcycle boots, completed the ensemble. She looked nervous, as if she was unsure she was in the right place. Her antelope guide perked up with interest at the new arrival and waved her over.

"Hi! I'm Dawn! Are you Maddy? Come on in and join us. You're in the right place!"

"Oh... yes! I'm Maddy. Celia asked me to come here and meet..." she turned her attention and scrutinized the horse. Then she smiled. "I mean, I guess we've already met? That one training seminar out in New Hampshire, hosted by the Granite Wall? I, uh... used to be called Heartforce, then."

The memory snapped into place. She hadn't spent much time with the Provincial Heroes' League. The Canadian teams did some cross-border training and team-ups, but most of those were either with the Bradley Group, or with neighboring state Hero teams. But there had been a couple of exceptions, and now she remembered the young telekinetic from the course. They hadn't interacted much, but their limited interactions had been cordial. She did recall that the rest of the Pegasus Phalanx had been very annoyed that she hadn't avoided them, but couldn't remember the details of why.

"Oh! Yes! You were part of... Ontario's Heroes? And... you're second-generation, right? One of your parents was a Hero?"

The sheep-bear nodded, grimacing. "Yeah. I defected last year. Decided I didn't like upholding Dad's *legacy* after all."

"You should talk to Starshade about that. Might have a lot in common. She... didn't want to uphold her mother's legacy either." Then an edge of black humor entered her voice as she continued almost unbidden. "I think her mom ended up getting the point in the end, though."

The horse felt bad about that last quip after saying it. She rubbed the back of her neck, trying to dredge up any other memories to help cement common ground, but both seemed to be falling into an awkward stage where there was just enough faded memory to establish connection but not enough to stand on.

The dik-dik piped up, clearly having been eager and too bubbly to sit the entire conversation out. "Maddy! Welcome to RIV. I heard you were staying with us for a little while after the ruckus. I'm Dawn, the local farrier, so if you need anything please don't hesitate to ask! ROSE can connect you. If you need anything done with your nails or horns, I'm happy to help!"

The Canadian looked embarrassed and shifted uneasily. "Oh, sure..." they trailed off, clearly intending to wave off the conversation. But they looked around and seemed to come to a decision. "Actually... Mom took me to a spa once when I was seventeen, and I saw their hoof girl with her, after the pedicurist who did claws couldn't figure out how to handle hybrid feet? And she was a lot better at it, honestly? So, uh, yeah, tell me more..."

The confession clearly had bothered the hybrid. Dawn looked delighted and moved to sit with Maddy. "There's no shame in not knowing something. That's how we all start and sometimes we aren't given the opportunity. What's important to understand is that hooves grow a lot faster, so shaping is more important. They are more susceptible to moisture but also that can keep them healthier. The focus needs to be more on forming the nails, not only to look good now, but with an eye to how the growth will happen."

The sheep-bear looked startled at the easy acceptance, and gazed down at her thick hands with new appreciation. "And look, here, hoof-nails like yours get a bad reputation, but that's because too many people just ignore them. But they have these amazing striations, and can take a lot more dedicated shaping than claws, for instance. What that means is that there are some extreme things you can do that just aren't possible for others."

The Percheron was secretly grateful that Dawn had taken over the conversation. She could feel it slipping away just as she had started to feel a profound interest in becoming friends with this Canadian villain. She just hadn't been sure how to start establishing that connection. Now that the ice was broken, it would be much easier to talk; with a start, she realized that the antelope had probably been planning to interject, for just that contingency.

She turned her attention back in time to see Volta groaning and holding her face while Ellen looked smug. The horse had clearly missed one of the punster's trademark quips. She was about to ask what she had missed when a column of smoke rapidly formed before her. Heroic instincts honed over years brought her to instant alert as the smoke coalesced into the form of a woman.

The catamount sat languidly on the table. One leg crossed the other clad in shiny leather pants that she had been poured into. A black racerback showed off her impressive figure and proudly proclaimed 'Hex The Patriarchy'. Black fishnet arm warmers and a black choker (complete with cracked gem) completed the goth look. She had an unlit cigar clamped between ebony lips.

The mare did not know this agent, but the easy confidence and clear use of powers clearly proclaimed her to be one. She reached up and drew the cigar out slowly, pink tongue darting out for a moment before she spoke. "Hey, sweetheart. I'm Mabel. Mabel Greysmoke. So *you* must be the pony that followed Starshade home…?"

The fallen hero nodded, remembering she was here to make friends and deliberately letting that combat alertness fade. "Yes. I suppose I am."

"Oh, *finally!* Well, here's the deal: you saved the bun, you have my everlasting gratitude. I'll be helping make sure you settle in, okay? Tell me what you need, and we'll figure it out, whatever it is!"

The horse blinked at the offer. The voice was filled with welcome and languid self-confidence. The mountain lion was clearly playing up the grace and smooth charm, but it had none of the slimy feel that Ethicoil had when he did the same. It felt... genuine.

"And Relly tells me that you haven't figured out a name yet?"

"Who's Relly?" she asked, but the expression on the catamount told her she was not focusing on the right part of that sentence. As did Volta's raised eyebrow. And ROSE helpfully scrolling text across her visor.

[That was not the important part of the question. I will explain Relly. Later.]

"Right. Sorry. No. I..." She trailed off. It was hard to fit into words. She wasn't sure how to encapsulate how *lost* she felt. She had carried the name Slate for her entire life. But it never *fit*. She had used it with vague distaste, always with a hint of a wish of a thought that she should find a better one. But she never had. It had always been *fine*. But it had never been fine. Not really.

She looked up, trying to put all of that into words. And she realized she didn't have to. Volta had done the same thing. As had Maddy. As had many others here. She saw understanding and compassion in the collected villains. Something she had never felt before.

It almost broke her, then. With titanic effort, she kept herself from falling apart. Tears threatened, but she could not unleash the deluge. Not yet. The only thing that kept her from passing that brink was the knowledge that she had finally found a place where she *could*. No one would judge her for it. Unable to speak for a moment as her throat closed and her vision swam, she nodded.

"Well then, sweetheart, let's figure one out for you. You can always change it later, but I think you'll be happier with even a temporary name." The depth of the compassion in those words almost undid her once more, but she took a deep, if shaky, breath and steadied herself.

"I… think that would be good. Yes." She was proud of herself for keeping the agony and desperation from her words. "I'd be happy to hear suggestions."

There was a moment of consideration as the atmosphere turned speculative. For her part, the horse was coming up blank. She had never undergone this exercise before and wasn't sure how to begin.

"Amethyst?" ventured Maddy.

She pondered the name, turning it over in her mind. Tasting it. Feeling if it fit over her… self. Finally, she shook her head. "It's too…" (*precious*) "… accurate."

"Rockbreaker." Volta seemed certain, but the horse shied away from how… rough it felt.

"Climbing Wall." Ellen was staring too intently at the Percheron when she offered the suggestion. Dawn gave her a suspicious glance, causing the punster to blush and study her nails.

"Gem? Or Gemstone? Maybe Opal?" Maddy had sat back in her seat, looking at the ceiling as they considered the question. The names did have some appeal and the fallen hero was warming to the suggestions. She quietly filed Gemstone away as a possible candidate.

"How about Krystal?" Mabel was clearly inspired by the sheep-bear's line of thought and her bright eyes were speculative.

"Krakatoa? Or Mount Fury?" Volta was clearly pondering fearsome names.

"Mount Hossmore." Ellen's cheeks remained pink as she tossed out the name.

"*No.*" Dawn batted down the suggestion with exasperation.

"Fine, Mount Hoss*less*!" Ellen's followup made the dik-dik bury her head in her hands.

Volta's eyes held a hint of amusement at the exchange and offered her own. "Bedrock."

"I suspect Ellen is down with anything that makes her Bedrock." Dawn quipped, deepening the flush that was burning so clearly on the demimorph's face.

"Grand Tetons," the giant wolf suggested with a grin.

"She hasn't gone to Empire yet," the antelope tossed back. "Might as well suggest Sugarcube."

"I suspect you're going to be calling her *that* soon, no matter what name she picks."

Unaccountably, the horse was blushing, as the suggestions started to travel further afield from her comfort zone. But it was Mabel who snapped her finger and pointed one clawed finger right at the mare's nose. "Geode."

Silence descended as the women pondered the suggestion. The horse pondered the name... testing it... feeling it...

"It's perfect. What's a geode? It's a giant stone egg that, when cracked open, reveals purple crystalline splendor. It's easy to say. It is intimidating on the battlefield but full of beauty in quiet moments. It's perfect."

"I don't know if it'll stick..." Geode said uncertainly.

"Oh, it'll stick." Mabel said confidently.

Chapter 7

Eruption Column

March 22, 2023

Fear raced through Jennifer as she sprinted down the street. As she desperately pushed herself to escape the alligator superhero behind her, she cursed her choice of heels, her aging body, how much she'd been slacking on cardio workouts, and how stupid she had been. Panic had gripped her in the opening moments of the flight, and she'd fled blindly, only to later realize that she had moved *away* from her car... with no easy way to circle back to it. Not without giving Everblades the opportunity to cut her off, *literally*.

The sound of heavy boots was growing closer. The heavy reptile might have been an old man, but he was a veteran of the streets, and still in excellent shape. A glance over her shoulder showed that infernal red glow, still burning fiercely in the gator's murderous gaze. His forearms had extended and lengthened into gleaming blades of bone-white, curved down to a killing point.

Jennifer pivoted and took a corner hard, trying to throw off her pursuer. The Hero (almost in a daze!) turned to follow too soon, and slammed into the brick corner. His blade arm seemed to reflexively slash into the wall, pulverizing a brick in a spray of red dust. Though Everblades stumbled, he resumed the chase with no signs of injury — or, for that matter, conscious thought.

The superhero that had starred in anti-drug commercials in her youth — who had even graced a poster on her childhood bedroom wall, when she had entered her rebellious phase — now seemed a rabid, mindless animal. That didn't stop his wicked organic blades from being any less deadly. As if to demonstrate, the Hero casually cut through a stop sign, with no sign of effort or concern. The red metal hexagon tumbled to the street with a foreboding rattle.

*Think, Jennifer, Think. Or he's going to **kill** you…!*

She knew deep down that she was going to *die*, if she didn't *do* something. But no immediate salvation presented itself, and she frantically continued looking for something, *anything*, that might offer her protection.

…He doesn't corner well, but he's faster than I am. I need to use that.

An abandoned construction site flashed past on her right, followed by her mind finally registering a slight change in the perimeter fence. Unbidden, her legs surged with a burst of speed. With a frantic desperation, and filled with half-remembered memories of her long-gone rebellious youth, she ducked through a gap in a chain-link fence too small for the gator to fit through.

Then, she was hauled up short, as her blazer snagged a ragged wire. She heard and *felt* the material of her favorite suit rip. Jennifer pulled against her trap, driven by pure animalistic desperation, knowing that death was mere moments behind her, but despite the sound of ripping fabric she remained caught.

With a cry of frustrated betrayal, she threw everything she had into forcing her way forward, terrified. Far too slowly, accompanied by a wet tearing noise, she pulled away. Just as she was sure she was doomed, the jacket gave out; she stumbled, and barely sprinted forward as Everblades fruitlessly slashed where she had just been.

There was a roar of primal frustration, though, as the berserker crashed his bulk into the fence, unable to figure out how to get past. Jennifer's frantic flight carried her precious meters before the maddened Hero began to take the path of least resistance, hacking into the chain-link barrier like a machete through dense foliage. Even though her back and shoulder alerted her to the stinging cuts incurred in the gambit, she cherished the precious moments she had gained as the mindless hero cut his way through the metal.

Okay, okay. I know this area. What can I do?

She thought about seeking help, but from *who*? If she found another Hero, they might lose their mind too, and then she'd have *two* murderous capes to escape from. The cops would be useless; they might even try to detain her before they realized the danger — or, worse, they might ignore her pleading desperation, and summon Heroes themselves. Civilians would just add their deaths to her conscience.

No. **No.** *I have to deal with this myself.*

She leapt over a long-abandoned pile of rusted rental bikes. Her landing was hard, and she could feel one of her heels shift worryingly; she wobbled, but kept running. The mindless hero had less luck as he tried to plow through, only to catch a foot and tumble forward. Still, superhero reflexes honed over almost fifty years had not faded. The fall became a roll, which turned into a sprint once more.

She had to *think.*

Then it dawned on her where she was. She had a destination…!

All her efforts to gain distance were being worn away, as she began slowing down unbidden from exhaustion, while the Hero seemed to have no such issue. Remembering his difficulty predicting and cornering, Jennifer's paw flashed out and wrapped around a passing sign pole, using it to slingshot her way around a corner at the last minute. The stitch in her side warned that she was reaching the last of her reserves, however, and that she would soon have to decisively *act.*

The yellow police tape on the doorway screamed WARNING — DO NOT CROSS, but instead felt like a beacon of salvation. She prayed to long-forgotten deities that the vague memories of her last visit had been accurate, as she threw her shoulder against the battered metal door numbered 329.

Her heart leapt as the door burst open, and banged against the wall loud enough to reverberate through the room. The interior was dark, with enough ambient light from the hole in the ceiling to make the catering kitchen a riot of gloom and shadow.

The same kitchen where she had been *branded*, mere nights ago.

The room was still a ruin, filled with twisted metal, broken appliances, and the increasingly-pungent stench of food left to rot; the nutria suppressed a gag as her sensitive nose picked up the damp scents of spoiled meat and mold. None of the lights were on, but the ambient light from outside showed that little had changed since Sunday. Sunday, the day everything had fallen apart…

But dwelling on her memories would not magically keep her pursuer from entering this place. With no time to get more than a vague impression, she stumbled to the side and grabbed the door's lever handle just as she heard the blue-and-silver-uniformed reptile reach the building. She slammed the steel portal closed as hard as she could. The metal slammed into the gator's muzzle with a crunch, but his blades still pierced the door, slicing through the too-thin material and ripping it from its hinges.

Jennifer stumbled backwards, trying to keep the debris of the central prep island between herself and the crazed hero. The last time she had been here, a dying elephant shrew had cursed her. She had seen that man die, leaving his brand upon her arm. Her cursed fate would be beyond cruel if she was to return here only to die herself.

The rodent shook off the panic that threatened. She didn't have *time* for it. Her breath whistled in and out through her orange teeth. The nutria felt trapped and outmatched, but she forced herself to think. This was a kitchen. A ruined one, yes, but her job, her *career*, had been all about public health and occupational safety. She knew a thousand ways someone could die in a kitchen like this.

Too bad the power is out.

Unfortunately, too many of those methods were far too slow to help her now. It wouldn't matter if Everblades died of salmonella, if she had been skewered two weeks earlier. Many of the others required a kitchen in operation; right now, there was no conveniently boiling stock pot on the stove, or sizzling grill waiting to sear the unwary. And though she was certain there was *dangerously* worn electrical wiring in the vintage appliances, it did no good without current flowing through it.

Still, there were things she knew about *this* kitchen. She reached behind her blindly, trusting her memory and instincts. Her clawed hand closed around a large plastic jug, and she pulled it out. The darkness was such that she couldn't read it, but the weight told her it was full, and there were only a few things it could possibly contain. Her claws raked through one side of the bottle, and then she hurled it at the gator.

Vegetable oil spilled out of the four neat holes she had punched, coating the floor between herself and the bladed protector. The instinct of the maddened Hero did the rest as he sliced cleanly through the container. Slick oil poured over him, turning his dull green scales glossy… and extremely slippery. The hero took one unwary step — discovering the hard way that traction was important to his pursuit — and his boot slid away.

Years of finely-honed instinct appeared to keep Everblades from simply tumbling to the ground, no matter how much Jennifer desperately hoped otherwise. Still, it was clear that he was struggling. She eyed the chef's knife near her. Her paw itched to wrap around the handle of the sharp blade, but the rational part of her realized that such a plan was suicide. There was simply no way she could match her opponent's skill and reach. She decided on another course of action.

Jennifer feinted towards the dagger, her face telegraphing her goal. The gator moved to intercept, but found his footing fouled by the oil that coated him and the floor. In the precious moments he spent steadying himself, she spun the other direction and ran to the wall. Though hidden by the gloom, she knew the metal rungs that led to the second floor might be her only escape.

Her lips formed desperate pleas that she did not have the breath to voice as she started to scramble up the ladder. The climb was much harder than she realized; her heels were a hindrance, and her left hand, too, was still slick with oil. But death was the only prize for failure, so she pulled herself up rung after rung.

The hero had not been idle. Though slowed down, he reached the base of the ladder and swiped at her. Only luck saved her, as the blade deflected off a metal rung. Still, she felt the metal trace a line of fire across the back of her calf. For a horrible moment she thought that it was the end —- visions of her limb simply falling away, like she had seen a hundred times in cheap action films, playing through her mind — but her leg kept responding.

She burst through the hatch at the top, finding herself in a dusty, forgotten second floor. Jennifer had never been in this part of the building before. By the years of undisturbed grime, it looked like no one else had either, lately. Fleeing into a pitch-dark, unknown building from a murderous hero was not something she felt, on balance, was a great idea.

Not that she had many good ideas left. Or *any* ideas left.

It was there, as she stared off into the darkness, that her heart fell. It was a terrible plan, it was a *dumb* plan, but she saw no other way.

Boots and hands on metal rungs told her that the gator was climbing after her. His arms had turned back into, well, *arms*, in order to climb. For this brief moment, the Hero was vulnerable. This was her only chance. Desperate pleas to the universe slipped from her lips, wishing more than anything that fate would take pity upon her and preserve her, despite her reckless plan. She took two steps and jumped... straight down the hole she had just climbed up.

Everblades looked up, red eyes glowing with murder, just in time to see eighty kilos of nutria spearheaded by twin high heels crashing into his face. There was a sickening *crack* as she tumbled a full story to the ground below, but the world was moving too fast for Jennifer to process anything more than a painful, chaotic tumble to the floor.

The impact jarred her to the bone; there were too many sensations, and the room was too dark for her to make sense of the situation. She tried to scramble away, but her body wasn't *working* and something was wrapped around her.

Then her arm *pulsed.* Fire shot up her left side as the entire scar lit up with molten agony. It was worse than when she had been branded the first time.

She screamed. She couldn't help it.

The pain intensified further. Her screaming stopped — not for lack of pain, but simply running out of breath. The line of torture continued up her arm, passing her elbow. Lights danced in her eyes in bright white flashes—

—Then, just as suddenly, the infernal torment vanished, leaving her panting for breath and blinking away tears. She whimpered in remembered anguish and fear. Somehow she was standing and backing away, blinded by the gloom and terror.

Arms grabbed her shoulders, and she gave a half-scream. She knew at that moment she was about to die. Her last thought was a desperate plea for justice in an uncaring universe. Her heart seized painfully as she tasted bitter betrayal.

But death did not come.

Instead, those arms pulled her into a safe hug. Through the roaring in her ears, she distantly heard someone whispering that she was okay, that it was *over*. It took a while for her to understand, and longer until her mind calmed down enough to believe. Tony was there, holding her close.

They were still in the ruined kitchen. But her brain was working again, even if she hadn't yet caught her breath; there just didn't seem to be enough air for her to fill her lungs. She didn't know how long she simply trembled, pressed against the cervine, before she found the strength to look behind her, towards where he was staring.

There, in the gloom of destroyed commercial cookware and appliances, at the base of a ladder, she saw... *something*. For a long moment, her brain simply refused to process what she was seeing. She knew it was protecting her; if she looked away, she would never have to acknowledge the horror. But she *had* to know. With an effort, she forced herself to see.

Only then did she take in the *skull*.

A full alligator skeleton lay crumpled on the ground. The remnants of a blue-and-silver uniform confirmed this was not just some random body. The bones looked old, as if they had been laying there for years. All the surrounding metal had rusted away, covering the area in a red dust. But she *knew*.

Everblades was dead. *She* had killed him.

She could also feel the brand. It extended further up her arm now, past the elbow, growth surging when she had killed the Hero. Her stomach twisted and the back of her tongue tasted sour. She didn't know what to do.

"Is... is that Everblades?"

She nodded mutely. She didn't have a voice. Not now.

"Did you kill him?" His voice was hollow and distant. Shock was clear in his voice.

A whimper escaped her, but she nodded again.

"Was he the one after you?" A sob wrenched its way out of her, but shook her head violently.

"Oh my God! What is going on?" he asked but shook his head as he took in the shock and horror on her face. "You know what, no, never mind, don't answer that now."

The silence stretched out. She had no energy left. No reserves. Nothing.

"Let's get you out of here."

Tony led her from the building, into the sunlight that seemed much dimmer, now, than it had moments before.

Chapter 8

Lithification

March 22, 2023

"Wait, you've *never* played *HeroClash?!*" Volta sounded shocked and indignant.

Mabel and Ellen almost looked affronted at the admission. After Geode had found her name, the gathering had fragmented into various conversations as the women got to know the newest horse and each other, including their hobbies — but her response to Mabel's casual question had apparently been a misstep, though she was confused as to why.

"They just licensed my likeness, from Teepa…? I never really thought about it afterwards."

Ellen looked almost wounded, though the tone of her voice suggested some of the bitterness was directed elsewhere. "But, you're a *major* character. You come in the *base* game. You aren't just a *region-locked DLC* character."

The horse clearly understood that she was missing something. But she couldn't figure out what. "Yeah? So…?"

"So… there are sixty-four characters in the base game," Volta patiently started to explain, her voice filled with import as if imparting essential, life-or-death information. "You appear alongside some of the biggest names in the world, like True North II. You may have started as a DLC character back in HeroClash 5, but you were such a fan favorite that you became a *staple* character."

Geode blinked. "But I am… I *was*… a mid-tier regional Hero. Why am I such a big deal in this game?"

"You're extremely approachable! Good stats, great reach, solid grapple game, durable. Anyone can pick up Slate and do *well*, but a master can be a *monster*. In HC6, you were honestly a little broken. HC8 rebalanced some other characters, pushing you into the mid-tier, and there's a lot of complaints demanding you be patched. Not so many Slate mains winning tournaments any more, but it's rare to see a tournament that doesn't have a few getting through the first couple rounds."

The horse was aware that all of those were words, and most of them were in a language she was at least passingly familiar with, but she had no idea what any of it meant. Though she hadn't considered it much, she suddenly realized that many of the autographs she signed *had* been on copies of the game, and those requests had been more frequent than the usual glossy headshots from the Teepa PR department. It slowly dawned on her that her teammates had almost never been asked to sign the slim game cases.

"I had no idea," she confessed, with an apologetic half-smile and a shrug.

"We have to fix this," Mabel declared — less to Geode than to the others, who nodded in perfect unison.

"Absolutely," Dawn said. There seemed to be a general consensus as a chorus of agreement echoed.

After a moment, Mabel asked. "So if you haven't played HeroClash, what games *do* you play?"

The Percheron shifted in her chair. The pause dragged out, turning uncomfortable before she finally answered. "Well… a couple of the guys had me try Madden in the Army, but it was confusing and the controller was so tiny… so I figured that video gaming didn't seem to be for me."

"Oh." The single syllable from Maddy seemed to sum up the collected sentiment.

"Video games… aren't all just like Madden," Mabel stated, with the careful tone of someone showing extreme restraint. "We'd be happy to teach you."

Geode looked for a moment at the catamount she had just met, surprised by the kindness she — and the others — had shown. It felt strange to be so easily welcomed in. "I…" she started to wave off the offer, but stopped herself. It took her a moment to realize how desperately she wanted these new faces to like her. "I would like that. Thank you." She frowned slightly, not able to really fit the meaning she wanted to convey into the simple words.

"If you don't play video games, what are your hobbies?" Dawn asked, genuinely interested. The tiny antelope had directed intense scrutiny towards the equine the entire meeting. She was surprisingly flattered, because she didn't get any sense of hostility; rather, just that the diminutive woman was simply trying to figure her out.

She opened her muzzle to answer, then paused. No words came to her. The moment began to stretch out, becoming uncomfortable. Lamely, she gave the only answer she could. "I was a superhero. That was a full-time job."

As the uncomfortable pause continued, Geode tried to explain further. "I mean... when I wasn't on patrol, I'd exercise. Extensive combat training. Reviewing intel briefs, studying threats, that was always important. Spending time with the nutritionists took up a lot of time every day, so I could look my best for the public. Taking my turn as the duty Hero at dispatch." She shrugged. "Crime never sleeps."

That last line hadn't been intended as a joke, but everyone else shared a look and a ripple of laughter filled the room. Volta slapped her shoulder, hard, rocking her slightly. "Look, sugarcube. Swing by Empire. When you get out of the tank, when you are finally *you*, I demand a rematch."

Geode blinked at the offer, memories of the pain coursing through her from their two fights. Electricity *hurt*. But the idea of sparring with this wolf was suddenly... exciting. Still, the outcome of those previous battles had always been part of her shame as a hero. Proof that she would never be more than a mid-tier powerhouse. "But... you beat me each time we fought. And I wasn't alone those times. We both know who's going to win..."

"First, it's not about finding out who's better. We both know that's me. Second, I want to see you fight when you aren't constrained by the chains of what the *Teepa* wanted you to be. But, really, sparring isn't about finding out who's best. It's about honing yourself. You *know* that, no matter what those jackasses tried to drill into you."

The warhorse was taken aback by the earnest eagerness from the younger wolf. Unaccountably, she wanted to cry once again; she'd wept more times in the past few hours than she had in decades. But her lips spread with a genuine, honest smile, muzzle aching at the unfamiliar sensation. "I'd like that."

Maddy chimed in. "I'd love to spar with you too, if that's okay? I've gotten a bit rusty, and would love to fight against someone in your... durability class."

The horse blinked, seeing the clear interest in the sheep-bear's expression. She found the answer remained the same. "Oh, yes. Of course. I'd be happy to." Moreover, she was surprised to find herself looking forward to staying, and learning about these people. Making *friends*. She was starting to get the sense that she had finally, *finally* found a place where she didn't have to carry the world. Maybe, just maybe, she could stop being the pillar of reality, if only for a little while.

"On the topic of sparring partners..." Mabel's bravado didn't quite hide a touch of desperation, and a touch of hurt, though she hid it well. "How is Starshade? They won't let me see her, but Relly mentioned you spoke with her earlier today."

A grimace pursed her lips but she nodded. "Yeah. They told me she'll be okay. That's the important thing. She's going to be fine. But... the fight with Manifest Destiny left her badly hurt. They're giving her cybernetic lungs, I guess? Was weird talking to her when she was a synthetic nurse."

The catamount had clearly been preparing for the worst, but the last sentence drew everyone's attention. Geode lapsed into silence as she was once more the center of attention. Slowly, after searching her face, Mabel asked carefully. "She was what?"

The horse rubbed at the back of her close-cropped mane, feeling the stiff bristles as she often did when she was nervous. She never quite understood why it made her feel a vague sense of loss. "She was too injured to fully bring her to consciousness, so they let her borrow the body of one of the fox synths, I guess? Is that common here?"

The incredible intensity of the collected staring told her that it was not, in fact, a common occurrence. After a long, uncomfortable moment, the other villains shared a look.

"How the hell does Starshade end up in these situations?" Mabel asked with bewilderment.

"I am more shocked that there's someone on this base who ends up in more trouble than you do. When can I meet her?" Volta half-jokingly shot back, though still clearly confused about the situation.

"Shut it, waff." Mabel started without heat, but whatever comeback she was working on was stepped on by further speculation.

"I've never heard of anyone else piloting a Nurse O chassis. I didn't even know it was possible." Ellen sounded disconcerted, not quite paying attention to the bickering between the red wolf and the catamount.

"Cybernetic lungs... do you think she's going..." Dawn started, but trailed off in speculation.

Mabel sighed heavily, shaking her head and taking a breath to settle herself. "So, Geode, how *did* you end up defecting? How did you know Starshade? All we knew was that you were a random hero who let her go after capturing her. Then all hell breaks loose and when we get back to base, we find out that Starshade is... in the medbay. And that *you* fought beside her to stop some undoubtedly heroic plan before following her home like a lost foal. Days later, we get a polite request to come help the new girl settle in. So, I will ask you, *hort*, politely, *what the hell happened?*"

Geode stared at the outburst. The catamount had clearly been dying to ask the question all day; she had hid the desperate anticipation well, behind jokes and a casual attitude. But more than anything, the realization of what had been simmering endeared her to the villain. She could sympathize with that curiosity, as she too had it denied so many times. None of that helped her answer the question, though.

"Oh... yeah. She... she helped me figure a few things out. We helped each other a bit. Now I'm here."

All the other women present stared at her with a collective mixture of mild exasperation and annoyance at the understatement. She blushed a bit, before offering a bit more. "I... uh... let her go after I caught her. And... when the Teepa tried to murder me for that, she saved me. We fought together. Took down Manifest Destiny. Stopped the Teepa plan. So I didn't have anywhere else to go. So... yeah. I really did... just... follow her home, I suppose."

The cougar glared at her for a long moment before she sighed and patted her shoulder. "There's more to that story, sweetheart, and I'm going to get it out of you one day." There was a silent threat to that soft spoken statement, but Geode took no offense. So much had happened that evening that encapsulating it all seemed impossible.

"I'm not sure where to even begin. I just did what any good Hero would do." She could feel it slip out, knowing it was the wrong thing to say to this group. It was just a phrase that she had uttered so many times for so many years that it was ingrained. She winced, waiting for the worst. And she was surprised when it didn't come.

Mabel smiled at her sadly and shook her head. "No, you did what a good *villain* would do. Which is what you *are*, now. Whether you like it or not. But I, for one, am much happier with you on this side of that coin."

Still embarrassed at her faux pas, she looked away, blushing. "Er... sorry. Just... a lot has changed for me. I'm still trying to adjust. Last night... er... earlier this week was a nightmare that never seemed to end. It's hard realizing that you're on the wrong side... and always have been."

"I mean... not *necessarily*." Ellen cut in, compassion in her voice, though with a touch of defensiveness. "Heroes aren't all bad. They do some really important things."

Volta and Mabel both bristled at the comment, turning to look at the demimorph. The giant wolf's voice held certainty and an edge of anger, though it was distant and not targeted at the punster. "Like hell, Standup. Heroes are just there to protect the rich. That's why we're out there fighting them. They stand in the way of making the world better."

The fox pursed her lips but didn't back down. She shifted, willing to defend her position. "Like... *yes*, the big Hero groups are bad. I know that. But... they still do *actual* good. There are real people out there who have had their lives saved by Heroes. They help out after natural disasters. And when the *really bad* villains show up, they're there to stop them."

Mabel snorted. "Most of which are caused by the wealth they protect. Natural disasters are worse because of rampant climate change, and because people are forced to live in vulnerable areas. The 'really bad' villains show up because they're mad with power that income inequality gives them, or got fucked up by the system the rich fucks made."

Desperate, clearly frustrated that she wasn't getting her point across, she turned to Maddy, who had been trying to look inconspicuous. "Not all disasters are caused by climate change. There are real, heartbreaking emergencies that hurt real people. Heroes are *essential* in helping with that."

But the sheep-bear shook their head. "Look, I've done that work. I've helped clear highway accidents, put out fires, that kind of thing. I once saved someone who tried to kill himself jumping off the Bloor Viaduct. But that's mostly not what my teammates were actually *doing*. They didn't like taking those calls from dispatch; they preferred the ones from the cops, or just patrolling for petty crime. Anyway, that's kind of gross as public policy, isn't it? Relying on the off-chance that a Hero with *exactly* the right powers happens to be available in the area, rather than the government funding boring, non-powered emergency response plans?"

The demimorph looked flustered. "I know Ontario's Heroes was using you for a shitty shield against calls for change, but being the LGBTQIA+ Champion *meant* something to a lot of people, didn't it? I read that interview! There were gay and trans-friendly reforms that happened because of it. And it meant other Heroes could come out with less fear of retaliation!"

Maddy squinted. "Did *you*?"

Ellen fell silent for a moment, ears splayed.

"I… was *hoping* to. Someday. Jack was…"

Maddy blew out a breath and pursed her dark ursine lips. "It's worse than that, though. It was just… *pinkwashing*. I was a stunt to distract the media, so they'd have cover to keep hurting or ignoring queer people, after they took all that flak for what happened with Sunrise. I let myself believe I could make a difference to that, somehow, do something to change minds in the Hero game. Just by being, you know, *one of the good ones*. Like, I knew, before I agreed to being their goddamn *Champion*, that queer people who encountered Heroes were a lot more likely to end up injured or arrested; so I tried to do things the right way, and educate my teammates. Diversity training and shit, not that it helped. But once I was out there trying to convince the community that, hey, OH is safe and isn't going to hurt you, and then the LGBTQ2+ people who believed me ran into the OH operatives who spent that whole training snickering about 'identifying as an attack helicopter'… what do you think happened then?"

Ellen looked deeply bothered by the revelation. It was clear that she felt that she wasn't being heard. "Geode, you were a hero for eight years. You've helped *save the world*. None of us would be here if it weren't for Heroes."

The room went silent as she opened her mouth to respond, then closed it, thinking the question through. Thinking over what she had just heard. Trying to come to terms with her own past. Finally, she looked back and shrugged. "The way I see it... there *are* good things that the Heroes do. We... *they*... *do* save the world. But what they're saving is the status quo; they're actively preventing that world from getting better. The good that Heroes do is... incidental to that goal. And if the corrupt Hero teams didn't exist, that doesn't mean no one would be around to do those very same things."

She shrugged massive shoulders, not really looking at the others. Her attention was within. "Other groups, like the Korps, could stand up. Be the protectors of a world *worth* saving. I look back at my life and... I can only see a single moment where I actually made the world a better place in all my time as a Hero. And that's when I let Starshade go. The best thing I could do as a Hero was to... *not* be one, anymore."

Everyone lapsed into silence after she finished speaking. Ellen was clearly troubled by the conversation but, to her credit, she didn't seem to take it personally or storm out. But the topic had Geode thinking about her time fighting crime. Finally, she ventured to ask a question of her own that had been eating away.

"What's been happening with the Phalanx?"

Maddy chimed in, evidently happy they could contribute. "From what I've heard, there hasn't been much word about your team specifically? You were listed as missing, which is unsurprising. It's hardly the first time there's been a delay in admitting someone defected; OH hasn't even reported me AWOL to the public, as far as I know, and it's been *months*. Anyway, most of the Dallas news is about the death of Fatal Thorns, and the sudden retirement of Manifest Destiny."

Geode sighed. She had expected the death of Starshade's mother, given her state, but it would not make things easy for the cottontail. But something bothered her about the explanation.

"The Phalanx lost two heroes. That's the signature Dallas team. That *has* to be making the news."

The others stared at her. Volta cocked her head to the side. "Two?"

A chill shivered down her spine. The Percheron figured that even if the Korps hadn't announced it, that the news would be filled with reports about the death of another member of her former team. Even if they were delaying the final announcement, the team would have to be benched for a while and that news couldn't be delayed.

"You know... Ethicoil. Celia... killed him."

A stillness spread across the room and the other villains glanced at each other. It was Mabel who spoke up. "Ethicoil isn't dead."

But she was shaking her head. "Celia petrified him. Turned him to stone. Tossed him off a roof. He's dead. He must be."

Ebony lips pursed. But there was certainty in her tone. "Ethicoil was on TV this morning, talking about the attacks. He was talking nonsense about how much an inspiration Manifest Destiny was and how he had earned his retirement. He doesn't *look* dead."

Geode stared back. It was always possible that death wasn't permanent, but the petrification and shattering of her erstwhile teammate had been pretty definitive. "Show me."

A window popped up in her vision, playing news footage. A coral snake in a blue and white uniform was happily telling a reporter that the higher than average number of superhero fights hadn't been anything more than just a busy night. But as she watched, a sense of cold foreboding settled over her. He looked like her former teammate... but something was wrong.

She had ROSE bring up other feeds, ignoring the looks of growing concern from the women around her. Finally, with haunted certainty, she paused the video on a still image showing the scaled Hero, smiling like the proverbial snake oil salesman.

"That's... not Ethicoil. That's someone else."

Chapter 9

Continental Shield

March 22, 2023

The air was cool and crisp in the sky over St. Louis. He always loved this type of weather. Others complained that it was bitterly cold, but it felt perfect to the reindeer as he soared above the city. So far, his visit had been mostly uneventful; his biggest annoyance was that the iconic arch was *absurdly* reflective, and would focus the sun like the defensive lasers of Doctor Oculus. He was quickly discovering the importance of adjusting his flight path based on the angle of the sun.

He privately thought that was precisely the lesson the National Hero Administration intended him to learn during his stop here. Since joining the prestigious national hero team the previous year, he'd been traveling across the country. He usually only spent a few days at each town, national treasure, or point of interest unless there was additional training or special activities scheduled.

The tour — the 'operational experience rotation' — was an essential part of joining the prestigious superhero organization. It let the Bradley Group evaluate their newest members, by putting them in a variety of real-world situations, ones that training scenarios could never match. Just as importantly, the Heroes learned more about the country and the cities they would be called upon to protect.

Up here, flying above the city, Rockfall couldn't keep the grin off his muzzle. He had been a provisional member of the NHA for almost a year now and it still felt unreal. The caribou had dreamed of this his entire life. But now, here, with the gold uniform shining in the spring sun, black cape flowing behind him, he *felt* like a hero. His reverie was broken when a chirp came over the radio.

"Rockfall, this is STL HQ. Be advised we are getting reports of an explosion on the Chain of Rocks Bridge."

Adrenaline flooded through him as his lazy, aimless flight became a sharp turn and swift dive. "Acknowledged. I'm en route. What happened?"

"Based on reports, it appears to be a terrorist attack. Witnesses say a bomb went off. The whole structure started to shudder before a loud boom. Dust sprayed into the air. It's nearly rush hour, and the bridge is packed with civilians."

A chill settled over him, and a shudder worked its way down his spine. If the structure collapsed… well, he wasn't going to let that happen. He poured every ounce of speed into his flight, heedless of the sonic boom that shook the city, hoping to make it in time.

The span came into view then. Dust hung in the air above the far end of the structure. He could see that side slowly, inexorably sliding downwards; a number of supports near the break looked shattered, threatening to plunge half the span into the Mississippi. He had moments before disaster turned into tragedy.

The fierce urge to save lives spurred him to find a new burst of speed. The river blurred beneath him before he shot under the bridge.

He saw it, then. Concrete fell like rain as the unimaginable weight of the bridge pressing against the support structure crumbled. Black gloves slammed into the underside of the structure, just before the break.

Thousands of tons of four-lane highway pressed down on him. The cold concrete was heavy enough that he could feel the grain through his gloves. It felt like he was trying to hold the *world*. For a moment, he hovered there in all his golden glory, in the air, holding the immense structure. But then he felt himself being forced downwards.

"HQ! Please! I can't hold it! We have to get the civilians off the bridge!"

"Platinum Blade is almost there. Just hold on."

The bridge continued to press him down. He could feel himself being forced toward the water, inch by inch. His fingers bit into the concrete, showering him in gray flakes of aged infrastructure, as every muscle on his massive body bulged. Breath whistled wetly through clenched teeth, fogging the air in front of him. The blood pounding in his ears shut out the rest of the world as his existence narrowed down to *holding on*.

A whimper escaped his lips when he felt his hooves touch the ground next to the pillar. He couldn't even muster the shame of making such a weak noise as desperation surged in his heart, feeling as he could the immeasurable weight bearing down upon him. Slowly, inexorably, his arms started to bend, as he approached the limits of his powers. If he let go now, the bridge would pivot into the water, dropping the people above into frigid doom.

The bottom of the bridge touched his broad antlers. Concrete chipped as each point of his rack was forced into the rough surface. The realization was distant at first, as one of his knees hit the ground. Some deep part of him knew this was how he was going to die, a pale shadow of the Atlas he styled himself after, but he kept struggling, muscles bulging, thews straining; still, it wasn't enough.

Then silver flashed in front of his eyes, and with a thunderous **CRACK—**

—Instantly, the weight lifted, just before a tremendous, eternal, world-ending crash washed over him.

It took a long moment before he could make sense of the world again. Rubble filled the river before him, sinking into the foaming water. He still held up a small section, but the rest of the bridge had collapsed into the Mississippi. He stared dumbly at the ruin for a long moment.

He only then realized that the break was perfectly clean; it hadn't broken, it had been sheared off, cut right through. Almost as an afterthought, he set the titanic chunk of road he still held down, to his side. The reindeer turned his head automatically when he heard a clapping noise.

Standing next to him on the bank was a scimitar oryx wearing a white and silver uniform. Her pale fur was offset only by those distinctive faded gray facial markings common to her species. White horns curved away gracefully. Though much shorter than the titanic reindeer, she still stood tall with the perfectly-honed body of an acrobat.

It was her featureless platinum eyes that bore into him and made him feel tiny, however. A new thrill of fear traveled through him and he reflexively swallowed. But his heroic mouth was moving faster than his self preservation could stop him.

"What happened?"

"I cut the bridge, *rookie*. Before it *killed* you." Her voice was ice and cut like the telekinetic sword that was her namesake. Platinum Blade held no sympathy in her expression. Rockfall might have been a meter taller than the NHA Regional Training Officer, but in the moment, he felt *tiny*.

"Oh. Did… everyone get off in time?" His voice was tiny and distant as his gaze turned towards the roiling river, still bubbling and surging from the immense structure that had just fallen into it.

"Mostly. A few stragglers didn't, but if they were too stupid to get off the bridge after all the time you bought them, that's their fault. Legal will quietly negotiate settlements and pay off the families, while the comms team drafts some big statement about the 'sanctity of life' and 'the tragedy that Heroes can't protect everyone.' That's how these things usually go."

With dawning horror, he stared at her. Then whipped his head back to the river, eyes frantically searching for survivors or cars or…

"Rookie!" The oryx snapped, a cold fury in her voice that managed to stop his impulse to leap into action. "What did you *think* you were *doing?*" Each word seemed chipped from a glacier.

"Uh…"

"The moment you felt your hooves touch down, you should have leapt clear. Had I not been here, you *would* have been crushed. You would have saved *no one*, ever again. You try your best to save civilians, yes, but the most important thing is that you *stay* alive, to *keep* doing it. *You* are more important than *they* are."

He flushed at the dressing down, but he couldn't argue. She was right. He couldn't help anyone if he was dead. Still, he looked over at the Mississippi river with a sick heart. People had just died, right here, because *he* hadn't been strong enough.

"Now, *rookie*, get out of here. I'll take over here for the cleanup. Patrol is over for today. Get a shower, and be ready to make a stoic, sorrowful statement to the press tonight. Command will send over your script."

With that, the scimitar oryx turned away, and started walking to the gathered police and media he hadn't even realized were here. He looked one last time at the muddy waters before soaring off into the sky.

Harrison Sturzstrom, known to the world as Rockfall, rested against the cool tile of the palatial bathroom. As was expected, the luxury hotel had been all too pleased to provide the visiting Hero a presidential suite, free of charge. (Free to him, anyway. The whole thing was part of some marketing deal between Bradley and the hotel chain.) The fact that it was the only room in the hotel that could reasonably accommodate the gigantic reindeer went unremarked upon by all parties.

He frowned as he stared at the ceiling. The death toll had been very low; only a couple people hadn't been able to escape the collapsing bridge. The news was happily speculating on the motives of the attack. But he had *been* there. He had been at the site of the break. There had very clearly been no blast damage, no smell of combustion. None of the surrounding area had been charred, or even really disturbed.

The concrete was old. The major supports had been rusty. There had been no 'terrorist bombing' that day. As far as he could tell, the bridge just hadn't been adequately maintained. The massive structure that so many relied upon had just been... *neglected*, until it finally broke.

When he had realized that, he reported it up to HQ, but they'd been uninterested in the observation. The response had been that it wasn't the NHA's responsibility to investigate further unless directed to by higher-ups — the Deputy Secretary, Secretary, or President — or other law enforcement agencies requested assistance. Federal Heroes only stepped in to help during the immediate crisis; it would be the responsibility of state officials to determine the cause, whenever they cared to open their own file, even though the media was still, speculating wildly about the motives of the 'attack.'

The whole response had seemed almost rote, as if HQ had been bored, having said the same thing a hundred times. None of it sat well with him, and the reindeer was left vaguely uneasy, as if he was seeing past a sparkling visage to the tarnish beneath. He struggled to reassure himself that this was just one of the difficult parts of being a Hero. He was tough. He would get over it.

After all, he *had* saved a *lot* of people today. He felt proud of that.

His musing was interrupted by the chirp of his communicator. With a quiet groan, he rolled onto his hooves and ducked through the door into the main living room. The communicator chirped again, as he plopped down onto the brown leather sofa. He propped one leg up on the table before triggering the device's Answer button.

The image of an older otter in a dark suit appeared. He was sitting behind a wooden desk, looking every inch the manager he was. He had opened his mouth to start before his eyes darted down. He flushed and barked "Good God, man. Put on some pants," Captain Anders exclaimed.

It took every ounce of effort he had not to burst into delighted laughter at the man's discomfort. He was proud of his chiseled body and generous proportions, and he *loved* making these stuffy desk jockeys flustered. But laughing would indicate intent, and *that* could get him in trouble. Instead, he pulled the innocent, earnest expression that he had learned to adopt for superiors long ago, when he got in trouble at the Academy.

"Oh, I'm sorry, sir! We were trained to answer the communicator as fast as possible. I assumed your message was too important to delay. Should I hang up and finish bathing?"

With a sigh of exasperation, and an obvious resolution to not look *down* under any circumstances, his boss continued with a strained voice. "*Rockfall.* Er... good work today."

Adopting a more serious tone, Sturzstrom nodded. "Thank you, sir. Just doing my duty as a Hero. I stand ready to protect this great nation with every inch of myself. How can I be of service?"

"What I'm about to tell you is highly classified. TS/SCI. But I need you to be prepared, because I don't want the NHA to look bad when this shitshow goes down." The otter rubbed his face. "You heard what went down in Texas last Sunday, right? The TPA clusterfuck that could have sparked a goddamn *war?*"

Rockfall blinked, surprised at the turn of the conversation. His playfulness vanished as he sat forward, focus sharpening intently. He had expected something routine. "Uh... yes sir. I got the classified briefing about it yesterday. I heard they lost some people."

"The Teepa is *wrecked.* They lost a lot of equipment, their reputation is trashed even with friendly media, and a lot of personnel wound up in the hospital. It'll take them *years* to get back to the strength they had two weeks ago, and politicians are starting to ask some serious questions behind closed doors."

He swallowed. The briefing had been very dry and clinical, so he clearly hadn't quite grasped the seriousness of the situation. "The TPA couldn't handle a few supervillains…?"

Anders tilted his head back and rubbed his face. "Their estimates of Korps strength were way, *way* off. Which is very bad, because their estimates weren't that far off from *our* estimates. The analysts are still scrambling, but it means that we've all severely underestimated this group. I don't know if there's anything we can *do* about it, but I wouldn't be surprised to see some focus shift to countering more of their influence. That's not something you need to worry about, though."

"Okay, then what should I be worrying about?" He asked the question, but he was privately convinced that the important thing to be worrying about *was* that a supervillain organization was strong enough to trash an entire state Hero group.

"One of the Pegasus Phalanx went missing. Their heavy. Big fella, Slate. Mid-tier bruiser. TPA isn't making it public yet, but they'll have to soon. They need to save face, which means blaming everyone but themselves. They're already pulling strings and whispering in ears in Washington, to make it known they want Bradley Group to come in and rescue their captured Hero."

"Wait, the Korps took prisoners? Do they even do that? Is there a ransom demand?" It wasn't completely unheard of for a villain group to snag a hero who'd stumbled in the field, and try to leverage the situation for cash or a prisoner exchange. But things always got dicey when that happened. A lot could go wrong in a hostage situation.

"Not yet. But expect Texas to start making a *lot* of noise about this, all wrapped up in demands for a bigger budget, of course. They want *us* to go find their little lost pony and bring him back. And they're going to have their pet pols claim that it's *our* fault, because *we* didn't step in when they called for help."

"For a fight *they* started, based on their own bad intel?"

"Precisely." The Captain continued to resolutely stare straight ahead.

The caribou frowned, thinking. He might have been new to the group, but he hadn't fallen off the turnip truck yesterday; he was a trained superhero. "Sir, what are the chances he defected?"

The question was answered with a long, slow exhale and a shake of the head. "We don't think so. Slate never showed any signs of sympathy to villains. He always seemed to be the good soldier. Served three combat tours in the Army, then spent the last eight years as a Hero. No blemishes until very recently, when he put Captain Alamo in the hospital."

The reindeer raised an eyebrow. "You don't think that might be a sign?"

"Listen, son, if you'd ever *met* Captain Alamo, you might have done the same. He's the sort of low-grade slime that could never cut it in the big leagues with us. With these... *undisciplined*... staties, though, they run wild. They positively *flourish*. You need to learn real fast that you can't trust state Heroes. They aren't *real* Heroes. And they *don't* have your back."

The young Hero swallowed. "Okay. Yessir. So... what do I need to do?"

"Continue your tour as scheduled. But you are to keep your bags packed, so to speak. You may get a call to fly down there with very little notice. If you *do* get that call, you get down there and retrieve their lost Hero. *You* retrieve him. Under no circumstance are you to let the TPA recover their Hero once you get there, or accept any kind of escort, support, overwatch or 'help.' When you find him, you don't hand him over; you report back for further instructions. There's a real risk they may even try to interfere."

"What... what if he did defect?"

"If he did? That doesn't change the mission. You *retrieve* the Teepa's lost hero. He's no match for you; that's why *you* were selected. This group loves its mind control, so just because Slate didn't defect doesn't mean he won't fight you. And remember, the Korps has some twisted fetish for torturing their 'recruits' with radical surgery. So just because he looks different doesn't mean it's not Slate."

Rockfall blew out a breath and leaned back, earning a soft grunt of annoyance from Anders. He thought through the implications. It was a dangerous mission. He wouldn't have a lot of support that he could trust. But he was a Hero. Not just any Hero, but a Federal Hero. A *Bradley* Hero. If anyone could, it was him.

"Understood. You can count on me. Anything else, Captain?"

"Yes. If you weren't paying attention, you need to make goddamn sure you start taking your psi-blockers — I checked with Medical, you were issued the standard sixty-day supply during your stop in Lexington — to keep those pink freaks out of your head. I do not *care* how shitty the side effects are. I'm not losing a Hero because he wasn't taking his pills, and some lucky drone slapped a visor on him, or a high-grade telepath puppeteered him."

"Oh." He hadn't considered the implication of the words, but he should have.

"And Rockfall? If they *do* grab you? We'll try to retrieve you. But after Sunday… we can't guarantee it. Do *not* get captured. Abort the mission if you have to."

The caribou gazed back, scared. But he shook it off. "You can count on me. I *will* retrieve Slate. The Korps can't stop me."

CHAPTER 10

SOIL LIQUEFACTION

March 22, 2023

Geode looked out over a lush garden that sprawled across the floor below. The air smelled crisp and clean, entirely unlike the recycled flavor she had assumed an underground base would have. There was even a stream burbling through the riot of greenery. The view was beautiful.

The tiny antelope stood beside her, enjoying the vista she had recommended. The afternoon had been one of the best she could remember. Meeting so many other girls who had welcomed her, so readily, was… humbling. The last thing she had ever expected was to be treated with kindness by supervillains.

They had chatted for hours, it seemed, until — one by one — they had taken their leave. Dawn had then shown her many of the amenities available. She was still in awe of this… this whole subterranean *city*. It all seemed so unreal. Too much had happened, and she felt adrift. This moment of calm was the perfect stop on their way to the quarters she'd been promised.

Geode wasn't sure how long she just stood there, gazing at the plants. When she finally shifted and looked up, her companion cleared her throat and indicated a bench nearby. Something was clearly on her mind, so the horse sat down gingerly.

"I need to apologize." Dawn's tone was contrite and serious.

The Percheron blinked at the statement, not sure what had prompted it. She opened her mouth to speak but was stopped by a gesture.

"I know you don't understand, which is why I'm going to explain it. Do you remember what happened when we met?"

—Before she'd known it, Dawn had one hoof standing on the mare's upper thigh and one hand stroking her muzzle, while she was making soothing noises; "Good girl," she'd said—

The horse blinked. The memory was intense and brought back a flood of emotions. With an effort, she shook off the feeling, and cleared her mind. "I don't know if I'll ever forget it."

"Consent is very important. That's not just about sex; it's about how we interact with people. It's about making sure we don't create an environment that someone else isn't comfortable in. ROSE acts as an amazing safeguard, but the thing about safeguards is that they shouldn't be relied upon to replace proper action."

Geode held up her own hand, causing the antelope to pause. "Celia spoke about some of this to me while you were talking with Starshade. She mentioned that if you made me uncomfortable, all I had to do was let you or ROSE know, and you would back off."

A delicate smile turned the corners of Dawn's bright pink lips. "I'm glad. And it's true. It leads into the point I was going to make. I apologize for dominating you when I first met you; it was wrong of me. I saw you as... well... a captured Hero. But, today, I've seen a lot more of you than I expected. And I like a lot more of the *you* I've seen than I ever thought I would." The giant Percheron blushed at the easy praise from the tiny woman, but didn't interrupt.

"I find myself wanting to continue... teasing you. Bending you to my will, occasionally. Nothing sexual. All my instincts are screaming that you aren't *ready* for that yet. Unless you're willing to tell me otherwise?"

Geode stared at the woman she had just met. She turned her head to gaze back at the garden once more as she thought back to their first meeting, and then the rest of the day. She had definitely seen a lot more... well... *everything*, just wandering around the base, than she'd expected.

She wasn't exactly innocent, to be fair. She had been in the Army, and working as a superhero occasionally led to some very seedy places. But there was a sense of... *wholesomeness* to the sexuality here, one that she'd never witnessed before. In her old life, it had always seemed shameful, even dirty. Objectifying. She had never been interested in it, when she had been expected to... do that... to a woman. As a man. Even now the thought made her shudder.

The fallen hero had assumed that the Korps — which had a reputation for being perverted and hypersexual — would be that, but magnified. Instead, she had so far found it quite the opposite. She would have to think about this further, but her thoughts had traveled far afield of the original question.

"Dawn, I don't know much about this place. I may change my mind in the morning. But... I think I'd like that. Maybe... maybe just a bit, though, for now." Her heart was pounding like it would before entering combat, and she felt nervous as she uttered the admission, but she forced herself to be clear no matter *how* much her body wanted to shy away from the admission.

A slow grin spread across the dik-dik's muzzle, and a mischievous glint entered her eye. But her voice remained serious and respectful. "Just a bit." There was a pause before a giggle filled her tone. "I can't wait for you to meet my husband."

Geode stared at the smaller woman, as her mind came to a screeching halt. "Wait, husband?"

"Orion! He's a smith and metalworker. I think the two of you would get along great. He's a bit tied up at the moment with a date, or I would have introduced the two of you already."

Each of her words had tumbled over each other, overflowing with glee. But each statement seemed to confuse the horse more. Finally, out of sheer self-defense, she put up her palms to slow the deluge.

"Wait, wait. I am *very* confused. I thought you were just flirting with me? But you're married? You want me to meet your husband? Who is on a date? I... what?"

The antelope looked almost giddy from suppressed laughter before she composed her expression. There was still a hint of it in her crystalline voice when she tried to explain. "Geode. Poor confused horse... Monogamy isn't the standard here. It's not even that common. It's respected for those who choose it, but very, very few people form exclusive pairs. Honestly, the idea that there is *one* person out there for you that will fill all of your needs — and, well, *fix* or *complete* you as a person — is incredibly toxic.

"I love Orion. With all my heart. He's amazing and sweet and funny. Watching him transform, these past few years, has been one of the best parts of my life. But we both have needs the other can't fulfill alone. For him, he loves meeting someone new, and going on first dates, and having those awkward first kisses. He *also* loves when I crash his dates, and take both of them home."

The draft horse opened her mouth, but closed it, not quite able to get her head around the concept long enough to ask a coherent question.

"He was on a date yesterday. It went well. Now the two of them are getting to know each other better. So, when they're done hanging out, he would love to meet you. He's been suggesting I find a new training project for a while."

"ROSE, are you there?"

[Yes, Dear. How can I help?]

"I'm really struggling to understand this. Can you help me somehow…?"

[Absolutely. Tomorrow, I was planning on spending some time talking over a lot of these very concepts and sharing resources.]

"Thank you."

She took in a breath and blew it out, then rubbed the back of her mane. "I'm sorry. This is all a bit much…"

Dawn grinned, showing pearly teeth. "Take all the time you need. ROSE just told me you were feeling a little overwhelmed. Honestly, it's time for me to show you to your quarters. It's still early, but you've had a very long day."

Geode thought back to the last time she'd slept, and stopped. She was sure she had slept, in a way, while… droned. Her body felt rested, or at least it had when she regained awareness. But the last time *she* had slept, she had still been a loyal member of the Texas Protectorate Assembly. The HUD showed her it was only about 7pm, but weariness was clearly fast approaching.

"That… that would probably be best. Could you show me to my quarters?"

"Absolutely." Instead of striding away, as the mare expected, she simply pointed a finger at the nearest door.

"Wait, what?" She blinked at the door. The door that had been built for someone her size.

"That's your quarters. If you need anything, I'm right next door." She tilted her head to indicate the adjacent door. Both opened onto this little sitting area, overlooking the garden.

It took her a moment for it to really sink in. This beautiful little space was where she would be staying. She hadn't seen the interior, but no matter how cramped it was, she could step outside here to rest and enjoy the view.

"Oh," was all she could say.

Dawn jumped up, full of energy and pranced over to the door… *her* door. "Come on. Let me show you around!"

In a daze, she followed the diminutive antelope into the apartment.

Geode had expected the interior to be spartan. She had still feared, somewhere out in the back of her mind, that it would be a cell or empty room. At best, she had imagined it would resemble the modest hotel rooms that the Teepa would put them up in when they had to travel to conferences, or for other national business. Those were rarely comfortably-sized for individuals of her stature.

Instead, she found herself in something out of a sci-fi show, one with too many lens flares and not enough character development. Everything was sleek lines and curves; dark chrome and magenta were the overriding color scheme, but offset with enough lighter, neutral colors. The result was a space that didn't feel like the customary dark, foreboding villain lair.

The living area was large enough to feel comfortable without being cavernous, though she suspected it edged into that latter category for the more modestly-sized, like Dawn. The cooking space was well laid out, with plenty of space and gleaming black appliances. A couch and loveseat, both sized for the gigantic mare, were positioned for easy company or entertainment; smaller chairs, self-evidently intended for smaller guests, were strategically placed around the room.

She smirked at the wall art. A couple were simply artistically-stylized helices. The rest were Korps recruitment posters, each a winking parody of historical propaganda. The closest one showed an incredibly busty wolf in a jumpsuit, holding a floating helix, the headline proudly proclaiming

"Join The Korps Today!" The mare shook her head with amusement at the studied and *expertly* articulated lack of all subtlety.

The bedroom, visible through the open door to her right, was similarly furnished. A smaller space, but still sizable enough for the gargantuan bed. The size was no doubt marketed as a 'Galactic Space Empress' or some other suitably royal appellation, with the result that it would be big enough for herself — plus another person of similar mass — to sleep comfortably.

The bathroom looked even more like a spaceship interior, if that were possible; the designer of the entryway's graceful, swooping curves had here clearly been given an even freer hand to be creative with shapes and materials, for the generous shower and sink. She was touched to see toiletries laid out for her, even if there… seemed to be too many of them? She would ask ROSE later, what all the little bottles were for, when she was alone.

Dawn was waiting for her back in the main room. The farrier was standing near the door, leaning against the counter that was almost as tall as she was. Both hands were clasped in front of her and she smiled with genuine warmth. "What do you think?"

Looking over at one of the many subtle helices worked into the design of the place, the horse frowned softly. She could see a touch of concern grow in the other woman when she saw it. "This is… too much."

The dik-dik's posture changed as she stepped forward. She reached up, capturing her hand with both of hers and waited until Geode reluctantly met her eyes. "No, Geode. It isn't. We aren't giving you special treatment because you were some big-name defector." She shifted uncomfortably as the antelope touched directly on the point that had been bothering her.

"You deserve a little place of your own, for however long you stay with us. This is the minimum everyone should have. One day, maybe, we can bring this reality to everyone. For now, we can bring it to *you*. Don't feel ashamed because you have a bit of comfort."

The mare opened her mouth to argue, but sighed and nodded instead. "Okay." She wasn't sure what else to say. After a moment, she continued. "Dawn? Thank you… for everything."

The antelope winked at her and grinned. "It's been my pleasure. We're *right* next door if you need anything. And ROSE is wired into basically every part of the apartment, all the appliances are connected on the RCG network; even if you have your visor off, help is just a word away. Get some rest, okay? I'll check on you in the morning."

She patted the horse's thigh and turned. The door slid open for her with that sound, the one — the one that even *she* knew — had been stolen from a TV show. Then... she was alone.

[You aren't alone any more, Geode. I'm here for you.]

The unexpected thought was filled with the feeling of a warm embrace; it almost shattered her, that love. But after a sudden, terrible moment where she felt like she would come apart, she shoved away the feeling. She centered herself, as she had learned to do, forcing herself through that brittle moment. The mare looked around the space... *her* space. She'd never had a space of her own like this before, and she wasn't sure what to *do* with it.

Those troubling thoughts were for another day, however. She was exhausted. Every hour of awareness had seemed to bring new, radical changes to her life. Nothing would ever be the same. But maybe... maybe that was okay.

"ROSE... *nobody's just going to walk in, right?*"

[Not unless you want them to.]

"*Okay. Good. Thank you.*"

With that, she peeled off the black t-shirt emblazoned with the magenta helix, and the similarly-styled bicycle shorts. She realized she wasn't sure where to put them.

[There's a chute in the bedroom. They'll be washed and returned to you, unless you specify otherwise.]

"*Of course, ROSE. Thank you. I—*"

She stepped into the bedroom and froze. It hit her, there, in the quiet stillness. Her heart started pounding. Her breath was shallow and quick and ragged as fear crashed over her.

[Geode? What's wrong?]

She stared at the bed. She was going to destroy it. She couldn't help it. The Teepa had stopped giving her beds, because she always destroyed them. *Always.*

[Calm down, dear.]

She couldn't calm down, not even with ROSE projecting soothing thoughts into her mind.

No, no, no, no, no, no, no—

The word was a mantra in her mind. The room swam through sudden tears. She couldn't sleep here. She would destroy everything. It would happen, and she simply couldn't help it. Nothing would be safe from her.

[*Geode, it's okay. I'm here.*]

The Korps would hate her, would fear her. She was dangerous and wrong and *broken*. That was why the TPA had ordered her into that vault: so others could be safe.

[*Dear, it's okay. People aren't going to hate you, I promise. That's not going to happen.*]

It *would* happen. It *would*, she was certain of it. Pain shot up her arms, as her clenched fists trembled. She always did this. *Always.* Only now, she didn't have a safe place where she wouldn't break everything, and hurt everyone. She would *lose* this beautiful space, with the beautiful view, next to her (*beautiful*) friend, who would grow to hate her. *Because of the screaming.*

[*Geode, listen to me.*]

Sleep meant the memories, and the screaming, and the great and terrible and brutal *breaking*. She wasn't even a Hero anymore, so now she couldn't even atone. Could never atone, never again be allowed to *hope* to atone. Oh, dear God, how she needed to atone—

[*Geode!*]

—She was *broken*. Soon they would all *know*. Tears rolled down her chest, soaking into her fur, staining them with her shame. She had to get out. She had to run. She had to—

[*Geode!*]

Everything stopped.

Her vision went black and her mind quieted.

For a while, there was nothing.

Quiet.

Still.

Calm.

Peace.

Dark.

Slowly, sensation started to return.

Slowly.

She was still in the bedroom. Her breathing was calm.

She couldn't move. Her body would not obey her.

She was still.

[Geode, I'm sorry.]

"W-what? What happened?"

[You were having a panic attack. I had to take control before you hurt yourself.]

"Sorry."

[Geode, there's nothing to apologize for. Nothing. You're okay. I have you.]

"Sorry."

[Geode, it's okay. Tonight, I will take away the nightmares. I will make sure you sleep. **Really** sleep. Tonight will be dreamless, and silent, and **restful**. You have been hurting for too long, and no one has been there to help. But I'm here now.]

"But—"

[No **buts**. Tomorrow, I'll introduce you to a therapist. They will help you start to adjust. To heal.]

"A therapist? But I'm… I'm not weak. I'm not broken."

But she *was* broken.

[You are **not** broken. You are **not** weak. You have been asked to do too much, with too little help, for far too long. Geode, we have you. You are **safe** now. Even in your dreams, if that's what you need.]

She didn't remember climbing into bed. She didn't remember laying down in the dark room on the comfortable mattress.

[Sleep, Geode. Rest.]

And she did.

For the first time in many, many years, she slept.

And the nightmares—

—The nightmares didn't come.

CHAPTER 11

GEOLOGICAL DETRITUS

April 2, 2023

The entrance to Knox-Henderson Station was unassuming, just a set of concrete stairs descending into the earth near the North Central Expressway. Designed to be forgettable and unremarkable, few people in the area knew that these stairs led to an artifact of the DART light rail system's frustrated 1990s subway initiative. The shell of a station had been completed at great expense, before complaints from locals shut down the project.

The subterranean structure languished, abandoned, after a wall was put up between the active light rail tracks and the subway that never was. The ruins mouldered, passing from local memory, until some enterprising individual realized the value in an underground, forgotten space, and it was expanded in secret. What was once meant to bring a more prosperous, interconnected city now hosted unsanctioned, illegal super fights.

Well past midnight, those stairs seemed to descend into the inky black void of hell. Apprehension filled Jennifer, as she strained to see the plain metal door a single floor below. The people inside were *bad* people. She knew, in her heart, that this was a hive of crime and vice. If they found out she was nominally an agent of the state, even if that was simply as a municipal health inspector, she would not walk out again. Her plan was a *bad* plan. But it was all she had.

There was no way she could stand up to a superhero. Everblades had been old and washed up; only luck had saved her. The memories of that fight haunted her nightmares. And there was this... *Master* out there, waiting to claim her. She couldn't be passive. She couldn't just wait. That way would be death.

Still, it took several moments before the nutria could bring herself to step down. For supposedly unused stairs, there was certainly a lot of wear and tear on these steps. Her heels clicked dully on the concrete as she descended, the echo off the bare gray walls growing as the walls rose to swallow her.

Just as she reached for the door, it opened on its own. She was left staring into the face of the bouncer.

"*Tony?*" she hissed as she stared into the face of the deer. "I thought your cousin was the bouncer?"

She hadn't seen the cook since he had helped her home almost two weeks ago. He had insisted on making sure she was safe after the... incident with Everblades. He had been kind, and surprisingly concerned for her. Far more than she had expected after she threatened to shut down his food truck. They had kept in touch mostly through text since, to arrange her entry.

"I wasn't going to let you go without backup. This way... I'm here. If you need me." He looked embarrassed by the admission and couldn't meet her eyes. She was deeply touched by his concern (and a bit worried he might have a crush on her). Nonetheless, she smiled warmly.

"Thank you, Tony."

"What's your plan? You never told me." He ushered her inside, where more stairs greeted her. While she could hear music and people deeper inside, they had a bit of privacy right now.

With a long sigh, she surrendered to the pressure. He wasn't going to let her go in without knowing *something*. "I need protection. I *know* I won't get that from anyone here," she said, immediately forestalling the obvious protestation building in him, "At least, not directly. But, one of the other... individuals... I know, put me in contact with someone." She was proud of herself for not saying her first impulse. No need to call Tony shady right now, when he was helping her. "I was told that I could meet Mr. Terrock here. He's willing to sell me something that I can use to protect myself."

Tony's eyes widened at the name. He blew out a breath and shook his head, not quite able to look at her. "Terrock is *bad news*. You need to be careful. But... he does sell protection from time to time. And he isn't cheap."

She shrugged. "It's a lot of money, but I don't have a choice. You saw the... you saw Everblades. There are more after me. I can't stop them without *something*. It's a huge risk, but... I don't have much of a choice right now."

Distress was written plainly on the younger man's face. "Can't you just... skip town? Lay low?"

But she was shaking her head, resignation and regret filling her words and written into the lines of her face. "Not from this. I *want* to. But... I can't. Not from this."

The whitetail looked away. "I'll be here. If you need me, I mean. Greg is inside, and he'll be looking out for you too. Just, I mean, we're here if you need us. And be *careful*."

She shrugged helplessly. "I'm *beyond* being able to be careful, but I'll try to do my best. That's why I'm here, frankly." She almost turned to go when she realized she was forgetting something. "Oh!"

The nutria pulled out a small card and handed it over. "Here's the contact information for Raul Garcia. He's the farmer I told you about. Just... if I don't make it out of this, please try to turn your truck around. You might be the only healthy meal many of your customers get."

Tony did not look like he cared about that at the moment, but he nodded. "Fine. I will. But... come back safe."

She opened her mouth to say more, but closed it and nodded. She was just delaying things now. Without another word, she turned and headed deeper into the theoretically-abandoned station.

When she stepped inside, she immediately felt out of place. There was a press of bodies. The place reeked of booze, body odor, and blood. The clientele was a mix of the sorts of people she would cross the street to avoid, and the type of businessmen she was *very* careful never to be alone in an elevator with.

She had *thought* she was dressing inconspicuously. She had been told that the attire was either rich businessman or punk. The thought of affecting the former turned her stomach, and was beyond her means in any event, so she had acquired a pair of ripped black jeans, a black racerback with a skull motif that was one size too small, and a black leather jacket. She had spent an hour teasing her lipstick into a black and white zebra pattern that popped in the blacklight. She hadn't really had footwear that matched, but settled on black stiletto heels. They were taller than she normally liked, but they gave her what she hoped was some kind of dominatrix vibe. Plus, she needed the height.

The music was loud, and *bad*, blasting over speakers long since blown. The crowd surrounded a roughly marked-out circle. Two almost-naked men were punching each other into submission to cheers and boos; she didn't see any obvious powers, since this was supposed to be a powered fight, but the crowd seemed happy. Ultimately, the thought of watching long enough to figure out what was going on was unappealing.

Instead, she made her way to a crude bar set up along one wall. Several others disinterested in the current fight lingered there, chatting or drinking. Few paid her any mind, though a cluster of jackals watched her with mild, predatory interest. She would need to keep an eye on them.

She waved over the scruffy golden retriever behind the bar, who wore an ill-fitting fancy suit. There was none of the welcome or cheer that was the hallmark of the breed. He looked at her with cold eyes.

"Boulevardier," she ordered without greeting.

The dog frowned at the request. "I don't know how to make that."

A stern, hard expression slid over her face. She wasn't usually a great actor, but she just had to let the stress of the past couple weeks — and the desperation that haunted the back of her thoughts — show. One glittering black claw pointed to a nearby table. "Yes you do. He has one right now. And if you are the regular bartender, there's no way you wouldn't know how to make one with *this* crowd." She punctuated her statement with a sweeping gesture towards the more moneyed-looking attendees.

The canine met her eyes for a long moment, then frowned and shook his head. He may have looked out of place, but the quick, sure manner he made the drink from memory said he knew what he was doing; he had been testing her. When he handed the drink to her, she already had a $20 bill on the table.

He stared at her as he took the bill, and offered no change. She made a show of looking away unconcerned; they understood each other. Jennifer's heart was beating hard enough to escape her chest, but she dared not let her real feelings show. Her contact had been very clear not to show weakness. She was winging it and hoping for the best.

She took a long moment to look back at the fight. One of the men was on the ground, bleeding; the other was barely standing (or, rather, hovering a few inches off the floor). The nutria also used the pause to rein in her near-panic. When she was ready — and without looking back at the bartender — she pulled out a small prepared card, and put it on the bar.

The retriever took the card and looked at it. Then at her. Then back at the card. Finally, slipping the card into his pocket, he spoke. A touch of concern entered his voice, though it was so faint she wasn't entirely certain it wasn't just her imagination. "… You sure?"

Jennifer found herself hesitating just a brief moment. This was her last chance to walk out. But reality asserted itself; the last chance had been long ago, and far away. She nodded.

With the look that clearly said that it was her funeral, he shrugged. "Head to the back hall. Third door on the right." He nodded at the unmarked metal door next to the makeshift bar. With that, he turned away to attend to another customer. Jennifer threw back her drink in a single, long swallow around the suddenly thick lump in her throat. With that meager fortification of her courage, she squared her shoulders and opened the door, stepping into a bare concrete corridor.

When the heavy metal door swung shut behind her, she was surprised at how quiet it suddenly was. She could hear muffled cheers and shouts, but she felt isolated. There was no way anyone would hear her screams for help, if it came to that. Tony and his cousin may as well have been in Canada. Still, it was simple: all she had to do was pay a bit of money to a supervillain-slash-arms dealer, and walk out of here.

Even in her harried state, she knew that was optimistic.

The hallway stretched and curved to the left, so she wasn't sure how long it was. The lights were behind grated metal covers, adding to the unfinished, industrial feel. The air was heavy with humidity, and condensation dripped down bare concrete walls. As she moved further, the dim sounds of the crowd faded away entirely, leaving her alone with the dull echoes of her ill-conceived footwear. In this liminal space, she was left alone with her thoughts and fears. Only her desperation — and determination *not to die* — moved her forward, even as every instinct screamed to just turn around and leave.

The third door was once again heavy, and seemingly solid metal. It swung open surprisingly easily to reveal a massive room the size of a warehouse; a single, giant hanging lamp in the middle of the space created a circle of light, but left the edges of the room in deep shadow. Centered in that pool of light was a podium with a silvery metallic briefcase.

This is a trap.

She tried to tell herself that clandestine weapon deals *obviously* just needed the same conditions as were ideal for murder, but she couldn't quite convince herself of that. Still, she had not come unprepared. She resisted the urge to pat her jacket, as that might alert an observer to her plan. Instead, she strode in confidently.

She was unsurprised when the door swung shut behind her with an ominous clang. Her heart was thudding in her chest as she kept walking. Her heels clicked one after the other, carrying her to her fate. She could see shapes in the gloom beyond the ring. Large crates — and other, less identifiable forms — clustered in the darkness.

What she did not see present was her contact. She stopped in front of the briefcase and peered around, but no shape stepped forward to greet her. Jennifer was sorely tempted to grab the case and run, but wasn't foolish enough to think that stealing from an arms dealer was a good idea. Instead, she called out.

"Mr. Terrock? I'm here, as per our arrangement. I brought your payment."

She waited as her words faded. Her heart pounded a staccato rhythm in her ears as she waited for something, anything, to happen. It didn't. But she had spent her career playing stupid power games with petty tyrants and kitchen despots; she knew how to handle them. So she waited. Even as her instincts told her to run screaming, she waited. She forced her face into a bored expression, and still she waited. Silence and patience would be her weapons now.

Jennifer used the time to get her breathing under control. As the silence stretched, she started to wonder if she was indeed alone in the room. But finally, a voice, gravelly and deep, emerged from the darkness.

"Open the case."

Controlling herself, she leaned over the podium and pressed two latches, which popped open with heavy clicks. The silvery lid was surprisingly weighty. Inside, inset into molded black foam, was a small, chunky pistol. Or something similar, at least; she realized that there was no barrel as such. Instead, the front curved down in a smooth arc to meet the base of the grip. It looked like a futuristic, weaponized letter 'D'. Made from some glittering blue metal and dark polymer, it was small enough to fit into a pocket, but she had no doubt it was sufficient for her needs. There was a dark hole where it was missing something vital in the grip, however.

Of course it's not loaded. She tried to convince herself that it was that simple as she turned back around. She knew she was way out of her league, but the only way forward was through.

"Okay. This looks to be what I need. Should I leave the payment here? And where do I pick up the... ammo?" She winced at the last word, uttered so casually in action movies, but knowing that it could clearly call out her ignorance.

"Power cell... and *no*. This projector is worth far more than the pittance you can offer."

A chill shivered down her spine as the voice confirmed her fears. This *was* a trap.

"I don't need your money. You couldn't afford the real price. But I had to set it high enough that you believed it was real." A shape moved in the darkness, but she couldn't quite locate it. Her hand shot to her jacket as she scanned the shadows frantically, trying to catch sight of it again. "Just high enough that you could reach it... if you *stretched*. But low enough that it was possible." Another noise... a scuff or a scrape, she wasn't sure. She turned around, trying desperately to locate the sound. "Something only a desperate person would gamble on. Someone with nothing left to lose. The type of person no one would miss..."

There! She caught sight of a figure moving towards the light. In one swift motion she pulled the cylinder from her pocket and depressed the button. With the distinctive hiss of compressed gas, a stream of pepper spray arced into the darkness, right into the face of the approaching figure...

... *Who did not react at all.* They kept walking forward as if nothing had happened. Even more terrified, Jennifer stumbled back.

"You see, you aren't here to buy a product from me." The voice started to change. The deep, gravelly voice of a man becoming distorted. Artificial. Green lights started to form where the figure's eyes should be. Then more, below them. The head finally entered the light and it was a smooth blackness with glowing points of light forming eyes and a crude mouth.

"You are here to help me calibrate my systems."

Chapter 12

Hydrofracking

April 2, 2023

Ethicoil slowly let his breathing even out. The air in the dim room was cool on the coral snake's scales, still damp with the alchemical mixture that had resurrected him. It took a surprising amount of effort to stand, causing more of the foul liquid to drizzle off him. He had to brace himself against the lid for a long moment, relearning his balance as if he stood for the first time.

He was naked, of course. Alternating bands of black, white, and red scales proclaimed his venomous nature to the world. He wasn't exactly tall for a superhero — certainly not compared to the lumbering Slate, that damned traitor — but his striking appearance made up for it, as he'd repeatedly had to insist to the Teepa PR flacks. He was lithe and sinewy, built like an acrobat, even if he was shaky at the moment.

The viper stood there for a long moment, breathing the unnatural fumes from the toxic mixture that had rebirthed him. Only once he was certain of his body did he step out of the sarcophagus. The snake shuddered, and though his gaze inexorably travelled to his masterpiece, the gloom only hinted at the eldritch carvings that covered it. A nest of tubes and pipes and cables attached to various points along the base.

The fog of confusion was slowly lifting, as his memories swam back to the surface in fragments. He remembered the giant viper. Pitch-black, as if carved from living onyx, suddenly looming behind him. A look into those soulless orbs. A shock of recognition as he realized who she was. Then the *pulse* of magic, and *wrongness*. The flash of some indescribable... *horror* in her eyes. Less seen, and more imprinted directly onto his soul — as if, for a moment, he could see outside the universe, and into something fundamentally *broken* with reality.

The memory brought a surge of sheer terror, making his knees weak once more. But the danger had passed, even though he could still viscerally feel the sensation of his body *warping* and *shifting* as it was consumed by stone. The sickening feeling of being warped into a statue would haunt him, but the fear was swept away by a wash of sheer euphoria.

It had *worked*.

He was *alive*.

He had conquered death itself.

He shouted his elation to the world, basking in the sound echoing through the dark room. Here in this secret chamber, hidden away, he had *resurrected* himself. Nothing could stop him, even if he had almost drowned in the process. He would, perhaps, need a better escape mechanism; the snake had not realized how disoriented he would be upon waking from the dead, and how quickly panic would rob him of his ability to operate a simple catch.

The squelching eldritch fluid was drying, and growing tacky on his scales. Finally, with a steadying breath, the snake opened the door, leaving the ritual room behind; he would need to restore it, rebuild it, replenish the material components, but that would be a project for later. For now, he had to clean himself up and announce his return to the world.

He quickly showered, watching the oily black substance wash from his scales and swirl down the drain, until the water was finally clear; perhaps it was even an effective scale care regimen, too, leaving him just as shining as if after a shed. The Hero finally stepped out of the bathroom, feeling like a new man. In some ways, he was.

I am Reborn, he thought smugly.

He picked up the spare communicator he had stashed in this secret hideout; the TPA would need to be informed that he was no longer dead. A glance at the clock on the wall showed that two weeks had passed since his death.

Ethicoil paused. That was a lot longer than the process should have taken, by his careful calculations. But since it had been impossible to truly test without… well… *dying*, it was all just magical theory work. Or maybe the magic of petrification had delayed the process in some way? It didn't matter.

I wonder if they broadcast my funeral? I'll have to watch it, and see what people said about me. Thankfully, my lawyer has instructions to delay any settling of my estate for quite some time. It would be amazingly hard to pry my money out of the hands of my relatives, if they already had their hands on it.

But pressing the button on the communicator produced an odd sound — a flat, atonal beep he had never heard before. Worse, it didn't connect to HQ; there was no immediate, faint hiss of a live channel, as he was used to hearing. Pressing the button again produced the same result. The communicator wasn't living up to its name.

Still, such a minor setback wasn't going to dampen his mood. He flung the device aside with a dramatic flourish, feeling satisfied as it skittered across the polished stone flooring. He wasn't about to let anything rob him of his triumph. Ethicoil took a moment to look around his hideout with a sense of smug accomplishment.

He had this place built in complete secrecy; contractors had been hired through shell companies with false (but plausible) cover stories, and well-paid for their discretion. No one who *mattered* knew of its existence, including the TPA and his family. Buried deep in a desolate area east of Houston, it was still suitable to his standards. The living bedrock had been polished to a mirror sheen. The walls were covered in exquisitely carved wooden bookshelves, interspersed with original artworks from a handful of highly-regarded contemporary painters. A high ceiling with recessed lighting helped brighten the room, leaving it feeling exclusive and luxurious, instead of... villainous.

Furniture of the finest leather, and rarest imported woods, added to the aesthetic. On one nightstand, carefully positioned in a charging cradle, was his backup cell phone. He snatched it up and plopped down onto the couch — one that cost more than many houses — uncaring that he was still drying after the shower.

As the device powered on, a warning flashed on the screen; it had no service. The line had been disconnected, though at least it was still connected to the wifi. For the first time, concern started to eat away at Ethicoil's jubilation. It shouldn't have been cut off so quickly, should it...? Nonetheless, the device still recognized his scale pattern, and soon he was greeted by the home screen.

A number of notifications started popping up. *Now* he was starting to get nervous. The email app was demanding he verify his username and password for every account. Ethicoil wasn't sure how, but all of his saved credentials now seemed to be incorrect.

When he entered the login for his primary email address — a password he knew by heart and had used for years, shrugging off the TPA IT department's passive-aggressive security advisories — it was rejected. He tried again, with the same result. Growing alarmed, he tried other accounts; none of them would let him in.

His pulse was starting to speed up. There was no reason his accounts should have been deactivated. Maybe one or two of the accounts associated directly with his Hero identity would have been locked, after widespread news of his death, but most providers would simply not have bothered. Other accounts were clean, *isolated*, connected neither to Ethicoil nor the name on his driver's license.

When he couldn't log into his most easily accessible bank account, one of several untraceable slush funds, Ethicoil started cursing. The invectives grew longer and louder with each subsequent failure. *All* of his financial accounts were locked out, and without access to the associated email addresses, he would be unable to recover the passwords. Something was seriously wrong.

Right. Don't panic. First, get in contact with the TPA. After the shitshow, maybe there was some massive lockdown.

By now he had migrated to the computer desk. His desktop here was also showing a number of account errors, but the browser still worked. Frantic typing and clicking quickly pulled up the news. The keys clacked with urgency. Then, his breath caught in his throat and his scales prickled: one of the Pegasus Phalanx was talking about Manifest Destiny's long planned retirement. And that Hero was... *him*.

He stared into his own face.

The figure on camera was in the middle of some public relations nonsense, but all Ethicoil could see was an imposter with his face. *Someone* had exploited his death to infiltrate *his* team. He wasn't sure how the identity thief had gained access to all his accounts, but here was the source of all his suffering... his *indignity*.

He barely registered the next hour as he frantically worked out how to place a call through the internet, with no functioning credit card or existing accounts. Finally, Ethicoil dialed a number that was not listed anywhere. Every TPA Hero was forced to memorize it, and recall it to superiors upon command, as part of their emergency protocols. The existence of this phone number was a closely guarded secret: it was a 24/7 manned hotline specifically to report infiltrators, imposters, and suspected mind control. In short, a countermeasure for a situation precisely like this one.

The line rang through to a bored-sounding man. It was with a vast and grandiloquent sense of vengeance that Ethicoil explained in *great* detail how he had been replaced. After spilling a number of damning details, the man grew very quiet. Finally, he was transferred to a supervisor.

"Is this the person claiming to be Ethicoil?" the voice asked with no preamble. He sounded stern and no-nonsense. Just the type of person that Ethicoil needed.

"Yes!" He couldn't keep the relief out of his voice.

"My guy here relayed everything to me. Did you have anything to add?"

"Be careful. I don't know what this imposter is up to, but I assume he is a Korps infiltrator. He appeared just after their attacks."

"I see." There was a long pause and the faint sound of typing. The coral snake waited with growing impatience as the silence stretched out.

Finally, the voice returned, this time with its own suppressed fury. His heart leapt at the tone. The infiltrator was about to rue the day he chose the wrong Hero. "We've looked into your story." He couldn't keep the smile from his lips. "I don't know who you are or how you got this number, but we will *not* tolerate attempts to smear the name of a good man and sow doubts as to his identity."

What?!

"Don't call this number again, or you *will* be prosecuted."

And the line went dead.

Ethicoil screeched in rage, looking over at the CBS Action 7 News report, still playing on the huge flatscreen. The figure wearing *his* face looked smug and oily, as he crooned mock sympathies for... for *the Traitor*. The footage was hard to watch — both because it turned his stomach, and because the imposter was hard to see through the spiderweb cracks covering the upper-right corner of the screen, radiating out from where he'd hurled his useless phone. The device remained lodged in the television.

Hours passed as he tried in vain to contact anyone who could help. Calls to his lawyer had gone unanswered, even on the firm's private line for elite clients. Attempts to contact Pegasus Oil to expose the imposter had been similarly fruitless. He had spent hours on hold, working his way through automated line after automated line, only to be politely told to go away. Subsequent calls revealed that his number had been blocked.

Rage and confusion and betrayal warred within him; at the moment of his greatest triumph, the triumph of *life* over *death*, he had been robbed of everything. Worse, now it seemed that no one would believe him. It was with a sense of dread that he finally, bleakly, pondered his very last option.

His father, Rodrigo "Rex" Alquitano II, was CEO of Pegasus Oil. He had held that position since *his* father had been murdered by a monstrous serpent in the late 70s. He was the last person on Earth to which Ethicoil wanted to admit failure, but he was out of options. He had to recover his identity.

He still stared at the dialing app as if gazing into the abyss. He could feel the thudding in his head when he finally, finally clicked the dial button. And waited. The phone was picked up on the third ring.

"*This had better be important.*" That voice sent a shiver down his spine. It was full of the ice and derision he had heard every time the stern man decided to take a passing interest in his son and heir.

"Sir, this is Ethicoil."

There was a pause. "No shit. Your lawyer called and told me you were back from the dead. I didn't believe it."

The scorn in those words left him feeling tiny. But someone finally believed him.

"Sir, I'm alive! I'm back from the dead! But someone's trying to replace me! Someone's fooled everyone into thinking he's me." There was a long pause, filled with disapproval before he meekly, and belatedly, added, "Sir."

There was an even longer silence. Finally, his father spoke with derision. "Are you expecting me to be *impressed* by your half-breed tricks?

Anyway, I don't know why you even bothered to bring yourself back. You were always worthless. Of *course* someone replaced you. I selected him myself. I wasn't about to let my investment in the TPA go to waste."

The bottom fell out of the universe.

Distantly, he heard his father continue. "When we got the call that they were sweeping shards of you into a dustbin, I finally did what I should have done years ago. I put a *real* coral snake in place, instead of a damned milk snake bastard."

Ethicoil blushed at the stark mention of his secret shame.

"Oh, I tried to raise you right."

That was a lie. You were never around to raise anything but your voice, he seethed, an echo of his bitter youth.

"But you were always fucking up. Never taking your duty to this family, to the *business*, seriously. When you lost *control*," — the erstwhile Hero flinched, at the disgust filling that word — "and revealed your alchemical prowess to the world, I knew it was the taint that your whore mother brought to this family. I never forgave her for sleeping with that... *commoner*. I knew I should never have taught you the family secrets. I *tried* to look past your mongrel heritage, but it was clear that you would always be *broken*."

"But I'm not—" Ethicoil tried to protest weakly, but quailed at the familiar snarl of rage.

"You put the entire family at risk and you dare speak back to me? When the world learned of your alchemy, powerful and *important* people started to whisper that perhaps the whole family shared your gift. Perhaps it had been more than business savvy that we had built our fortune upon. You risked robbing us of our greatest advantage. When your foul mother tried to protect her traitorous whelp, it was time for her accident."

Father... had mother killed? The world felt distant and hollow. Or, perhaps, it was just him.

"So I found a new son, just in case. One who isn't a *milk snake*. A properly *venomous* son. Not one who has all the bite of a... a common *gecko*."

"But..." he tried weakly, but even he didn't know what he was going to say.

"Oh, but what about the TPA, you ask," the man whined mockingly. "*They* were all too eager to hide the shame of losing a star member of the Dallas team. It was very *synergistic*, you see. Pegasus Oil certainly had no interest in losing their investment. Nor did I."

"But…" he tried again, barely audible.

"This is the last time we speak. If you know what's good for you, you'll just slither away into some dark hole. If you try to go public, we will fight you. Try to air the family's dirty laundry, and we will *bury* you. For good, this time. DNA testing won't lie; you *are* a milk snake, after all, and when that comes out, no one will ever believe you. The real Ethicoil — my *real* son, natural-born fruit of my loins or not — is the one wearing the cape, and protecting revenue-producing citizens."

With that, the line went dead.

The man who had been Ethicoil, moments before, stared blankly in shock. He had been the son of an important CEO, scion to one of the nation's largest oil companies. He had been a *superhero*. He had *conquered death*. Now… he was alone in a hole, in the middle of nowhere. No money. No purpose. *No name.*

He cried for hours.

He would have his revenge.

The new Ethicoil sat in his uncomfortable plastic chair, staring across the desk at the giant bull. The *mean*-looking bovine glared back with cold disdain. The snake had been called over to the Fort Worth Division HQ to meet with their new Division Chief rather suddenly, and he couldn't quite quiet the nerves. He had trained his expression into one of polite disinterest. He was, indeed, an expert at hiding his true feelings.

In the week since he had replaced Ethicoil, he had been terrified of slipping up. It didn't matter that he had been training for this for years, ever since his… father… decided to improve upon his lacking heir. Now that it was *real* and *happening*, he had everything to lose if he stumbled. He didn't know who *knew*, so he had to keep up the act at all times. The Holstein frowning at him did not look amused.

He was a giant of a man. Not quite as big as his supposed former teammate, but close. Lone Steer was a legend in the Texas hero community; he had made his name in the 80s as a lone vigilante. When he joined the burgeoning TPA, he had founded the Musketsteers, a legacy team venerable enough that none of its original members still remained.

Though now much older, Lone Steer wore his age like battle scars. Lines were etched into his face, and the gray fur on his muzzle made him look grizzled, but this was no weary retiree; hard muscle still shrouded his bulky frame. Broad horns had been painted like the Texas state flag, an affectation the aged Hero would no doubt have derided as vainglorious in any other man. But it wasn't his size that made the coral snake feel tiny; it was his beady red eyes, and his *scowl*.

When he finally spoke, the strand of hay that projected from the corner of his lips bounced in emphasis. His voice was deep, like rocks falling down a well. *"Ethicoil.* You hold that title, you wear that name — for the moment, at least — because we *allow* it. No matter how much your Daddy thinks he owns us, it is by our will alone that you replace the first failure."

He swallowed, nervous at the secret being so casually discussed. He honestly hadn't thought this slab of beef knew, but the complete lack of tact, or subtlety, was alarming. He tried to speak, but the steer quelled him with a glare.

"Nothing I say is to leave this room. I have a mission for you, one that only you can complete. And if you don't complete it… well… the TPA will soon discover, and reveal to the world, that one of their *beloved* heroes was replaced by an imposter. An imposter who was brutally mauled to death, while trying to sabotage our operations." The threat was abundantly clear. Those red eyes bored into the imposter, and left him certain that it was not an idle one.

"Ethicoil died in the shitshow that claimed my predecessor Fatal Thorns… plus some others I don't really care about, to be blunt. And it also seems that our stupid Heavy wandered off at some point."

Ethicoil knew that, of course. He had been briefed about the disappearance of 'his' former teammate, not that he had to be; the kidnapping of a major superhero by the Korps was big news these days. The supervillains were getting bold.

"To the point: we have *one* chance to salvage this shitshow. The TPA is in bad shape. We lost a *lot* of stuff we can't easily replace. Equipment. People. The public's *confidence*. The Korps is a lot stronger than those jackoffs in Intel led us to believe."

The snake blinked at the blunt assessment, but his input was not required, as the bull barrelled onwards to whatever meandering point he was trying to make.

"We've been forced to tuck our tail between our legs, and beg for help to rescue our captured Hero. Whispering in the right ears to send backup." Ethicoil knew all this, of course. "But that's all a lie. It's a cover."

Wait, what?

"No, we need to show those ungrateful, sniveling *bitches* that only *we* can protect them. We need to show them that the Korps are killers, who will stop at nothing to achieve their evil ends. But we can't *do* that the way we need to. That's where you come in. Slate wasn't kidnapped. He defected."

Ethicoil gaped at the old Hero.

Slate... defected!? None of his files indicated that was a possibility. He was just a dumb Heavy!

"Close your damn mouth, snake, and listen. I'm only going to say this once. The only way we can pull our tails out of the fire is to show the world that they *need* us. The goddamn Bradley Group is sending one of their newest, finest Heroes here in the next few weeks. Rockfall. *He* is going to be officially tasked with rescuing Slate."

Rockfall was a major hero. New, but already becoming a big name at the national level. If he was coming here...

"We can't allow him to succeed. We can't allow him to capture Slate."

Oh.

"You," Lone Steer emphasized by pointing a thick finger at his chest, "are going to kill Slate *and* Rockfall."

Ethicoil stared in open-mouthed disbelief. His mind short-circuited as he tried to process the order.

"W-what?" he squeaked.

"You heard me. *You* are going to stop Rockfall from capturing Slate. They both die. You're the perfect person to pull that off; an expert in poisonous alchemy. You don't need to fight fair to kill with a bit of venom, do you?"

The snake shook his head mutely.

"That's what I thought. With Rockfall dead, we can show that even the Bradley Group can't keep handling modern villains with kid gloves. More importantly, with Slate dead, we have a *martyr*. Together, they will ensure our funding will flow like wine on one of your Daddy's cocaine-fueled sex yachts. It will mean that we were *justified* in attacking the Korps." The division chief paused, standing up and peering into the trophy case behind the desk, still filled with the previous chief's mementos.

"We will have a *mandate* to crush these villains, and maybe even get some legislation passed, untie our hands. Terrorists don't get 'due process,' and it'll be open season on those queer fucks. Might even bring back the good ol' days of bounties," the steer mused wistfully. It would have been more concerning to the snake, if he wasn't still reeling from his own orders; he felt like he couldn't get his footing.

"You are being detached from the Pegasus Phalanx, effective immediately. Your only job from now on is hunting down and killing Slate and Rockfall, preferably at the same time, to avoid any loose ends. They both go in the God-damned *ground*. Do that, and you will really be Ethicoil. Fail, and you won't be around to worry about how we deal with *Daddy*."

Lone Steer stepped up, towering over the still seated snake, those red eyes boring into him with dread finality. *"Do you understand me?"*

It took him a moment to answer. His life was on the line. But... the wheels were starting to turn. Ideas flitted through his mind. Now that he was thinking instead of reacting, he was starting to see the angles and the opportunities. After a moment, a sly grin spread across his face.

"Oh yes, Chief, I understand. They both die." He didn't bother concealing his excitement.

CHAPTER 13

EXTENSIONAL TECTONICS

April 2, 2023

Morning came with a start. The Percheron's heart hammered away in her chest; she was gasping for air, panting heavily, but hadn't quite sweated into a lather. The myriad horrors that plagued her memories were distant and vague today.

Most importantly, she wasn't entombed in the wreckage of a bed... as she still feared, each day, in the brief but seemingly endless seconds before fully regaining consciousness.

Geode had been in the Korps base for two weeks, and she was still unused to waking up without screaming. ROSE had to hypnotically knock her out the first few days, but she could now sleep through the night without needing to wear the visor. The RCGs influence — and the aid of the therapist Tori, had finally allowed her to *rest*. The troubling dreams hadn't disappeared, but they weren't as frequent or as powerful.

Still, her hand groped for the visor charging on her nightstand. With a moan of relief, she slid the sleek pink interface onto her face, and felt the warmth of love flow through her, settling her nerves. When had a Korps mind-control device become *comforting*?

[When you realized that you preferred it to the nightmares.]

"Are you...?"

[No, dear, I'm not imposing this calm. I'm not forcing you into acceptance. I am sending mild comfort, but that's simply helping you settle your nerves; nothing that would override your will or influence you into feeling things you wouldn't want, just a light touch to take the edge off. I can stop, if you like.]

"I... no. That's okay."

The Percheron stared around her. The bed was messy, as if she had tossed a little, but there was no visible sign she had ruined it. Nor were there the usual signs of damage to the floor, or to other furniture within flailing distance of powerful equine limbs. She still felt a sense of wonder that she had slept through the night without an episode.

The digital figure of a fox appeared, sitting on her bed, kind eyes and pointed muzzle tilted towards her. Geode pushed herself up on her elbows to look over the translucent image. The vixen was about average height, with a shock of short pink hair. She looked friendly and welcoming. She rarely chose to appear visually to the former Hero; it seemed that she usually preferred to use text scrolling across the HUD, and a mix of words and feelings projected directly into Geode's brain. Still, the horse appreciated the visual approach at quiet times like this.

"Thank you."

[You're welcome.]

There was a beat, a moment of calming relief at seeing the AI's avatar, before ROSE spoke again.

[Dawn sends her regrets. She has a rush commission to complete, so she won't be able to join you for breakfast. However, Zala wants to meet you, finally.]

"Zala?"

[A dear friend of Starshade. She also acts as Starshade's overwatch on missions. We had wanted to introduce you on your first day, but ultimately decided that she might be one new face too many. She's been dying to meet you.]

"Oh. Okay."

[You don't have to meet her if you don't want to. But she'll be at Starshade's decanting today, and she wanted to meet you first.]

Geode sat up in a rush at the words.

"Wait, that's today?! How could I have forgotten?"

[Time moves differently when you aren't working yourself to death, dear.]

"Oh."

The draft horse mulled over the words. She couldn't remember the last time she'd simply had time to herself. She had been too important to the Teepa... though, admittedly, even that wasn't quite right. She hadn't been important at all. What she represented was what had been important. She had been a tool, a weapon system, and what had been important was keeping that weapon in peak condition.

[Get showered and dressed, dear. She'll be outside when you are ready.]

ROSE's words shook the warhorse out of her reverie and she tossed the sheets aside.

"Let's not keep this Zala waiting, then."

Geode stepped out of the apartment with a soft smile. The quiet overlook smelled fresh, heavy with the riot of greenery just below. Intellectually, she knew she was in an excavated cavern deep below Austin, but the air was fresh and alive. The mare was still giddy with the knowledge that simply stepping 'outside' was enough to brighten her spirits, in a way she hadn't believed possible, until she came to live among Supervillains.

Her thoughts were broken by a soft, rumbling purr. A jaguar, with midnight fur liberally speckled with teal rosettes, was languidly sprawled across one of the nearby chairs. She was curvy and soft, but still possessed of a predatory confidence. Silver eyeliner framed golden eyes filled with mysterious and undoubtedly-scandalous secrets.

She was wearing what could generously be called a dress. The neckline of the shimmering silver ensemble plunged far below her generous chest, coming to a point perilously close to revealing *all* of her peaks and valleys. The garment did nothing to hide the large Korps helix tattoo across her heavy belly. The sides had been cut out, replaced with sections of lacing that further accentuated her voluptuous physique, and her thigh-high stiletto heels were propped up on the arm of a second chair.

The feline clearly loved her jewelry; her wrists were adored with a panoply of bracelets, and heavy earrings dangled from those pointed ears. Other gold piercings dotted her face or were ill concealed by her clothing. Most spectacular was the heavy gold torc around her neck, along which she was idly drawing a sparkling blue claw. The necklace seemed ancient and complicated, as if the figure before her were the priestess of some long-forgotten goddess.

"You must be Zala?" Geode ventured uncertainly.

"I suppose I must be! For now, at least," the feline said with a playfully cocked brow. She then tilted her head to regard the massive draft horse.

A speckled blue claw tapped at one of her prominent fangs before she smiled. "I've seen you once before, you know. Though you were in no state to meet me at the time."

"Oh." Geode blinked before the memory resurfaced. "You were on the transport when we were evaced from the Teepa headquarters."

"Give the girl a sugarcube, got it in one. I've been dying to finally meet you, you know? You saved one of my dearest friends, and brought her back to me. I don't know what I would have done if you hadn't been there."

"It was…" but Geode trailed off. She had reflexively started to wave off the thanks by saying that it had been nothing. But it hadn't been 'nothing;' it had quite literally cost her *everything*, and it hit her that Zala was trying to acknowledge and appreciate *that*, too. The thought was unsettling. After too long a pause, she finally continued. "It was my honor."

The jaguar gestured imperiously at the seat across from her, inviting the Percheron to sit down. Awkwardly, Geode sat down gingerly, as she was bid. She still didn't trust furniture, as such things had a habit of betraying her.

"Starshade means a lot to you. Are you two… er… lovers?"

"Oh, we've been together many times, but that's usually at the command of someone holding a leash or a whip. You'll find us frequently tied up together in the Dominion Club in one predicament or another. So while there is *certainly* a sexual aspect of our interactions, we're not directly in a relationship, as such."

Heat rushed to Geode's face, and she was certain the insides of her ears were beet-red. The horse had no idea how to process the frank statement. Her pure embarrassment was met with delighted laughter.

"Oh, teasing you is going to be *fun*," Zala crooned with mischievous amusement. "But ROSE has asked me to go easy on you, so you can relax. At least, until you're *ready*." The last was said with such anticipation that Geode's blood ran cold… though some secret part of her whispered interest.

"Er…" Geode managed eloquently.

The languid feline looked incredibly tempted to continue teasing but, with visible effort and a soft frustrated sigh, she changed the topic. "You've been here a couple weeks now. How have you been settling in?"

"Well… it's been tough." With effort, the warhorse pulled herself back to the conversation. "Everything is so… different here. I'm not sure what to do with myself. Without a job, without *responsibilities*, I don't have anything to *do*."

"In my experience, RIV is filled with opportunities and activities. Have you not been able to get involved with those?"

Geode blew out a long, frustrated breath. "I'm used to having direction. With the Teepa, my whole life was laid out. I knew what I had to do, and when. Here, I usually meet with Dawn for breakfast, then I spend a couple hours talking with ROSE. She's been running me through classes. Helping me understand the world in ways I never considered. But then I find myself at loose ends, and just start working out."

Zala tilted her head. "Really? Have you not made any connections with people in the gym?"

Geode rubbed the back of her neck, unable to meet Zala's gaze. "I… haven't been to the gym here yet."

"Oh?" The midnight jaguar looked concerned, leaning forward for the first time. "Why not?"

"Because…" the mare started but stopped. She finally dropped her head and sighed heavily. "I'm not sure."

There was a long pause as Geode struggled for more but wasn't sure what to say. Finally, Zala broke the silence. Her voice was soft and compassionate, filled with understanding. "Because you are in a new place, and feel vulnerable in a way you never have before. You feel overwhelmed. An outsider."

The warhorse looked up in surprise. "That's… exactly it."

"So? Let's fix that. You have super-strength; bodyweight exercises are pointless. Time to hit the gym. Let's go," she said perkily.

"What?" Geode looked up, blinking.

"You heard me. Let's go."

"Right now?" she asked, not quite certain what had just happened.

"Yes, right now."

"But—"

"No buts. ROSE will make sure there's appropriate exercise clothing waiting for us in the locker room, by the time we get there. If you *want* to wear clothing, that is."

"Uh—"

"We're going to go, now, or you'll never go. This is the party cake problem."

"The... what?"

"You bring a cake to a party. You set it out all nice and fancy, excited for people to sample this thing you brought. How much of the cake gets eaten?"

"I... don't know?" Geode ventured weakly, entirely lost.

"None, unless *you* take a slice. Otherwise, at the end of the party, there's a full cake left over. You feel bad, because no one enjoyed your cake. But the trick is that no one wanted to be the first person to take a slice. However, once one slice is gone, the whole thing is suddenly fair game and is devoured like a defenseless demimorph at a K-BURP luncheon."

"K-BURP?"

"Not important right now. The moral is that, when you are at a party, you need to make a conscious decision to break the seal on food, so that others feel welcome in eating it. Also, that it's time to go to the gym or you'll keep putting it off."

"Okay...?" Geode said uncertainly.

In a fluid motion the feline stood up and held out one paw to Geode. "Great, it's agreed. Time to go to the gym. Oh, and if you don't want to see public sex, you can ask ROSE to filter it out of your perception."

"I have no idea what just happened."

"That's fine. You'll get used to it."

As she stood up, Geode feared the jaguar was right.

[**Did** you want me to filter out any perceptions of nudity and/or sexual activity?]

Geode stared at the entrance to the gym as the text scrolled across her visor. The question brought her up short. She started to reflexively agree but stopped herself. While Zala looked over, questioningly, the warhorse really considered the question.

Sex did make her feel a little uncomfortable, but how much of that was wanting to be polite? Clearly, these people wanted to be seen — or at least, didn't care if they were — so it wouldn't really be *polite* to ignore them. How much of this aversion was simply what had been drilled into her by her staid upbringing, and then the culture of the military and Teepa? She had been learning just how flawed society was regarding sex and sexuality. How much of that was distaste for her own body?

She shied away from the last question, refusing to let her mind ponder it.

"No, that's okay, you don't need to filter it out."

[Are you sure?]

No, but I'll stick with my answer. It's such a common situation here that I might as well get used to it rather than putting the blinders on. I need to see this place for what it is, not just for the version of it that would make me most comfortable.

With that, she squared her shoulders and strode into the locker room.

She had been expecting to walk into a massive, unending orgy, but she found herself in a remarkably common changing room. Rows of metal lockers filled the space. Fine wooden benches dotted the room. The concrete floor was covered in rubberized mats for traction, dotted with drains.

The air didn't smell nearly as musty as she was used to. It seemed clean; cleaner than any gym she'd ever experienced, actually. But it was clearly well used, as evidenced by the activity in the place. No attempt had been made to separate genders here, but most seemed to be just going about their usual routine. Admittedly, the people were in various stages of undress, but there wasn't the lewd atmosphere she had been braced to expect.

Zala walked by and looked at her with a wry smile.

"Where's... the sex?" Geode couldn't stop herself from asking the question even if she did feel remarkably silly for it.

A slow, languid smile spread across Zala's face. "What? Did you expect a non-stop reefer den hypno-slave orgy?"

The fallen hero shifted uncomfortably.

"I thought as much. Now, don't get me wrong, sex *happens* here. But it's still primarily a *gym*. People are mostly here to work out. Also, in point of fact, Clarion is getting eaten out just a couple of rows over."

"Wait, what?" Geode's head whipped around, but couldn't see anything from where she was standing. "How... can you tell?"

"Because I can hear her ultrasonic moans. The point is that this isn't a porno. Well, not at the moment; that's scheduled for later." Zala licked her lips in clear anticipation. "I'm getting off-track, sorry. The point is that most of the time, most people are just living their lives. Sexuality is *encouraged* here, sure, but it's not everyone, everywhere, all at once, doing nothing but the kinkiest sex imaginable, like the propaganda would have you believe. You've seen how unrealistically *lurid* Heroes' ideas of us are on other counts; is it really surprising to find that here, too?"

"Oh."

"So, let's get changed and work out."

"Okay. Er... thank you." Zala was already turning away to lead her to a set of lockers. ROSE helpfully highlighted one; inside she found the same helix-branded workout clothes she had in her apartment, helpfully sized for her enormous bulk. A magenta towel hung from a hook.

[For future reference, there are gyms here with no horny stuff allowed. Zala just doesn't set foot in those ones.]

"Oh. Thank you. Er... why not?"

[She feels she gets a better workout when she's showing off for potential partners.]

"Oh. I... don't know what I expected. But thank you."

She changed quickly, trying not to think about the environment, but that was an exercise in futility. On the one hand, she felt skittish, almost *afraid*, knowing that others might be interested in her body. But on the other, for the first time she could remember, there wasn't any level of toxic masculinity.

She hadn't even known the name for it until ROSE taught her the concept, but she had always experienced it, even if she had never been able to explain why it made her so uncomfortable. Here, there were none of the rampant homophobic 'jokes', or insinuation that anything feminine was weak if not despicable.

In a matter of moments, she was prepared and already feeling more at ease. She *had* missed regular workouts, and was looking forward to spending the next several hours losing herself in honing her body. Zala took longer to change, leaving Geode several minutes with just her thoughts.

Was Zala joking about Clarion? Or... is she really...

The mare desperately wanted to know what was happening. Zala's knowing smirk was proof enough that she knew what impact that casual remark had left on Geode... such that when it was finally time to head into the gym proper, she could not help but glance down the aisle. Then she turned away, blushing furiously.

Sure enough, the fruitbat was splayed out across a wooden bench, a sabertooth tiger's muzzle fervently lapping between her legs. She could hear the faint rasp of a rough tongue, but the flying fox's moans were apparently far above Geode's hearing range, so there was no sound. It was nonetheless *extremely* clear that Clarion was lost in the pleasure of the moment.

[I can censor out the horny content, if you like.]

But she was already shaking her head.

"No, ROSE. Thank you. *It's part of life here, and I need to get comfortable with it happening. Even if I don't participate.*"

[Okay. Just remember that it's an option. And I will continue offering it as long as you show physiological signs of distress.]

"Thank you, ROSE. Truly."

[Of course, dear. We're villains. That means we take care of each other.]

"That sounds so backwards."

[It does, I suppose, unless you know exactly what the Heroes do.]

Any response she would have offered was lost as she stepped into the full gym. The place was massive; a myriad of machines and stations were set up throughout the space, all clearly heavily-used but well-maintained. What really caught her eye, though, was that several stations were clearly designed for those with enhanced strength.

Then, she realized, one of those very stations was occupied by someone she knew. A gigantic red wolf was working on the bench press. The weight was set to an impressive 1000kg. Despite the immense weight, the bar rose and fell with perfect precision, just barely brushing her massive chest before rising once more.

Spotting her was another gigantic individual: a shaggy bovine that stood just shy of Geode's own height. Thick red fur covered the cow, and she sported a truly incredible pair of horns. She was heavily muscled, though with plenty of softness layered over the powerful core, and a long braid draped over one shoulder and down to her titanic chest.

Geode had taken two steps over to greet her friend when she froze dead in her tracks.

The cow wasn't just spotting Volta. As the bovine pulled back, a thick pink shaft slipped out of the red wolf's muzzle before slamming back in. The supervillain's eyes were half closed in pure bliss as her lips were locked around the intruder. Volta's throat bulged from the sheer girth of the cow. Throughout it all, the barbell rose and fell in perfect form.

The horse flushed furiously as she realized she was staring open-mouthed at the public display. She felt cold and hot and lightheaded all at once. Slowly, she looked down to see Zala grinning with delight.

"Did you...?" Geode trailed off, flummoxed.

"Of course I knew. That could be you, you know. If you wanted."

"What?" the horse asked, distantly.

"There are hundreds of people here that would love to be on either side of that for you. If you wanted it, of course."

"Oh," she managed, eloquently.

"But at the moment, we *are* here to work out. While you wear out your body, you can think about whether you want what she has. And that no matter what your answer is, it's valid." Zala tugged one of her hands, leading her over to a clear area so they could begin stretching.

Numbly, Geode started going through the familiar routine of warming up, but her mind was far away. Zala's question bounced around, never quite finding an answer. Geode couldn't quite understand why she felt vaguely jealous.

Hours passed, as she began to challenge her body in ways she hadn't been able to for weeks. So lost was she in the reverie that it took her a moment to realize ROSE was speaking to her.

[Geode? It's time.]

"Time for what?"

[*You need to get cleaned up. It's time to go to Starshade's decanting.*]

"Wait, Starshade's awake?"

[*She will be shortly! Get ready. It's time to meet your friend again.*]

Chapter 14

Lava Spike

April 3, 2023

Jennifer backed away from the approaching figure. Her heart was pounding like a jackhammer going in all directions, as if trying to escape her chest to save itself. Each step brought more of *it* into view, all gleaming metal and black polymers. Softly glowing LEDs dotted its chest and limbs. But its legs seemed to have too many joints and moved... unnaturally. *A synth.*

She had heard of them, but had never seen one. Artificial life. Sapient robots. *Killbots.* That last was an uncharitable thought, but right now it seemed apropos. The advancing bot had no obvious weapons, but she suspected it didn't need any; maybe that was the point.

As she passed the plinth with the briefcase, the synth paused. With a flourish, it drew out a small object from behind its back. She had never seen it before but she instantly recognized it. It would fit perfectly into the hilt of the pistol in front of her.

The power cell!

But the android was toying with her. With a flick, the item that might save her flew off into the darkness, where it skittered and bounced around with a dull clinking sound. She would never find it without being caught. With that, she turned and ran towards the door.

Fear threatened to fog her mind and steal her ability to plan; the only thing that kept her from blind panic was the realization that the machine wanted her to do just that. Even then, her body screaming to *run*, she almost gave in. But as she reached the darkness, she turned away — away from the door, away from the power cell, away from the synth; she didn't know where she was going, but she had to buy herself time.

The android had begun to chase after her, only to stumble when she veered off unexpectedly. One foot was clearly stepping askew, and the creature wobbled.

He said something about 'calibrating'? I wonder if this is some test for new legs…?

Now it was time for the highest-stakes game of hide-and-seek in her life. She cursed the racket her heels were making, as each frantic footstep seemed to telegraph her location. She might as well be sending up signal flares. She weaved between half-seen crates and around tarps covering unknown hazards.

I have to stay in the dark.

She didn't know what to do. All her self defense plans had assumed a flesh-and-blood attacker. Pepper spray had done nothing, and the stun gun she could still feel hidden at her back was the projectile kind; those spring-loaded probes would find no purchase on steel. The hour she had spent sharpening her claws seemed wasted. She hadn't planned on having to stop a *Terminator*.

Jennifer dove between two crates, hoping to hide while she *thought*. She could hear that… that *thing*, casually strolling towards her. Something about that stride told her that the synth was cruelly toying with her. She was going to die.

No! Focus. What's the first problem?

Sound. Her heels were too loud. Each step was a beacon that signaled her doom. But barefoot wasn't an option — there was too much that could cut up her paws, and stumbling would lead to her quick death. She had to improvise.

She quickly slipped off her shoes. They were her nicest heels, usually reserved for (sadly rare) special occasions. It was with a twinge of regret that she cast them into the darkness, hoping the sound would distract or delay the mechanical monster. She needed the time.

Those sharpened claws sliced through her jeans at the upper thigh as she gave herself impromptu Daisy Dukes. Fashion was no longer high on her list of priorities; with blood pounding in her ears and every instinct screaming to *hurry*, she wrapped the fabric tightly around her feet. She would just have to hope that several layers of denim would save her from the worst of the metal debris, or other sharp hazards she might find.

Not that it'll stop a nail.

The nutria shoved away the dire prediction. Good enough was all she could hope for. She didn't need to dwell on disaster; it would find her soon enough anyway.

*Okay, I should be able to move quieter now. Not sure how that **helps** me, if this thing can see in the dark. I have to assume it can. Now... how can I even the odds?*

Suddenly, with a thunderous CRACK, splinters rained down on her as the crate above her head exploded, and a short scream escaped her. She couldn't help it. She looked up, to see a metal fist slowly withdraw from the hole; it had missed her by mere inches. A stinging in her scalp and wetness down the side of her neck told her that one of those wooden shards had sliced open her cheek.

She was sprinting again. Quieter now, she hunched over, desperately trying to make herself a smaller target. There, against the wall, was a massive metal shelving unit. Shrouded in gloom, she jumped, catching the edge of the second shelf... and pulled herself up with strength she didn't know she possessed.

Heart pounding, she wedged herself behind the unknown boxes cluttering the shelf, trying to work her way further along. She wanted to whimper, but swallowed the noises as she tried to move stealthily. She almost jumped out of her skin when her finger touched a smaller metal cylinder, almost knocking it over.

"Poor lost little beaver. Doesn't know she's already dead." The voice was fully synthetic now. There was a discordant note in it that caused all of her fur to stand on edge. The words were full of cruelty and anticipation.

A bad plan formed in her mind in an instant. She found herself calling out in response before she could stop herself. "Big talk for a glorified cell phone. How's it feel to know you'll be obsolete in six months when the new model comes out?" She spoke down, behind the shelf, hoping the words would sound like they came from the bottom level.

The response was an electronic growl and an unsettling *crunching* noise as the synth started stalking towards her hiding place. She couldn't see him, not without peeking over and possibly giving herself away; she had to judge from the echoing footsteps.

Her heart was beating loud enough she was worried he could hear it.

The steps grew closer.

She slowly drew out the object she had hidden.

The steps grew closer.

Her instincts said *now* was the moment, but she waited.

The steps grew closer still.

It sounded like he was right on top of her. She had moments. She let the taser fall from her fingers, down the gap at the back of the shelves. The heavy plastic made a clatter as it bounced off hard concrete. Instantly, the steps stopped.

She braced both of her denim-wrapped feet on the wall, her back against a heavy crate, and *pushed*. For a heartstopping moment, nothing happened; the crate was much heavier than she had anticipated. Panic surged, driving her body further, and somehow she found the strength. With the screeching protest of wood, the entire crate toppled from the shelf, crashing down upon the metal form below.

The racket was incredible, as the impact vibrated through her. But that had only been half her plan; she already had that metal cylinder in her paw, popping off the cap from muscle memory. Jennifer jumped down after the crate, shaking her prize with distinctive clicking.

Pain shot through her left leg as something sliced through her improvised footwear. The synth was splayed out under an avalanche of shattered wood and unknown metal parts. Wasting no time, she pressed the nozzle atop the spray can in her grasp, and heard that distinctive *hiss* as hi-vis Hunter Orange paint coated the figure's head.

Her surge of triumph was cut short when one arm shot out, bending at an unnatural angle; she felt the impact on her side, forcing her to stagger back. The pain wasn't immediate, which she knew was a bad sign. Then it roared into her central nervous system with a vengeance, turning the world white with agony. Jennifer staggered back, feeling a great gash in her side that was already coated in blood.

As her back hit another wooden crate, she watched with horror; the synth stood up as if the remnants of the crate were but styrofoam packing peanuts. Her ears were assaulted with another cascade of metal as nameless spare parts bounced away across the concrete. Shrouded in darkness, the android slowly turned to face her, unbothered by her attack.

Despair gripped her heart as she watched him step forward. Her attack had left a long crack across the chest of the machine, but otherwise he seemed unharmed. Those green LED eyes were dimmed by the paint, but clearly locked right on her. She had managed to do nothing.

Jennifer willed her body to run, to continue to fight, but her knees gave out instead. She slowly slid to sit on the floor. She sat there, watching, as her foe stepped forward. There was no urgency in the stride. She never had a chance. They both knew it now. There was no rush.

"Please..." she found herself begging. She hated herself at that moment for being so weak. For being so stupid. The crunching of unhurried steps punctuated her hopelessness. Then, the figure towered over her.

Instinctively, she raised her arms to protect her face from a blow. Instead, a metal hand was clamped around her throat, lifting her effortlessly. Her paws kicked uselessly as she struggled to breathe. Her hands scrabbled against the mechanical paw, trying to pry it free, but even adrenaline-fueled strength couldn't budge the digits cutting off her air.

She looked down at the green LED smiley face. She hung there a long moment, slowly choking. Her kicking and tugging grew weaker as she dangled from her neck. Finally, she felt herself moving. The synth was slowly pulling her down, bringing her face to face. He was *right there*, and there was no mercy in that digital face.

"I hate your kind." The voice was synthetic and cruel, filled with disdain. She couldn't exactly argue, as the edges of her vision started to be eaten by a narrowing ring of static. "So squishy and messy. I despise having to work with *vermin*. But you? No one will miss *you*. You will die here, alone, and no one will remember your name. What do you have to say to that?"

She couldn't exactly answer, but perhaps her death was to be answer enough. Some instinct, some buried desperation, caused her to brace her left hand on the chest of the synth. She could feel the crack under her pawpad.

Despair blossomed in her. She was going to die. Anger bloomed too, at the unfairness and the cruelty of this monster. Desperation then spiked, seeking some way, *any* way, to survive. Suddenly, burning agony shot up her left arm unbidden. She felt as thought the entire brand was being rewritten into her flesh.

All that maelstrom of emotions seemed to drain through her arm. She would have screamed if she had air. She had to settle for the tears pouring down her face. But the molten torment magnified further, stealing the color from the world and causing stars to explode in her vision. Jennifer started praying for death just so it would *stop*. Then it all *poured* out through her palm.

There was a heartbeat of stillness before the synth suddenly dropped her. She fell several feet to the ground, gasping around retching. Air, precious *air*, flooded into her lungs too fast. A new pain, as if her body were pierced by a million needles, flashed through her. Only fear and confusion forced her to *look* at Terrock even as her body fought her.

His chest *rusted*, in real time, as she watched. The armored metallic casing turned into brownish-red flakes as it was rapidly eaten away. The machine had staggered back a step before its joints seized with a screech; the polymer components seemed unaffected, surrounded by the rapidly decaying metal.

"What… did you… *do?*" The voice, sounding like a child's toy with a dying battery, emerged. The bewilderment and panic was so stark and *naked* that it twisted a knife in her heart, even for someone who had just tried to murder her.

But she could not find a voice, not when she was still gulping desperate breaths. She never got a chance to answer — not that she *had* an answer — as the LEDs switched off unceremoniously.

The synth that had been Terrock, supervillain and arms dealer, was now nothing more than a rusted statue, slowly flaking away. Jennifer stared at the still form for a long time as she relearned how to breathe… and how to feel pain. She could have sworn she saw a ball of reddish-brown light flicker above the machine's head for a long moment, but then it was gone.

Jennifer whimpered as she pulled herself up another metal rung. The hatch above her was finally drawing closer. Climbing a ladder with one badly gashed foot was a new nightmare, one she had never before contemplated, let alone wanted to experience. But she was finally closing in on her goal. More than anything, she was praying that it wasn't barred or blocked.

The door to the room had remained locked, contrary to every comic book she had ever read. She had no idea how long she had been trapped in the room, but she had spent a long time just... *hurting.*

Another rung, another agony. It had taken her a while to crudely bind her wounds and even longer to find the power cell for the weapon. She didn't know if it worked, but she had almost *died* for this... she *had* *killed* for this. She wasn't leaving it behind. She just hoped that it wasn't a fancy paperweight.

Tears stained her brown facial fur as she finally, finally reached the top of the ladder she had found inconspicuously bolted to the wall. With trembling fingers, she slowly reached up and touched the rough metal. Up close, she could see a latch painted black and yellow, though it was hard to make out in the darkness.

With a silent prayer to forgotten gods, she pushed the latch. Nothing happened. Her heart stopped. Desperately, she pushed harder. She cursed the heavens and the gods for their betrayal as she pushed with everything she had. After a moment, the handle moved. There was a loud metal *pop* as the door above her shifted open a couple of inches. The nutria wept with relief, tears streaming down her face to join the previous stains.

She had always assumed that that had just been a turn of phrase, but the release of stress was so sudden and complete that she literally cried. She could feel the exhaust-filled air against her face, and it was the most beautiful thing she had ever smelled.

With a shaking paw, she pushed open the hatch — which swung up with a little effort, and a lot of protesting screeching — until it tipped over and *crashed* into the ground. She clung to the ladder, her ears ringing, briefly panicking at the thought of anyone hearing. After a moment she realized that she was being silly, and forced herself to climb up to the surface.

The escape hatch had been an unassuming metal plate in the grass near the freeway; at this early morning hour, only the occasional headlights flashed by. Jennifer looked around in a daze, blinking in the night. She felt a shock at just how *normal* everything suddenly seemed. It took a moment to figure out where she was. Her car wasn't far away. She looked at it with hunger and desperation. She slowly pushed herself onto her bloody paws, limping through the grass.

Then she stopped. She had forgotten something. If she left now, Tony would not know she had left. He was waiting for her. It would be cruel to leave without telling him, leaving him to wonder about her fate. With an audible whimper, she turned her head back to where the entrance to the supposedly-abandoned station was. It was almost in the opposite direction.

But she wasn't going to abandon the one person who had shown any concern about her in… too long. *Far* too long. Each limping step towards the unassuming stairs felt like a mistake. Halfway there, a couple came out: two ferrets dressed in punk attire, who took a couple steps towards her before they registered her presence.

Jennifer froze. She was easy prey if they chose hostility. For a long moment, the taller ferret looked at her speculatively, as if appraising how much her kidneys might be worth. But the shorter one, with a nasty scar across her left cheek, elbowed her companion. Her expression was more compassionate as she looked at the blood-covered older woman.

The tall one looked sheepish as her companion glared. With an apologetic smile, the shorter ferret grabbed the other by the paw and pointedly pulled her along into the night. The danger having passed, Jennifer continued her limping journey.

It seemed to take forever to cross the distance. She almost cried when she reached the stairs, and stepped onto the concrete instead of the softer grass. She was breathing heavily by the time she reached the bottom of the stairs. The thought of having to climb the stairs was almost unbearable, but she was here.

Her paw rapped dully on the thick metal door. After a moment, it swung open to reveal the suspicious face of a deer. Tony was clearly annoyed at the late arrival… until he saw her, and she saw the color drain from the inside of his ears.

"Holy shit, *Jennifer?!* What happened?" He stepped forward, hands out but not quite touching her. In the dim light of the stairs, he was staring openly at her blood-covered face, neck, body… well, *all* of her. For some reason, she felt oddly ashamed at being so dirty.

"Oh my god. You're bleeding. Fuck!" The concern in his voice was touching. He hit a button she hadn't noticed on his belt, before he took her by her less-injured arm and guided her to sit down on the steps.

"We need to get you tended. Did… did Terrock do this to you?" She nodded, unable to find her voice. Suddenly, she was *exhausted.* Her thoughts felt foggy and distant. For some reason, the thought that struck her was that she was in no shape to drive home. A chilling image flickered through her mind, of disastrously veering off the road as she fainted in this moment, slumping over the steering wheel; had she gone to her car instead of seeking out the deer, she might have survived the synth only to die in a stupid *accident.*

"Oh fuck. Did you, uh, *escape?* Is he still after you…?" Tony looked around frantically, as the implications struck him.

But she was shaking her head and squeezing his hand. *When did I take his hand?* It took her a moment to speak. She had to swallow, finding her mouth dry. "He's dead." Her voice was hoarse and flat. It sounded alien to her ears, as if it was someone else speaking. Someone colder.

The deer stopped and stared. For a long time, he just *looked* at her. Finally, he hissed his question in fear and concern. "You *killed* Terrock? You killed *Terrock?*" She hadn't thought he could be more pale, but he managed somehow.

She nodded confirmation. She was beyond caring about consequences. She was just so tired. After a minute, she spoke again. She didn't know where the words came from. "He started it. I finished it."

It was only then that she realized the two of them weren't alone. Another whitetail — this one a little taller and a little older-looking than Tony — was staring at her like she was a pair of approaching headlights.

"What's… going on, Tony?" His voice was guarded and concerned and distant, clearly (and not unreasonably) scared of the crazy lady, covered in blood, who had just admitted to killing an infamous criminal arms dealer. Tony jumped at the words, having been too focused on her to realize their company.

The cook looked back and flashed a tight, humorless smile. "You heard the lady. She… killed Terrock. This is Jennifer, my friend."

The cousin, whose name she couldn't remember, gazed at her like she was… like she was *a supervillain.* He then glanced at Tony, and his shoulder fell slightly. He muttered softly though her ears were sensitive enough to pick up the invectives. Louder, he asked, "Are you sure about this?"

With a sigh, Tony nodded. "Yes. She's going into shock. She came here to make a purchase. I guess Terrock decided otherwise. We need to get her somewhere safe."

Jennifer was having more trouble following the conversation. It seemed distant. Irrelevant. She shook herself a bit, forcing herself back into the present.

As the taller deer headed downstairs, Tony kneeled in front of her.

"You need to tell me what's going on. You've killed two people in two weeks. Please. Tell me. What is going on?" His voice was urgent. Pleading. She couldn't say no to that.

"Some... *thing* branded me. Makes Heroes go berserk and try to kill me. Some villain is coming to *claim* me if I survive them. I'm... I don't want to die."

"*Branded you?!*" Tony asked in an admittedly reasonable tone of voice.

She held out her left arm and spread the fur in a spot that wasn't covered in blood, grease, grime, or other mystery substances. (There weren't a lot of places to choose from.) Tony peered down, seeing the scars, then up at her. She could see the white ringing his sapphire eyes.

"Oh fuck, this is serious. *Fuck.*" There was disbelief in his voice, and she was wondering if this would be where he abandoned her to save himself. He turned away, pounding his fist on the concrete wall. His shoulders fell in a great sigh, as he turned around.

"Okay, we're going to get you cleaned up. I know a guy that *might* be able to help. But he got mixed up with some serious criminals. I haven't spoken to him in a while, but he owes me. If anyone can help keep you safe, it's him. But... it might take time. And we need to be careful. *Very* careful. These are some *real fucking dangerous* people he's mixed up with."

With that, Tony helped her up and supported her so she didn't have to put much weight on her gashed paw. He surprised her by taking her down the stairs, back into the station. She didn't have the strength to argue. She didn't have the strength to think much more at all, for a while.

CHAPTER 15

TECTONIC UPLIFT

April 2, 2023

...

...

...

...

[Welcome Back, Starshade!]

Starshade gasped for air. The deep breath felt... wrong. Her eyes flew open, and she found herself staring at the inside of a Korps medical tank, already drained of its fluid recovery medium, with only a few streaks and droplets still lining the transparent pane in front of her. Microfans mounted around her quickly evaporated the liquid left on her body, leaving her clean and (mostly) dry. She could see outside into the larger room beyond, filled with identical tanks and various other medical paraphernalia. She had woken up in this situation often enough that she didn't panic at the confinement.

But her breathing was another story. Air came easily, but it didn't feel quite right; it didn't feel like *breathing*. Her lungs felt *wrong*. Her breath started to quicken, which drove the alien sensation further. It was like some *parasite* was inside her. Her pulse pounding in her ears, she started to reach up to her chest.

[It's okay, dear. You're okay. Those are your new lungs. We have you. You're safe.]

The wave of soothing mental contact cooled her panic, and she was able to let the spiral of anxiety go. She swallowed, forcing herself back into control. Her memories were resurfacing: the strange dream she had with ROSE, the unnerving time spent inhabiting the Nurse O chassis... her decision. But still, she couldn't help but think about her breathing, even if she was no longer panicking.

ROSE didn't appear to her often in full-body avatar mode, but she always left the cottontail blushing when she did. Her appearance was never quite the same. This time, she appeared as a vaguely feline shadow, tall and graceful, with a notable hourglass figure. Her iteration of ROSE always took the shape of a shade; an *almost* distinctive silhouette. Never quite identifiable, but always tugging at the back of her mind, a memory she couldn't quite place... because it was the shape of someone who had fucked her when she was tied down and blindfolded in the Dominion Club. She was always teasing with that tempting, suggestive, *almost-*knowledge. It was a *very* effective way to derail any line of thought the bunny had.

This time was no different. The shadowy tail of the augmented-reality overlay lashed languidly as the digital feline slinked towards the tank, and trailed one phantom claw down the glass that separated her from the world. Starshade was flushing furiously and squirming, trying desperately to figure out who ROSE was hinting at this time. But, as always, she couldn't quite place it.

... And in the process, she had *entirely* forgotten about her breathing.

[There we go, dear.]

What?

She asked, but realized the answer immediately. She had started to hyperfixate on her breathing and was working herself towards a panic spiral — but now, she was breathing normally. The lungs still felt slightly odd, but no longer like the unnatural *wrongness* she had first encountered.

Oh. Thank you, ROSE.

The figure vanished, but the presence in the back of her mind did not. She could still feel ROSE there, like a warm hug on her soul. Panic broken, her memories snapped into place. She had chosen the cybernetic lungs, and would now have to learn more about them. ROSE had offered details, but she hadn't been in the headspace to process any of it; she just knew Adam had made them for her. That was enough, at the time.

A synthetic fox walked into the room, as proper as ever, but Starshade saw her differently than before. She *knew* more about the mysterious medical synth now. It was both eerie and comforting; Nurse O was no longer an unknowable enigma. Still incomprehensible in many ways, yes, but the rabbit saw her and recognized her in a way she couldn't quite describe. The demure medic was friend now, and the sight of her striding into the room brought a smile to Starshade's lips... even if the tips of her pierced ears still stung in memory.

The hiss of air releasing heralded her imminent release, and the entire front cover of the capsule-like medical tank slid open smoothly. The whole thing had inclined so that she could step out, whenever she felt she had her legs under her. (Which was immediately, because she was still Starshade.)

The rabbit bounced out as soon as she was clear, stumbling slightly — her legs weren't quite under her yet, after all — but she didn't care. She caught the lip of a nearby table to steady herself. A couple careful hops on her bare paws, and she felt ready to sprint across the state. She looked at the nurse with bright eyes and eagerness.

"Nice to see you, Nurse O! Thank you so much for all your help. I really appreciate it."

The synthetic arctic fox paused and looked at her, slowly tilting her head as if seeing her from a different angle might reveal something. Starshade had never seen the always-composed nurse be surprised. She realized that, perhaps, she had not been so understanding and thankful the past few times she had left one of these tanks. But she hadn't been that bad, had she?

[Dear, I'll remind you that last time involved a great many novel invectives, pushing yourself too hard, and some very creative whining. You're lucky that Nurse O found the whole thing more amusing than exasperating.]

A flush spread up her long ears as they splayed back. Perhaps she *had* been a bit overeager to escape the medbay. But it was the glimpse she'd had into who Nurse O was that had changed all that. She resolved to be kind to the hardworking medic, and also to try and spend some time socially with the synth. But her thoughts were interrupted, by the nurse gesturing to the full length mirror nearby.

"Starshade, now that you are operational, please do not be alarmed. There have been some minor cosmetic changes to your appearance that you should be aware of."

With a touch of trepidation, she stepped closer to get a look. She remained the tall, lithe rabbit she had been, though why she thought a change to that would register as a 'minor cosmetic change' she wasn't sure. Her pelt was still the complex brown of a desert cottontail. The black shorts she'd worn in the tank were looser than she generally liked, but the magenta racerback (with obligatory helix symbol) was stretched over her large chest in a pleasing display. It was her *eyes* that stood out.

Her breath stopped for a moment. Her eyes were no longer the dark brown they had always been; they were now a bright purple. The reflection reached up with one trembling paw to touch the side of her face. The other paw reached out towards the mirror as she stepped closer.

The shade of violet shifted as the light changed. Her irises glittered and sparkled, like a precious gem. Like *amethyst*. Starshade peered at herself in pure, open wonder. Another realization crashed into her: for the first time in her life, she didn't have her mother's eyes. Part of her distantly noted that her new eyes *shined* when she was at the edge of tears.

"What… happened?" she asked distantly, unable to look away.

"It happened during the fight, when your companion used her powers on you. We're still not certain of the extent and function of her abilities — stress-induced breakthrough manifestations of novel powers can be unpredictable — but your eyes appear to be perfectly normal, from a functional and biological standpoint. The color change seems purely cosmetic. If you like, we can of course change your eyes to anything you choose."

"No!" She was surprised at the vehemence of her own reaction, but immediately sorry that she snapped. "No. Sorry. I… *like* it. It's just a surprise. But… what happened with Sl—… the horse?" she corrected herself quickly. Her mind was still on her eyes, but she would need to be better about that. She hoped her friend had a *name* now. That would make the process so much easier.

"She is waiting for you with the others, just outside. I know how much you would rather go to them than the alternative, so they are still waiting in the gathering room. And she has chosen the name Geode."

"Geode… Geode…" she tasted the name, rolled it over in her mind, and eventually grinned at the synth. "It's perfect. So she chose to stay?"

The nurse gave one gracious nod, the waveform pattern on her mask pulsing with her words even as she gestured for Starshade to precede her out of the room. "Technically, the decision has been delayed until she speaks with you, but yes. We believe she will stay with us. Her two weeks awake here have not been without incident, but she is settling in well. Further details are hers to share."

Geode is a good name. Suits her.

[She seems very happy with it.]

Geode's defection to the Korps had been so sudden, and so prompted by traumatic urgency, that Starshade had worried that the horse would choose to leave once the crisis of the moment faded. It was not easy to abandon your previous life, your entire *world*, as she knew all too well... even when the world you were leaving was destroying you. With that thought, she proceeded through the door into the gathering room.

Then a black-and-glittering-blue missile *launched* itself at her with a squeal.

Starshade staggered as Zala crashed into her, and wrapped her tightly in two strong arms. Then the jaguar was *crying* and *laughing* and Starshade was too. They embraced for a long time, with the cat's face buried in Starshade's cleavage and the rabbit's chin resting between those triangle ears.

Finally, as Zala started to relax her grip, the cottontail opened her eyes. A true smile spread across her muzzle as she saw other friends. Adam was there, looking smug; he had every right to be, having built bespoke lungs on short notice for her. Mabel was there, looking disgusted at the display of affection between the two friends, but they both knew it was an act. The glint in her eye and the quirk at the corner of her muzzle showed her true feelings.

She was surprised to see Celia coiled in a corner. The viper was always so hard to read, but seemed happy to see the rabbit. Her purple tongue flicked out, tasting the air in... greeting? She guessed?

The tiny pink-clad dik-dik was sitting in a chair, looking delighted. Starshade was always happy to see Dawn, though she was surprised she didn't see Orion with her. The two were often together, and she liked the dour Giant Eland. Instead, sitting next to her was Geode. The Percheron was clearly trying to look as inconspicuous as a half-ton of sparkling purple mare could manage.

The cottontail froze. She didn't know who to greet first. Zala had taken initiative. But who would she greet next? Who would she greet *last*? Would her friends get jealous, or think she didn't value them, because she greeted someone else *first*? Or what if they thought she was greeting them first so she could get her obligation to them over with? How would she—

[*Calm.*]

They were her friends. It was *okay*. She turned to the nearest, and smiled brightly to Mabel. Somehow she was unsurprised that the catamount had positioned herself nearby. She wrapped her arms around the shorter agent with a tiny squeal. "I'm so happy to see you Mabes!"

The cat burglar relaxed into the warm hug. "You really scared us, Glitterdust. I am so, *so* glad you're okay. Please, be careful next time? And this is coming from *me*." Though she had tried to add a bit of humor at the end, Starshade could tell her friend was deeply relieved to see her up and about.

She returned a weak smile. "I shall strive to follow the example of Mabel, the Paragon of Caution herself." She squeezed her friend tight, trying to show how much she cared about the catamount through hugs alone. "Thank you, Mabes. And thanks for passing along my stupid tweet. You saved my life."

The cottontail finally stepped back, seeing Mabel wipe away a tear before grinning back. "And you gave me the perfect gift with Jordan's password. I can't wait to use it." The two supervillains shared a conspiratorial look of anticipated mischief. Then Starshade turned to greet her next friend.

Adam was standing there. The diminutive lion was much shorter than she was. He was an engineer and tech whiz. One of the few in RIV trusted to work on RCGs and other extremely sensitive Korps equipment. The lion specialized in keeping existing tech operational; his inspirations tended to be about enhancements and iterative upgrades, rather than building new devices. Of course, there *were* exceptions, like her lungs.

She swept him up into a hug and kissed the top of his head. The maneuver smashed the poor lion's face into her chest, and the poor base techie squirmed in the embrace until she put him down. Starshade couldn't help but giggle at the blush that had turned the inside of his ears bright red, but Adam played it off by fussing over the mane that was finally starting to fill out.

"I'm so glad you're okay, Starshade," he said, after a moment of regaining his composure. "I was honored that you chose to accept my offer to build you new lungs. I'm curious, though — which feature was it that sold you on my proposal, over bioidentical replacements?"

"I didn't pay attention to the features." She said it casually, but suddenly every eye in the room was fixed on her in a mix of shock and alarm.

Adam looked confused. "But... what?"

"*You* made them. That's all I needed to know at the time. I'm going to need you to run the features by me again at some point... !" She said the words casually and brightly. She did, however, take delight in the reactions around the room.

The lion stared in a mix of confusion and horror, evidently unable to comprehend someone not *fully* understanding the specs of a new gadget — to say nothing of a cybernetic organ replacement! — before becoming an early adopter. Zala looked entirely unsurprised, if exasperated... not that she had any room to complain, given her own plans for *her* next Empire visit. Geode looked faintly alarmed at the prospect, though Dawn smirked and rolled her eyes in resigned acceptance. For her part, Mabel had thrown her paws up and was beseeching some goddess or other for patience. Conversely, Celia looked like a terrifying, unknowable monster who would be very annoyed at finding inedible bits in her next meal, or so the bunny guessed; she still hadn't *quite* figured out the lamia's expressions yet.

She took the opportunity afforded by Adam's consternation to approach the massive serpent. The two of them watched each other for a moment, before Starshade gave an awkward half wave. She immediately felt like an idiot and smiled more genuinely.

"Hi... er... I'm surprised to see you here, Celia. But... thank you for coming for me." She rubbed the back of her neck, feeling her ears growing hot. "Both times."

"My dear Ssstarsssshade, it wasss my pleasssure." The snake then paused for a moment. The next words seemed more difficult for her, a touch of uncertainty entering that self assured voice. "In truth, I wanted to make sssure you were awake, and in good health. It isss true that I could have sssimply have asssked ROSSSE. But reportsss do not reassssure the heart quite asss well asss one might hope."

The cottontail gaped at the lamia. "Wait, you were worried about me?"

The viper swallowed and bobbed her head back and forth. "Of courssse. You were gravely injured. I care about all thossse basssed here in RIV. I worry over each perssson asssssigned here, essspecccially the agentsss who are ssso often in harmsss way. Ssstill… I will admit that I have a particular… *fondnessss* for your anticsss."

Is she…

She was certain the large woman was holding back, wasn't telling her *something*. Starshade looked again at the serpent with appraising eyes. She was gigantic and scary and hard to read. But she was *here*, and expressing concern.

Does she just feel bad because I almost died when she was there? Or… ROSE, what's going on?

[*I'm sorry, dear. You know I don't share personal thoughts without explicit consent.*]

Personal thoughts…

Starshade would need to think about the implications, *later*; now was not the time. What was important now was that the base commander herself wanted to make sure she was okay. Whatever the reason, it was currently immaterial, whether guilt or something else. With a smile, she forced herself to stop diving down that particular rabbit hole.

"Thank you. I'm glad you came."

ROSE, do you think it would be possible to talk with Celia privately at some point? I know she's always busy with base… stuff. I know she doesn't have time for every field agent.

[*More than possible. I'm happy to arrange a time that fits her schedule.*]

Thank you, ROSE.

Then, she turned to the remaining pair. She eyed Dawn and Geode closely. Dawn was watching her with bright eyes and an easy smile; she was lounging a bit, at ease. Geode, however, was sitting stiffly and nervously. Still, the closeness of the two, the way the mare's body language deferred to the dik-dik's, was obvious. She wondered how far things had gotten; Dawn was well on her way to owning the poor horse. The cottontail secretly thought that might be good for both of them. Even if things didn't progress the way she suspected, she was delighted that the former Hero was developing a social circle of *some* sort in her absence.

"Dawn, I'm so happy to see you again. Where's Orion? I figured he'd be here too."

The dik-dik rolled her eyes in bemused exasperation. "When he heard that your knife broke in the fight with Manifest Destiny, he was mortified. Three days ago, he woke up at 2:00am and immediately started working on a new project like a man possessed. When I asked him what he was doing, he said only, and I quote — 'Dagger.' — before returning to work. I suspect we won't see him for a couple days, at which point you will have a new toy."

Starshade shook her head. Orion was a master smith. When he wasn't tied up by... *with* other obligations, he was often crafting particularly unique, or personalized, or *intricate* items. While the various super-science fabricators filled most of the base's needs, there was still call for personal attention on special projects. The Giant Eland prided himself on quality. Thanks to the Korps, he was able to dedicate himself to his passion; many of the blades carried by agents had been created by the gruff antelope. (Also, much of those same agents' *specialty* bondage gear.)

"I look forward to seeing him in a few days, then. Thank you for coming! I'm so glad to see that you and Geode have hit it off." The satisfied hint of a smile and slight blush from the draft horse told her that she had hit the mark.

"I've been showing her around, and helping her settle in. We put her in the empty apartment unit next to mine."

"Perfect! So I can visit you both at the same time." She almost, but not quite, suppressed the sly grin and knowing tone as she continued. "Has she been behaving?"

Geode sat up straighter at the question, but Dawn looked and sounded satisfied. "Oh yes. She's been a *very good girl.*"

As the giant draft horse blushed furiously, she was met by a chorus of giggles. Dawn stood up and wrapped herself around Starshade. "I'm so happy you're okay."

The cottontail hugged the tiny woman back, blinking away the sudden urge to cry. The dik-dik always seemed to fill any room with her cheerful demeanor and force of personality; it was moments like this, when Dawn's head only reached her belly, that Starshade remembered just how *small* the woman was. The thought of how close she had come to... *not being here* for this moment... threatened to overwhelm her. But here she was, surrounded by people who cared about her. That was enough.

After a moment, with the farrier settling into the hug, Starshade finally smiled at Geode. "And you! I'm so glad to see you here. I was worried you might choose to leave before I woke up."

The horse looked sheepish. "Part of me was wondering if you really wanted me here."

Starshade understood, then. She patted Dawn, who stepped back as compassion spread across her face. "Geode... of course I wanted you here. I want to finally get to *know* you when the stakes aren't life or death. I want to show you the brighter world you were always trying to find." The rabbit stepped forward and took one of the fallen hero's giant hands in her own. "You are my *friend.* Let's talk, privately. Later. But for now... so, you've decided to stay with the Korps, then?"

Geode glanced at Celia, who remained silent and inscrutable, before frowning. "It's not official yet. I wanted to talk with you first. But... I think so. At least for a while. Still trying to... figure things out. What I *want* out of life. *Who* I want to be." She shrugged helplessly.

Patting the horse's hand she smiled. "You finally have time to find yourself." She then turned to address the entire room. "But for now, I'm starving. Feels like I haven't eaten in weeks."

The joke was met with soft groans and polite chuckles. But underlying the expected reaction to the expected joke was... love. It was not something she had ever *expected* to feel, until the Korps. Something she had never really even understood. She hoped that Geode would learn that same lesson; the poor girl had been wounded so deeply and so often that she didn't even know she was hurting.

She just hoped that Geode had time enough to heal, before the world tried to hurt her again.

CHAPTER 16

TRANSVERSE STRAIN

April 2, 2023

Geode leaned over the railing, gazing across the peaceful garden below. She had done this a lot over the past week, and there was always something new to see. The lush greenery wasn't in the strictly regimented plots she'd expected. At first, it seemed to be completely wild, but she had started to realize it was carefully tended that way; there were hidden paths that twisted and intersected harmoniously, and the plants complimented each other. She was certain that she could spend years staring at this space and always see something new.

That seemed true for the Korps as well. Her first few conscious days here had been difficult in many ways. Lacking the strict structure of the Teepa, she had struggled; she had gone from no choices at all to *endless* possibilities. Tori, her therapist, had been helping her try to integrate. That had helped more than she cared to admit. (She still felt shame that she needed a therapist, but she was working on that too.)

It had not helped that she didn't really know anyone here. She had only known Starshade briefly, during that horrible night, and the rabbit had at least been *someone* familiar. But she had been so injured that even that comfort was gone, leaving the horse alone.

Well, not entirely alone. She had started to make... friends? Dawn, Volta, and Maddy had all made it a point to spend time with the Percheron. She liked them, and had started to find things in common with them. She and Mabel were still feeling each other out, though. They were so... *different* that it seemed at times they had no common ground, but that was slowly changing. Ellen, she had barely seen since that first day. It troubled her, because she was worried she had done something wrong. Geode hoped she hadn't offended the demimorph in some way.

The horse stared into the riot of green below her as she pondered her place here. The choice was rapidly approaching... as was Starshade. Geode had slipped out of the rabbit's reunion tour, overwhelmed by the gathering. The horse had felt terribly bad about doing so, but Dawn and ROSE had both encouraged her to act on her needs, and assured her that withdrawing from overwhelming social situations *was* in fact a real and valid one. Now, the lithe cottontail was jogging down the corridor to meet her.

The mare felt oddly nervous. The pair had faced down the entire TPA, it seemed. They had each saved each other's lives. They had gone through *hell* together. But they didn't really *know* each other. This would be the first time they had to just... *talk*... without the stakes being life and death.

The bunny loped gracefully towards her. Her long stride ate the meters easily, and the smile on her face showed how much she loved the act of running. Some of the tension in Geode eased, as the smile grew brighter when she saw the amethyst horse. Then she...

JUMPED...

... *and was suddenly wrapping two arms around the mare, leaving a fading starry afterimage behind.*

Geode easily withstood the impact, even unexpectedly, but had to enfold her own arms around the bunny so the supervillain didn't fall. The cottontail couldn't quite get her arms all the way around her massive form. They hugged for a moment before the mare gently put the younger woman down.

Starshade took a seat in one of the nearby chairs, if that was what one could call the position; the rabbit was twisted in the seat, with one leg folded against the arm and the other sticking straight up. Her back was lounging against the corner of the chair. One hand was folded, elbow against the back of the chair and hand on the back of her head, while the other was splayed out over the arm. She was clearly committing serious crimes against sitting. Geode had no idea how she even managed the pose, much less how the woman could be comfortable in such a position.

After giving the bunny a long look, the Percheron sat down, *correctly*, on another chair. A moment passed as they both wondered how to start the conversation. There was so much between them and yet so very little.

How does one introduce themselves to someone they already share a bond with?

The warhorse started slowly. "Thank you... for saving me. In the warehouse. They would have killed me. I would never have been able to stand up to my entire team, plus Fatal Thorns. I was... too surprised to run, before it was too late."

"I mean, it's only fair. You saved my life in the first warehouse. That day, when you cornered me." The rabbit gave a sympathetic shrug.

"Not killing someone isn't the same as saving someone's life, is it? You had every reason to suspect that that first encounter was a trap. And I am... I *was* a Hero. Walking away would have meant one less person to fight." The thought had plagued Geode. She felt better having finally voiced it.

"Seems to me that there's one less person to fight now. With the added bonus of one cute girl to fight *alongside*." Starshade's wry grin accompanied the easy compliment.

Still, Geode found herself blushing. She gazed down into the garden, trying to get her brain working again. They lapsed into silence, still trying to figure out how to *talk* with each other.

As usual, it was the rabbit that jumped into action. "So, ROSE has told me a lot about what you've been up to since you woke up. But how are you settling in? Really?" Her words were gentle, but genuinely, concerned.

Geode blew out a breath and looked over at the garden below. "It's... been tough. Everything is new and confusing. Every day I see villains I know from briefings, or even those I fought myself. I encounter what feels like a *surprising* amount of public sex, even for... here. It's very chaotic. But it's... good? Everyone here is so *genuine*. People are taken care of instead of... being forgotten. I'm finally starting to see that more is possible than I ever imagined."

The rabbit took a minute to consider the words. "Are you going to stay?" The words were asked casually, but the fallen hero knew they were nothing of the sort.

At least the horse had an answer now. She nodded. "I'm going to stay. I don't exactly have a choice, honestly; while the Teepa seems to be claiming I was kidnapped instead of defected, I have no doubt they'd kill me if they got me back. But... that's not why I'm staying. The Korps is the only place I've ever seen that seems to want to make the world a better place. I don't know if... *we*... will ever pull it off. But... I can dream... now. And, well, saving the world has always been my thing."

The admission had taken a lot from her. To finally stop her running from the inevitable. To acknowledge that now she was *part* of the Korps, instead of just a guest. But it felt right.

"I'm going to tell Celia later today, officially. Though I'm sure she already knows."

Starshade chuckled. "I'm never sure if ROSE feeds her intel or if she's just better at seeing the shape of events than we are. Probably both."

"She is one of the most terrifying people I've ever met. But I get the sense she cares deeply about everyone around her."

"She's base commander for a reason. The Overlord trusts her." Starshade was replaced by a statue made of the night sky as she was suddenly...

STANDING...

... at the railing overlooking the garden. Geode rose to stand next to her, realizing again just how much she towered over the agent.

"So, enough of the heavy stuff. Has Dawn fucked you yet?"

Geode sputtered, caught completely off guard. "W-what?" Her voice squeaked and she looked down at the rabbit with shock.

Starshade giggled and smiled. "I'll take it from your scandalized tone that it hasn't happened yet. I expect to hear about it when it does!"

But the Percheron looked away, frowning. She felt her shoulders hunch a bit. "She's just being... friendly."

The comment was met with a snort. "Bullshit. That girl might as well have planted a flag on you that says 'I'm going to fuck this horse.' She is *definitely* interested. The question is, are you?" The rabbit's tone turned concerned and serious at the end, sensing something.

Geode swallowed. "I... don't know."

The rabbit turned around and hopped up to sit on the railing, perched precariously over the drop to the lower level. But it gave her the angle to look into the draft horse's face. "Geode, it's okay. If you aren't interested, it's fine. I just... saw how close you two seemed."

Self-hatred boiled up within her. She couldn't shake the feelings of inadequacy that always accompanied these thoughts. Finally, her voice emerged, tiny and distant. "I don't want to hurt her."

The rabbit cocked her head to the side, looking concerned and confused. "How would you hurt her?"

Geode distantly wondered what the loud, shrieking noise filling her ears was, until she realized she had crushed and twisted the metal railing tube in her hands. With a sob, she pulled away as if she had been burned, hugging herself and turning so she didn't have to see the cottontail.

"Like I just did. I'm... too strong and too heavy... and too... *big*." The last word came out as barely a whisper.

The warhorse almost jumped when she felt a paw gently touch her back. "First, it's *adorable* that you think that you'd be on top. Second, she sleeps with *Orion*, so I would be shocked if she couldn't fit you. But I'm starting to think this isn't about Dawn."

Hunching further and hugging herself harder, she didn't realize she was crying until the damp fur of her muzzle started cooling in the air. She felt monstrous and ugly. She had always tried so hard not to think about her body. But considering the idea of actually having sex? Then she couldn't avoid it.

[Oh, my poor Dear. It's okay.]

As ROSE projected soothing love into her mind, Starshade let out a soft "Oh," before gently but firmly guiding Geode to sit down. There was no resistance in her. The supervillain then hugged the giant horse from behind while silent sobs shook her massive shoulders.

They stayed there for a while, as waves of self-hatred and revulsion cascaded through her. But, finally, the tears ebbed. She realized that Starshade was gently stroking her broad muzzle and whispering "It's okay..." over and over in her ear. Her heart ached, as did her throat. But she felt a little better.

Only when Starshade sensed Geode was ready, did she change her mantra. "It's okay, Geode. It's okay. *You* are okay. You are *safe* here. And you don't have to be stuck in a body you don't like. Not anymore."

"I..." she started, but trailed off. She didn't know what to say. She wasn't sure what she wanted to say.

"I always knew I was trans. I always knew my body was wrong. I couldn't *wait* to go to Empire and fix it, make myself more me than I'd ever been. It wasn't just..." Starshade trailed off, blushing a bit as her next words were more tentative. "It wasn't just my bits that I needed to get rid of. I shaped my body into one that was really *mine*. I *knew* what I wanted, even if I never thought I could *get* there. But you didn't even have that, did you?"

Starshade's long sigh warmed the damp fur along her neck. "If I had to guess, you're like a lot of others here. You always hated your body, but you didn't know why. Do you even know your sexuality?"

The question caught her completely off-guard once more. Shame blossomed in her chest; how, at thirty-five years of age, could she not know something so fundamental about herself? But she shook her head slowly. "No." Her answer was tiny and tinny and distant, as if muffled by the blush that filled her ears.

Those paws stroked her muzzle gently, not stopping from her admission. "It's okay, Geode. It's okay."

Unbidden, she couldn't stop herself from admitting something she had never told anyone. The depths of her shame. "I just... when I get... when I *think*... when my body... *reacts*... I just want it to go away."

"Oh. Oh, *Geode*." The words were so filled with such heartbreaking compassion that Geode couldn't stop the tears from flowing again. Again, ROSE and Starshade wrapped her in love as the shame and fear and self loathing worked their way out of her. She cried until her throat ached and her eyes hurt and her shirt was sodden.

But the tears were not endless. Though exhausted, she felt better. The rabbit slowly let her go to step in front of her. Both her paws wrapped around her right hand, rubbing small circles. "Let me take you to Empire tomorrow. First thing. We'll get you the body you can not only be comfortable in, but feel sexy in. Whatever that is."

Geode could only nod. "I... think I'd like that." The idea of doing it was so... daunting. But she had faced bigger stakes than her own happiness. She was not one to shrink from battle, even if it did make her heart race with fear.

Starshade clearly sensed the direction of her thoughts, guiding her away from dwelling on it. "So, you clearly like Dawn. Tell me about her."

"But you already know her," she said with a frown.

"Yes, but I want to know her through *your* eyes. Tell me how *you* see her."

The fallen hero let herself be led away from the treacherous thoughts, willing to see where the rabbit led. "Well... Dawn has been a tremendous help. She's just endlessly cheerful, and always willing to take time for a wayward horse. Even if she does occasionally just... uh... 'bend me to her will,' as she describes it." She broke off with a blush, and her voice grew weaker. *"Maybe especially when she does that."*

Patting her hand encouragingly, the cottontail had a knowing smirk. "Because when Dawn exerts that power over you, *you* can surrender control for a little bit, right? Gives you the freedom *not* to have to choose anything."

Geode flushed harder, but nodded. "Er... yeah. Maybe."

"Listen, it's clear you don't know much about bondage."

The warhorse jolted in startlement, staring wide eyed at the blunt question. "Er," she managed bravely. Rallying, she tried again. "I got the primer from ROSE on the second day...?"

"... And you thought it was purely academic and would never apply to you, because you weren't expecting to get in that kind of a relationship, *right?*"

She couldn't help but flinch as the supervillain hit exactly what she was thinking.

"Listen, Geode. Dawn is an experienced Domme. If you are going to end up in a relationship with her or, frankly, if you are going to survive around here without imploding, you really need to internalize the concepts. Consent. Safewords. Traffic light system. Power dynamics."

The horse shifted uneasily. "I don't know..."

"... if you want to end up in a relationship." Starshade finished for her. "And that's entirely fine! But a lot is changing about your life. When you get into something, you should go in with your eyes open. Even if, after considering it, that something turns out to be nothing."

The mare bit her lip, unable to quite meet the rabbit's eye. "Sex is so... complicated here. I'm not sure... how it even works. How do you know... you aren't hurting someone?" The words came haltingly as she struggled to understand.

"The best place to start, when you're ready, is a long conversation with ROSE. She can share the situations you're likely to come across, and help you understand if those are the sorts of things that might interest you. You can work with her to figure out the kinds of things you would or wouldn't consent to — or that you'd want to have a discussion about first! — and then you can set that list to be automatically shared with a partner's ROSE. What's more, if there are things you don't want to see *others* engaged in, you can tell ROSE and she can filter the, uh, *explicit* parts out of your vision. You'll still know they're *there* — we don't want you tripping over people you don't see — but you won't see those things that would cause you distress. There are people here that filter out *all* of the sexy shenanigans the rest of us get up to."

Geode ruminated on the points for a long moment. Starshade was right. Going into a situation where you knew your partner's interests… made the whole idea more palatable. And now that she really thought about it, she *did* like Dawn. If she could think past the obstruction of her own vile body, she could admit to feeling… *something* for the tiny farrier. But she shied away from thinking about intimacy; she didn't want to cry again. Instead, she changed the topic.

"Mabel and Volta have been teaching me to play video games."

The rabbit looked over with shining, violet eyes. "Oh! That's excellent. Which games?"

With a rueful smile, Geode shrugged. "HeroClash. It's not much like the video games I played in the Army. I got to borrow Volta's controller to start, which helped. I'm not very good."

"Are you having fun, at least?"

The horse waffled a bit. "I think so? It's… hard."

"Is it the video games that are hard? Or is it the relaxing and playing that's hard?"

The Percheron opened her mouth automatically, intending to clarify, when the depth of the question hit her. As was too common these days, she felt a yawning chasm open within her as her world shifted, and a concept she had never before considered seemed to instantly crystallize within her as undeniable truth. She felt unmoored in some fundamental way.

The silence stretched out, while the rabbit simply waited for Geode to work her way through her answer. Finally, her voice distant, she found her words once more. "Both, I suppose. Relaxing feels wrong. I feel I should be *doing* something. But for the first time in my life, I don't know what to do."

Starshade pursed her lips. "What the Teepa did to you was *wrong*. Not just morally, I mean, of *course* it was repugnant, but..." the cottontail frowned, gesturing about with her paws as if she could pluck the idea from the air. "Strategically, maybe? Logistically? Depriving you of leisure was both cruel and short-sighted. They were *using* you up, instead of *building* you up. People *need* time to decompress. To make connections, and to pursue their own desires. Without that, they get worn down until they break. You were *expendable*, in the long term, because they only saw you as a machine.

"But a car isn't more capable if it's constantly redlined. Why would people be any different? Each day that passed was grinding you down. You had no reserves to pull from; no social reserves, no emotional reserves, no physical reserves. Hell, not even *body fat* reserves. So even a small break would cascade into a system-wide collapse."

"I guess you could say I suffered a hare-line fracture?" Geode asked with a weak smile.

The cottontail's mouth fell open for a moment in shock before she groaned. "*Goddamnit*, Geode. But... yeah? Yeah. All I'm saying, is that relaxing? Socializing? Those aren't wasted moments. Those are *essential* to being a complete, happy person. Purely from a tactical standpoint, that time for maintenance is necessary for you to be able to respond to disaster."

The mare frowned as she thought through the implications, tried to square it with her past and with what she had seen. She didn't like what it revealed... but she couldn't actually refute the statements, either.

After a long moment to let the horse digest the ideas, the lapine supervillain walked back over to the railing, blessedly away from the shameful, twisted portion. It was her turn to sigh deeply. "I'm sorry I missed your first couple weeks. I should have been here."

Instantly, Geode stood and moved to stand next to the rabbit. She didn't touch the bunny, but made sure she was near enough to share closeness. "That, you don't need to apologize for. It's not your fault."

That tiny tufted tail wagged in agitation. "I still feel bad about leaving you alone, though. And now, if you go to Empire tomorrow, it'll be weeks before we can finally start… being friends."

The warhorse let the silence linger as she thought through her response. Finally, she started tentatively, "When I was deployed, I would occasionally hit it off with someone not in my unit. The thing is, in war you have very little control over where you go, and what you do; so you'd never know when, or *if*, your paths would cross again. You had to seize upon those moments when you could.

"When you saw each other again, you'd still be friends. Nothing had changed just because you hadn't seen each other in a while. Time and distance don't sever those bonds. There will be time enough for us to be friends."

The rabbit pondered for a while. "Did you have many friends in the Army?"

The horse snorted in frustration. "Not many. Most people didn't like me, because of my powers and my size. I was *useful* in combat, but not in day-to-day operations. More of a logistical hindrance, really. There was… a lot of resentment."

"You weren't with other supers?" she asked with some surprise. She looked up at the warhorse with confusion.

"No, I was regular Infantry. While the Army does have specialized super units, the 'War on Terror,'" she scowled — she had never liked the phrase, and couldn't argue when Starshade rolled her eyes at it — "Changed things. The Pentagon decided it would be better to integrate some of the supers into regular units, to build camaraderie and familiarity. It wasn't particularly successful, at least for Heavies like me. I… ended up pretty isolated."

A warm paw covered her own. "That'll be different here. I'm glad you're staying."

Geode smiled softly. "So am I. Just… try not to get in too much trouble while I'm out?"

"I'm a supervillain. Getting in trouble is my *job*."

"I just wish your job involved getting out of it too."
She couldn't help but laugh at the cottontail's wounded expression.

Chapter 17

Orogeny

April 3, 2023

The image of a sparkling purple mare waved down at Geode. The 'storefront' facade of Empire Enhancements was covered with posters and screens. Each was animated, and displayed a figure running, lifting, dancing, or some other activity designed to show off their bodies. Each was a different species, showcasing a different body type, all women... but it was the central screen the warhorse couldn't take her eyes off, the one with the mare.

The woman on the screen had a bodybuilder's physique, with a modest chest. Though muscular, her build was undeniably feminine. Her fur was identical to Geode's own crystalline pattern, leaving no doubt as to who was being targeted by this particular advertisement.

The fallen hero could not explain the aching *hunger* she felt looking at the figure. There was a deep longing in her for that woman. To *be* that woman. Beside her, Dawn giggled and tugged at her wrist.

"That's just the demo. It gets even better inside. Celia sent a message ahead, so they should be expecting us!"

"Oh. Celia didn't... I'm not cutting in line, am I?" Geode's voice held a hint of desperation at the thought of being delayed — especially when she was standing *right here* — but she couldn't bear the idea of being given special treatment that caused someone else's dream to be deferred.

"Not at all! They do a lot of walk-ins. The only time I've seen a delay is when they run out of tanks, but that's rare and usually quickly remedied. Worst case, they overflow to another base, then bring the tank back here before you wake up." The antelope pulled her in through the sliding doors as she put the horse's fears to rest; Geode had no choice but to follow the brightly colored dik-dik. Today, Dawn was wearing pink jeans and a pink hoodie that proclaimed 'Life Is Merrier With A Farrier' encircling a print of two overlapping horseshoes.

Starshade was waiting just inside for the pair, with a grin. For her part, she was wearing her favorite high heel combat boots. Above, she was wearing a *very* low-cut tank top emblazoned with a logo for something named 'Night Of The Lepus.' Her pants were the most eye-catching part of her outfit; the shiny faux-leather looked painted on. Geode couldn't help but think that the rabbit was trying to show off Empire Enhancements' capabilities with her own, clearly *very* satisfactory results.

The interior lobby was sleek and bright, with gleaming chrome and clean lines. The center of the room was clearly the front desk. The furniture had clearly been designed for form rather than function, looking more like an intricate art project rather than a workspace. Anyone attempting to place a laptop — or, heaven forbid, write anything — would have been quickly stymied by the bafflingly ergonomic surfaces. The only item on the desk was a carefully tended potted plant, the shape of which made clear that it must have been part of the design specifications. The limited functionality of the desk *qua* desk was no impediment to the Nurse O behind it, who had no need of a functional work surface.

But it was not the odd desk, welcoming synth, or bright lights that were Geode's focus; it was the soft-looking carpet, with the intricate helix pattern, that stretched between the entrance and her destination. A carpet that was currently *unmarred* by hoofprints crushed deeply into the soft surface.

It took Starshade a moment to realize why her companion had stopped. Then comprehension spread across her face. "Geode? It's okay. The carpet is tougher than it looks. And the tiles are easy to replace. They, uh, have to be, with some of the... wear... they get."

Dawn smirked at the supervillain. "*You* would definitely know about unusual wear patterns on the carpet."

The rabbit blushed furiously at the comment, but Geode was too distracted to pay attention to the casual banter between the two friends. She swallowed, and glanced worriedly at the synthetic fox. "Are you... sure?"

"Absolutely. Now, please, stop worrying so much? The Korps builds stuff to last."

With that, Starshade pulled the giant horse forward, who winced as one steel shoe sank into the soft material. But a glance back didn't show the utter ruin she was used to seeing on office carpets; her hoofprint was clearly *visible*, but not irreparable.

Finally, she stopped and looked at the nurse. She waved hesitantly, suddenly very nervous. She couldn't help but feel like she was intruding somehow — as if she didn't have a right to be here, and she would somehow be turned away for her deception. She knew the feeling was silly, but that knowledge didn't help her chase away the butterflies suddenly fluttering in her stomach.

"Welcome to Empire Enhancements, Miss Geode. Miss Celia said you would be stopping by."

"Oh. Yes. Er. Thank you. Nice to, uh, see you again." She could feel her muzzle warm at her embarrassing display, but she suddenly couldn't form a sentence.

[*Easy, dear. It's okay. You are safe and you are welcome here.*]

"It is wonderful to see you as well. I am happy that you have come to see us. Would you like a refreshment before we begin?" The nurse picked up the plant and offered its leafy end to Geode.

"No. Thank you. But… that is very kind. I think… I'd like to begin. If that's okay?" Her words belied the need that had suddenly roared to life. She didn't want this taken away, somehow, by some sudden disaster. She hadn't been allowing herself to hope — or fear — this moment. Now that it was here, her feelings were conflicted and contradictory; it was with great effort she kept her tone respectful and moderate.

"Of course, Miss Geode. Right this way. We have a review room ready for you."

Geode turned around to find another Nurse O there, already turning to lead her away and carry on the conversation, as if no change had taken place. The synth had already pulled this particular stunt when Starshade was decanted, but it still took her mind a moment to catch up.

"Er… thank you, Nurse O."

"I've been told that you have had some reservations about this process. That is normal, and there is no shame in self-doubt. I want to assure you that you may back out at any time, and return when you are ready. I am here to serve you when you need me, whenever that may be, however many *times* it may be. My job is to make sure that you are the *you* that makes you happiest."

The warhorse was already trying to keep anxiety in check, and the gentle speech by the fox did ease some of the tension that threatened to overwhelm her. She kept moving forward — that was, forever and always, just who she was — but each step was a little easier, thanks to the soothing words.

"Thank you, Nurse O."

The nurse paused to open a door and gestured the trio inside. Geode was surprised to find that it looked very much like a normal examination room. A little nicer, perhaps, and built with better materials, and with a little more care paid to layout and design. The walls were a creamy tan. A counter and shelves were stocked with medical supplies. But the exam table was pushed to the corner; instead, the room was dominated by a large chair with a giant screen.

The horse hesitated for a moment, but Starshade tilted her head to indicate she should take a seat. Decades of mishaps made her hesitate again as she gingerly sat down, but the chair had clearly been built with individuals of her size category in mind. Reassured, she settled into the soft cushions.

The antelope gently touched her shoulder and caught her eye. "Do you want us to be here for this? It can be overwhelming, or even embarrassing, to let someone see you design yourself. We're happy to wait outside, and neither of us will judge you if you only want the other present with you."

Geode opened her mouth to dismiss Dawn's concerns, but then paused. She thought about it, really *thought*, and considered. Nerves were eating at her. Another person in the room might make her reluctant to select certain options. (Nurse O would be able to answer any questions, wouldn't she?) But then she shook her head.

"I'd rather you both stay. Thank you."

Starshade beamed and pulled up a chair while Dawn stood behind, looking over her shoulder. The synth stepped forward and slid the door shut behind her. "So, now for my *favorite* part. Let's see what you want to *make* of yourself!"

The display flashed a rotating magenta helix before a 3D model walked onto the screen. It was the same amethyst mare that had sauntered across the display at the front, only now, she was in her underwear. The interface began to fill with options, and then *kept* filling with options. A bewildering set of menus appeared. The complexity took her breath away.

[It's okay, dear. I'm here for you too. I'll highlight specific areas based on your needs and thoughts. You have all day, if you like to dig through everything.]

The 3D model took a fighting stance — her *own* fighting stance — then started working through one of her common routines, letting Geode see how she moved and flowed. The stats indicated she was a few inches shorter than her inspiration, with slightly narrower shoulders.

"This is the best character creator you'll ever see!" Starshade was clearly excited.

"Character whatnow?"

The rabbit deflated quickly. "You don't know... Oh, of course not. Sorry, video game thing. Er... this will help you perfectly design yourself. You'll use sliders, dropdown menus, and other things to help tweak who you will become!"

It was very overwhelming. But Geode turned her attention back, and let ROSE highlight several key areas. First was name and pronouns and other biographical information. She got a bit of a thrill when she saw She/Her filled out, but it all looked right.

"I can change all that later if I want, right?"

[Absolutely! How you want to be known is up to you. None of that is set in stone when you leave here. You met Zala; she comes in here every few months and changes everything. You can too, if you like.]

That was comforting. She looked back at the horse on the screen as she moved through the common routine. Geode wanted to *be* her so badly.

[That's what we're here for. You could hit accept right now and become her. What's stopping you?]

When ROSE put it that way... there were little things that stuck out. First, the mane. It was cropped short, just like hers was now. It was that way for combat but... she had always longed to grow her mane out. The option menu highlighted itself. She found she could select hair styles, though there was a note that hair would grow naturally and could be styled at will. But she didn't *want* to wait for it to grow out.

After some adjustments, the long, dark purple mane cascaded over one eye. Long strands draped down her back. Her tail, which had been docked for ages now almost brushed the floor in a long waterfall of silken hair.

As she expanded color options, an error flashed on the screen, surprising her. Starshade also squeaked in startlement.

> ERROR: Unusual User Fur Detected. Existing Characteristics Of Fur Are Of Unusual Origin. Empire Enhancements May Not Be Able To Restore This Setting If Changed. Alternatively, As Fur Color Was Caused By A Power, User May Find Fur Reverting Upon Power Usage.

The pair looked at each other in startled confusion and then to Nurse O.

"As indicated, I regret that we simply don't know enough at this time about the crystalline color and texture of your mane and fur. I recommend not changing away from it unless you are sure you don't want it. Temporary dyes might be a better option, for short-to-medium-term alterations."

Geode looked back at the warning. After a moment, she cleared the message. She *liked* the crystal look, so she wasn't interested in changing it now; she had just been caught off guard by the warning. But the hair had just been a hoof in the water. Now she was seeing other things to change.

The next option she selected was Height. This brought up a simple slider. Several silhouettes appeared for scale, including Volta, Starshade, and Dawn. She ticked the slider up a couple inches to her current height. But then she paused.

All her life, she had been a giant. Many buildings were simply not constructed for her; while more modern buildings were often up to code, older ones were problematic, and some, she just couldn't fit into at all. Vehicles presented a similar problem, and equipment was often awkwardly small for her massive hands, as if she was holding scale models. How often had she wished she could be shorter?

She clicked, ticking the slider back down a notch, then a few more times. She had always wished to be... tiny. *Dainty*. How many times had she stared at women like Dawn and hoped, in her next life, she could look like them?

The slider slid down until the mare on the screen was the same height as Dawn; no longer an Amazonian draft horse, but a pony. Part of her longed to click accept, to solve so many problems she faced just… living. But then she stopped. Sure, she had super strength. But her size mattered there too. If she chose to be so much smaller… she wouldn't be able to fight as well. She'd lose reach, strength, and toughness. She wouldn't be able to be the Heavy she had always been.

Which brought her to the question that she had yet to confront: what did she want to *do* with her new life? Did she want to be a *supervillain*? Did she *want* to go out and fight heroes? Rob banks? Do crimes? She couldn't do that effectively if she halved her size. Not the same way.

She had to sit and think for a long moment. Did she want to be a villain, or did she want to do something else? Become a Korps civilian, maybe? Help the cause in some other way? She didn't *have* to fight. And the only conclusion she could draw was that… she wasn't sure.

So, she ticked the height back up, up to where it started… then clicked a couple more times, to raise the slider to her current height. She didn't know if she wanted to fight for the Korps. Not yet. But she wasn't going to walk away from the option yet. She sighed softly; maybe someday, when her fighting was done, she could come back here and live *all* of her dreams.

Still, it took her longer, and much more effort than she cared to admit, to confirm the Height options and click through to the next category. She was grateful that the two women with her had said nothing.

Next, she moved onto hips. The figure was fairly blocky, like she was now. She had a fighter's build. She wasn't sure what compelled her, but she moved the slider, expanding her hips; the model's waist grew, adding curves. This caused the figure to adjust her stance, drawing a soft noise of appreciation from Dawn. Then a look of embarrassment flashed across her face. "Oh, sorry."

Geode looked at the antelope with curiosity. "No need to be sorry. What is it?"

Dawn flushed slightly. To see the dik-dik — usually so confident and worldly — actually *bashful* caught her by surprise. "Oh, just… Er…"

Starshade was thoroughly enjoying her friend floundering, but took pity. "She likes a thigh gap."

The horse looked in question between the two ladies. Starshade pointed to the thighs on the screen. "As the hips widen, a gap is formed right here. Dawn has a huge *thing* for a lady with a thigh gap."

The antelope squeaked, clearly blushing hard even as she buried her face in her hands to try to hide it. But, almost unbidden, and muffled by her hands, she whimpered, "They have their uses."

Geode smirked and looked back at the screen. She could see what they were talking about now. The thought of Dawn finding part of her attractive enough to get flustered was... intriguing. Intoxicating, even. She adjusted the slider a bit more, trying to find the right balance between emphasizing the gap and becoming absurd; finally, satisfied, she moved to the thighs.

These were already massive, matching her own. With the hip adjustments, they almost seemed bigger. A couple tweaks here was all it took to be happy. Her stance looked incredibly powerful, but now... feminine in a way she couldn't define.

Panning back up, she paused at the waist. While she had zero body fat — the slider was already at the minimum for that — she could still adjust the diameter of her waist a bit. Frowning, she just took a couple clicks, narrowing her waist by a small degree. The change was minor, but it really helped emphasize the curve of her hips. Still, she needed to address the chest. She was looking a bit bottom heavy.

The mare on the screen had a very modest chest. She just didn't have the fat necessary for more. But... Geode wasn't satisfied with a minimal chest. It still looked... masculine. It was uncharitable, and she would never think of another woman like this as mannish. But... it wasn't for her. She needed more. She clicked a few times to add a bit more, then blushed.

"That's it?" Starshade asked.

Geode stared at the question. Then back to the model. "That's... not too much?"

The cottontail lost it. She laughed and shook her head, struggling to breathe. "Geode, that's barely anything. Think about Volta, and then tell me that's too much."

The horse felt her ears burn, but she had to admit that the figure was nowhere near the... *volume* of many of the other villains she'd seen.

Including Volta. She still felt discomfited, but clicked much higher up on the slider.

The 3D model *expanded*. Her chest filled out, and spilled over. But... she looked wrong. With a frown, Geode moved the slider back, a little bit at a time — the model lost the massive mammaries slowly — and then back up. It took longer than she'd expected to find the right balance. Dawn, Starshade, and ROSE all had to assure her once again that she had all the time in the world, and that it was important to get it right for *her*.

But... she thought back to Volta. That fearsome villain who was so much... *woman*. With trepidation, she set her chest to be the same size as the wolf. She stared at it for a long, long time. Then, she clicked the down arrow. *Once.* That would do. She could always come back if she needed to adjust.

Dawn was strangely quiet, but Starshade was making appreciative noises. Geode looked at the display, trying to see it with fresh eyes. Other than the heavy chest, there was no body fat. She had spent a decade of her life ensuring that she was in perfect shape; she had to be, for the cameras, and to be the Hero the media and the public demanded. While other categories of Hero didn't have quite as strict standards, the Heavy was expected to be muscled perfection.

But... she looked... underfed, like this. Volta had quite a bit of fat on her, and it added... softness. It took *nothing* away from her strength and fierceness. She still looked like she could rip a tank in half.

Dawn and ROSE had both been after her to let up on her strict diet. She had spent a decade of her life in the endless pursuit of the perfect body; the Teepa marketing team had been testing her every day, and adjusting her diet and exercise to shape her figure. But who had that body been perfect *for*? She certainly hadn't liked her body. The Hero-adoring public? She was a villain now — by affiliation, at least, even if not presently a *practicing* one.

Minutes ticked by as she stared at the body fat slider sitting at zero. It took everything she had to click the up arrow. Instantly the 3D model filled out slightly, losing a small amount of muscle definition. But she suddenly looked more... complete? More like a person, and less like a perfect, airbrushed model. It took her another long minute before she could accept that it made her look... *better*. And clicking away from the category with that softness on the body was one of the bravest things she had ever done.

[That took a lot of courage. I'm proud of you.]

The thoughts were accompanied by a wave of compassion and love. Geode blushed at the praise and acknowledgement. She still had regrets, but... she moved on. She could be okay with this. ROSE would help her.

At ROSE's prompting, she moved to facial features next. She still looked very much like she always had, with a little more femininity. She was tempted to leave it. But she started tweaking things — first, her lips, adding a bit more here, adjusting the shape there. Dawn and Starshade started offering advice when she stumbled.

After a few moments, Geode realized that she had changed a lot more than she realized. She looked... feminine, and beautiful, but unquestionably fierce. Like some pagan warrior goddess. She smirked as she imagined herself in some kind of Viking war paint. Then the smirk faded, as the thought stuck; maybe... maybe she could really consider something like that.

She looked at her obsidian-black eyes. This too had a warning that changes might not be reversible. Geode pondered for a long time, but decided she liked the drowning pools of onyx and left them as they were.

She sat back and considered the... *her* before her. She looked... fierce. Dangerous. Powerful. But... undeniably feminine. A goddess of war and fertility made flesh. She was gigantic still, towering over the silhouettes; Dawn could (*would?*) practically get lost in her cleavage. But... it looked... *right.*

The mare shivered at the thought of *being* this woman. She wanted it so bad she could taste it. But there were a lot of options she hadn't even touched yet. She was trying to figure out what they could be, when she glanced at Starshade.

The desert cottontail looked positively gleeful with anticipation. A glance back at Dawn showed a similar expression. Slowly, suspiciously, she asked the question that had begun to form. "Why are you both looking like that? What's next?"

Twin feral grins spread across muzzles, but neither voiced an answer. Feeling a real touch of fear, she turned back to the options. One highlighted. Breast Functions. Considering she had just spent a long time playing with breast size, which was a wholly different option set, she was confused as to what this was. But she clicked on it, like a Hero — one who was now blushing furiously.

The plain black bra the model was wearing vanished, showing everything. Then a *host* of options popped up. Sliders for nipple size and diameter, sliders for the areola size. Lactation. *Sensitivity.*

Geode felt faint, as all the blood seemed to rush to her head. She could feel it pounding in her temples, and her breath was quick. Then a hand was stroking her muzzle and a head filled her vision.

"Whoa, girl. Easy there." Dawn was kneeling on her thigh, running her hand through the soft fur of her muzzle. She felt herself relaxing, almost unbidden, as the dik-dik soothed her with quiet words and gentle hands. When the antelope let her go and jumped down, Geode had calmed.

There was a touch of embarrassment in her comportment still, but not the overwhelming, almost panicked version that had started to spiral. With a bit more objectivity, she could see how important these functions were. She started to approach it once more, serious and thoughtful, so as to shape herself towards her ideal.

She slid the nipple size slider and stared at the sheer size possible, then did the same with the various diameter sliders. After some adjustment, and some more blushing, she settled on a size that felt right: large, but healthily in proportion with the rest of her. She expanded the areola diameter the most, but all the sliders were increased.

Then, she turned to the dropdown for Lactation. It was currently set to 'Off'. She could see a huge number of options grayed out below it; clicking just to see what the other options were, Geode was surprised to find it was more than just 'On'. There were a *lot* more options available.

There was, in fact, an option for 'On,' but there were options for 'Induced,' 'During Pregnancy,' 'During Orgasm,' 'Cyclical,' and more. The system also made it clear that multiple options could be selected. She started to select 'Off,' but stopped.

Did she want to lactate? She had never thought about it until this very moment; the idea was utterly foreign to her. But… the more she thought about it, the more it appealed to some part of her. As she was trying to work out her feelings, she just started clicking around on the menu, to see what other options would unlock. Then something caught her eye under 'Induced' that caused her to do a double-take.

The options *there* were for induction by 'Partner Orgasm,' 'Pheromones' and 'Remote Control'. Hovering over it indicated that a remote control would be provided to the patient, or someone else designated; that remote — or the functionality of it, securely loaded into a single authorized user's RCGs — would allow all these settings to be changed by the holder. The idea was so kinky she couldn't believe anyone would select it... but the idea stayed in her mind, haunting her.

She clicked out of the entire section without selecting lactation (though a small, traitorous part of her wanted to revisit the idea). The next category, she had seen earlier; the horse hadn't let herself focus on it before, but now her eyes were drawn to nothing else. Her heart ached to click on it. Taking a deep breath, she finally let herself move to the category she had wanted most of all.

The cursor moved over the 'Genital Options' and clicked. The panties of the 3D model vanished, showing her the current settings. Both her companions turned and stared at her, as they took in the sheer size of the member on display. Geode was blushing once more, but this time in shame. She hated it. *Hated it.* She hated it so much that it made her *ill.* Her next click made it go away. The other ladies said nothing.

Something unclenched in her heart. With a rush of giddiness, she selected a more... receptive option. The sight that greeted her felt so right it hurt. Instead of the *thing* she had never wanted to even think about, the model sported an equine vagina. Dark, plump lips seemed to *invite* exploration. Then her eyes bugged out at the host of options that had suddenly become available.

There were selections for External Genital Structure, Vaginal Canal Structure, Cervix Structure, Womb Structure, Heat Cycle, Egg Count, Fertilization Probability, Menstruation, Species Compatibility, Oviposition Options, Live Birth Options, and more. She was suddenly confronted with a host of questions she had never realized were possible, much less could be *applied,* to *her.* Geode had to hover over several and ask ROSE follow-up questions before she even *understood* some of them. In the process, she learned a lot more about reproduction, and sexual pleasure — and the woeful inadequacies of the Texas education system — than she'd ever known in her entire life.

The default Genital Structure specifications indicated that she would be able to accommodate… *insertions*… that were roughly equivalent to her current size. That seemed more than sufficient. She eyed some categories like 'Knot Capacity' with some suspicion, but tweaked them up a little bit, just in case.

She kept 'Fertility' off. She could always come back to EE later to change that, if she decided to have kids. She doubted her lifestyle would ever allow such a thing, and she hadn't even considered them before now. The mare was simply being practical, even if part of her was awakening to other possibilities.

Then she eyed 'Heat Cycle'. Embarrassed, she looked over at her companions. "Er… What are your th—"

"*Yes.*" Starshade hadn't even let her finish the question before snapping out her affirmative. "Absolutely. Best thing ever."

Dawn giggled a bit, patting the horse's shoulder to draw her attention. "Starshade is a bit… overeager. Heat can be *incredible*, but also inconvenient. You become unbelievably aroused, more than you ever have in your *life*. Every thought is focused on sex. Orgasms become even more potent and blissful. But it can be a problem if you find yourself in a situation where you don't actually *want* to have sex with anyone you have access to… or if you have anything urgent to do *other* than getting fucked until the heat cycle ends."

Geode gaped, blushing, at the thought. She was tempted to just select 'No,' and move on. But she hesitated. She would still have a body that would let her be happy. But, maybe… maybe heat would make it *ideal?* She was torn.

The antelope watched her, and a soft smile played at the edges of her lips. "Look, here's my recommendation." She reached over and changed a couple options. "Here, this is a regular monthly heat cycle, with the option of deferral. Your heat cycle will happen like clockwork. Perfectly predictable. ROSE will be able to display it at any time. Deferrable, at the option of either you or ROSE.

"For example. If you feel like you shouldn't go into heat tomorrow because you're likely to be in the middle of combat and it would be *really inconvenient* to want to fuck the enemy, you can choose to delay it. Or, ROSE can decide that you really shouldn't go into heat now just because *you* forgot to defer it, she can do that for you. Finally, a three day heat is the most I recommend for a newcomer, though I really prefer two days. Long enough to have the best marathon sex ever, but you can still lead a perfectly normal life."

The mare stared with wide eyes at the explanation, but it all *seemed* to make sense. She glanced at Starshade for confirmation. She nodded. "She's right. Deferrable and Regular Cycle is the way to go. I... tend to prefer a longer heat, but she's right. Two days on a monthly cycle is the right call for now.

"ROSE, what are your thoughts?"

[I think it's a fine recommendation. You can always adjust if it doesn't suit you after your first. And remember, I also have an emergency override. If I feel you are in distress, I will cancel your heat. I won't let you violate your boundaries just because the hormones are riding you, and interfering with your ability to think rationally.]

That safeguard made her feel a lot better about the whole thing. Then Geode paused, blushing at the next question. She felt she should know the answer already. "Can I *only* have sex during Heat?"

Starshade snorted. "Oh *goddess* no. You can have amazing sex all month long. Heat's just... better."

Dawn nodded. "I almost prefer sex outside of estrus. I have a lot more control, so I can get more creative. But then my next Heat comes around, and I remember why I love it."

Heart pounding in her chest, she selected the recommendations and closed out those menus in a rush. She sat for a moment, re-centering herself and letting her pulse slow. When she felt ready, she started clicking through a few more setting options for minor body functions and features she hadn't thought about; she really could adjust *anything*. Geode settled in to start exploring all the features available to her.

The next section that leapt out at her was Voice. The layout changed slightly, filling with various waveform displays and a host of audio editing tools she didn't have the first clue how to understand, much less use. The horse froze, paralyzed by the overwhelming nature of trying to change the way she spoke.

Dawn was suddenly there, stroking the fur of her neck. Geode tensed at the touch, but quickly relaxed, feeling part of the tension draining out of her. She wasn't sure how that simple touch had suddenly become so soothing for her, or so *important* to her, but she couldn't deny how safe it made her feel.

Part of her felt shame that she was a gigantic, nigh-unstoppable juggernaut… and yet, it was the touch of a tiny, fragile woman that made her feel safe. But that feeling also faded, as Dawn simply stroked her neck.

"We're here to help, sugarcube. You don't have to face this alone, and there's no shame in not knowing how to adjust something."

Geode's eyes snapped open. She hadn't even realized they were closed. She felt better, and smiled weakly in thanks. "I… don't know where to even begin."

"Red, could you please generate a couple preset options for Geode to pick from or tweak?"

[Yes, Mistress,] the voice emanated from several RCGs.

"Wait, your ROSE calls you *Mistress*?" Starshade squeaked.

"Of course! She does everything I ask, takes care of my every whim, and is a Very. *Good. Girl.*" Dawn's voice was filled with delight as she emphasized the last few words.

Geode felt her muzzle burn and saw a similar flush creep up Starshade's ears at the comment. Before she could say anything, several new buttons popped up on the screen. Curious, and immensely grateful for the distraction, she clicked on 'PRESET 1.'

The model's lips moved as she spoke. Her voice was no longer the gravelly basso she had always carried. The words sounded feminine and cheerful; not too deep or too high-pitched, as if she were a news anchor. It took her a moment for the actual words to register.

"I am Dawn's obedient pony, and I am a *good girl*."

There was a moment of silence as waves of smug amusement radiated from the dik-dik. Geode's blush roared back to life; a cascade of confusing emotions smashed through the horse, leaving her unable to quite process the world, or stop the small squeak from escaping her lips. Then Starshade roared with laughter. As the Percheron buried her face in her hands, Dawn patted her back and the rabbit's delighted laughter filled the room.

Finally, blessedly, ROSE's familiar mental voice slid into her head, cooling the roiling mix of emotions.

[Too much, dear?]

"… No. It's okay. The teasing is, um, a lot but… not bad?"

[Good. We want to make sure it doesn't go too far.]

Before she could figure out how to respond, the strangest sensation filled her as the model spoke the words again — except, this time they sounded different. They sounded like they were inside Geode's *skull*. It took a moment for her to realize that this would be how she heard her voice in her own head, rather than what others would hear.

She'd never really considered that her voice sounded different to her than to anyone else. She knew it intellectually, of course; that was why so many people hated hearing a recording of their own voice. But it hadn't dawned on her how important that would be to adjusting how she sounded. She had to consider *both* aspects.

It was with those thoughts that she clicked on the second preset. This time the voice was high-pitched and girlish. The type of voice that haunted cartoons whenever the director decided a character's voice should be 'Girl'. She hated it immediately, and the option disappeared from the screen.

The third was sultry. Low and deep, but richly feminine. That option sounded like a lounge singer, or an earth goddess; it was *resonant*. The version from inside her head vibrated through her in even more complex ways.

It was perfect, and Geode knew she didn't need to hear any other variations. Instead, she simply selected and confirmed it, satisfied. She didn't know how to tweak it, and she didn't *want* to. She had found her own voice. Somehow, this choice made her feel even more desperate to *be* the person on the screen before her.

With that submenu's options locked in, ROSE drew the horse's attention to a small icon of a yellow triangle with an exclamation mark. She had assumed it was simply part of the GUI, but upon selection, it expanded into a warning.

NOTICE: Empire Enhancements Has Made Small Changes Throughout Your New Form To

ADDRESS GENETIC DEFECTS. CHANGES ARE LISTED
BELOW AND CAN BE DECLINED AT USER REQUEST.

Below that notice was a long list of items related to organ function, hormone levels, memory encoding, and much more. She clicked one to see a notice that liver enzymes were being adjusted slightly to improve efficiency and long term health.

"ROSE? What's this?"

[Everyone has tiny genetic defects or oddities that can impact the overall function of your body. EE tries to adjust these to optimal parameters; this reduces, or eliminates, long-term health concerns that might one day arise. Additionally, by perfectly tailoring the chemical levels in your blood, you'll find a host of tiny quality-of-life improvements.

[You'll have improved memory, energy levels, mood, and overall well-being. Think of it as a general health upgrade. You won't have to worry about developing conditions like gout or diabetes. You'll live longer and healthier.]

Geode stared at the list with new appreciation.

"What about... mental conditions?"

[Those, we don't touch automatically. That treads perilously close to changing who a person is. If there is anything you specifically want to address, that can be done, but it would be done by your choice, not ours. Even then, we tend to lean heavily towards a feather-light approach. Neurodiversity isn't a collection of flaws; they're simply traits, and don't need correcting. They need understanding.]

The warhorse pondered that, for some time, before turning her attention back to the myriad options available to her. Some she tweaked; others, she left the same. She'd be roughly as large and as powerful as she already was.

The cybernetics option list was interesting, but she wasn't quite ready to consider that route. (There was even a big notice about 'full synth conversion' options, but she dismissed that idea immediately.) Still, she added skeletal durability enhancements and subdermal nanoweave armor; she was already tough, but this would make her a juggernaut. It wouldn't impact her appearance at all, not like some of the more protective options; combined with her natural gifts, she would be very difficult to take down. She was about to click away, when ROSE highlighted the option for Nanite Colony.

[*You should really consider healing nanites.*]

"Oh, I missed that option. Talk to me about them? What sort of capability do they have here?"

[*A colony of healing nanites, tailored to your unique biology, will live in your blood and collect in strategically placed reservoirs. When injured, they will start repairing that damage automatically. They have their limits, though. They can be used up in a long fight, or knocked out of commission with certain powers or attacks. They rely on the RCG network for command and control, though they can also operate independently on autopilot, with decreased effectiveness. The downside is that you'll need to consume a lot more calories after using them. You'll be ravenous while the colony replenishes itself.*]

"That sounds very useful."

[*You wanted to be a juggernaut, dear.*]

Geode grinned. This would be a serious upgrade to her fighting capability, being able to shrug off injuries that would have been crippling. Plus, she wouldn't have to rely upon medics and healers nearly as much, which made her feel less of a burden.

[*You are **not** a burden.*]

The warhorse flushed at the rebuke.

"Sorry."

[*It's okay dear. Just remember, you aren't a burden. You are Korps. We take care of you as you take care of us. We lift each other up. Together.*]

"Er… thank you, ROSE."

To distract herself, she went back to looking through the myriad options before her, but though she tried to focus on new areas, her eyes kept wandering back to the breast options. The thought of lactation kept insistently, lasciviously urging its way back into her head, unbidden. Reluctantly, she opened that option back up.

First, she scrolled down to an option she'd hardly paid attention to, the first time. She had planned to keep it at the default, but now — after the discussion about Heat — she was reconsidering. The cursor hovered over the option for 'Breast Sensitivity'.

She saw Starshade smirk, while Dawn showed only stringently polite interest. The current setting was very low; when she asked, ROSE indicated that it was a little less sensitive than average, but not much. Her eyes were drawn much higher up the slider, where there was a warning at about 60%:

WARNING: Breast Sensitivity Above This Level May Impede Day-To-Day Activities

That warning seemed ominous, especially as it was barely over halfway to the maximum. Just how sensitive *was* that? Feeling the familiar heat in her ears, Geode turned once more to her friends.

"Er…"

"Don't go over 60%." Starshade answered flatly before she could even ask the question; considering her eagerness for Heat, the caution surprised the horse.

"Oh?"

"I… made that mistake on my first trip to EE." Now both Dawn and Geode were staring at the rabbit. She rubbed the back of her neck and shifted, embarrassed. "I… er… thought it would be funny to set it to 69%."

The expression on Dawn's face was one of concerned anticipation. "What… happened?"

The rabbit blew out a breath and turned away. Her ears were splayed as she continued. "Damn things were so sensitive that accidental contact could bring me to orgasm. I couldn't wear a bra because it hurt too much. I lost *hours* playing with them, creaming myself sodden. Then my Heat kicked in, and ROSE activated the failsafe to shut it all down, or I would have lost my damn mind. If you *want* to lose yourself in an endless breeding cycle, then it's great… but if you aren't going to join the Breeding Division full-time, don't do it. Trust me."

Dawn and Geode shared a look. Then the antelope walked over and hugged the taller cottontail from behind. "Thank you for sharing. I'm sorry you had to go through that."

Starshade chuckled. "It wasn't all bad. I mean, a lot of it was amazing. Part of me *still* wants to crank it up to a hundred and lose myself in forever orgasms. A *small* part. But I still have villany ahead of me, and I really don't think Geode is ready for that level of horniness."

Geode frowned. "So… what level *do* you suggest?"

Her two companions looked at each other.

"I'm now at 31%. Damn sensitive and I love having my tits played with," Starshade offered.

"I've never been to EE. But if I *had*, I would tell you that I was at 25% because that's what ROSE recommends, and I'd never had reason to change it." Starshade rolled her eyes at the comment, but didn't press.

"ROSE?"

[*I still recommend 25%.*]

With a nod to herself, she moved the slider up to the quarter mark. Then her eyes were drawn back to that lactation option she had pondered earlier. She knew she should just skip it and move on. She didn't want to leak milk... did she?

But that small part of her decided that no, she wasn't going to get off that easy. Almost against her will, *almost*, her hand dragged the cursor to click several options. She set Lactation to Remote Control, High Productivity Cycle, and hovered over Regular Milk. She was flushing hard enough that her ears and face almost hurt.

But as she stared at the default flavor option, she really started to wonder what she was doing. Why did she want to *lactate*? The thought of producing milk seemed so... alien. But she just couldn't bring herself to move on. Some small part of her screamed to her that it was something she wanted, somehow. Then her eyes went back to the remote control option. That was her safety net. She never had to actually turn it on. And if she *did* and she didn't like it, it would never have to bother her again.

With that, she found she could put up a wall of separation. This was purely academic, after all; more importantly, it meant she could get a little *whimsical* with it. Clicking the dropdown for the flavor, she saw the expected options at the top, but a mind-boggling list below, many that she had never even considered. Then one caught her eye. Maple Pecan. Long ago, before the Teepa took over her diet and everything approaching flavor left her life, that had been something she had loved. While she couldn't *imagine* drinking her own milk, maybe she could share that treat with others?

Her heart was pounding in her chest. Geode couldn't quite focus on the menu, but she managed to click the option. Then, blushing furiously, she closed the menus, trying to ignore the raised eyebrow from Starshade (and the even more worrying predatory look in Dawn's eye).

Flushing even harder, she went back to genital options. There was a sensitivity slider there too that she had ignored the first time around. Her chest felt tight and her breathing was quick. Thinking about the previous discussion, she set this to 25% as well.

I should keep everything the same... shouldn't I?

But then she started to think about all the time she had lost. She'd never been comfortable with sex, or even thinking about it. Now... maybe that would be different; maybe she should make the most of it? She knew she was being stupid, and probably wasn't making sense, but that tiny part of her that was pushing for more forced her to click a few more times. Soon enough, the slider was at 31%. Just like Starshade.

When she closed that menu, she sat there for a moment, breathing hard. She felt like she had run a marathon and her fur was tingling. Regrets immediately flooded through her; the nagging thoughts that she had made a *mistake* and set things *too high* and she probably didn't even *want* sex anyway chased each other through her mind. But she didn't go back.

Dawn's hand rubbed at her shoulder and she leaned over to murmur in her ear. "It's okay. You're a brave girl. Good girl. You're so strong and tough. *Good girl.*"

The words sent a shiver down her spine. A lot of the tension in her chest eased. She managed a weak smile, though she was still embarrassed that her friends had watched her tweak those settings. She smiled weakly. But there was no judgment in the others. They instead looked... happy. Happy for *her.* That helped, a lot.

While she was being brave, she clicked over to Oral Options. She hadn't intended to explore this area at all. She was generally happy with her teeth and throat, wasn't she? The first thing that greeted her was another note

> NOTICE: Change To Oral Structure Does Not Change Dietary Restrictions By Default. Any Setting Mismatch Should Be Addressed Prior To Finalization.

Idly, she changed an option listed as Dentition. Instantly, the figure had sharp, powerful fangs. A row of viciously pointed teeth filled the model's face as she snarled menacingly. Geode could imagine the terror those canines would strike into the hearts of her opponents; she would be a nigh indestructible beast, saliva dripping from a wicked grin as she stalked her prey. She could almost feel those teeth clamping down on helpless prey incapable of outfighting, outrunning, or outhiding the ruthless killing machine.

But the idea didn't sit well with her. She didn't mind being feared; ultimately, being able to cow an opponent meant you didn't have to fight them. But she found she was more intimidating as the unfeeling, unstoppable, unknowable machine. She had fought many slavering beasts in her time, and they were usually too predictable, even shortsighted. She didn't want to be that. Granted, she could still be the stoic, implacable wall *with* a set of sharp teeth, but then the benefit of such an intimidating display would be lost.

With a shake of her head, she set the teeth back to standard equine. She was distracting herself from what she really needed to do here. Further down the list, she couldn't help but pause again. Gag Reflex. As a horse, she didn't currently have one, but there was the option to *add* one. Twice during her time in the Army, she had too much to drink, and the absence of that particular biological trait had sent her to the hospital instead of the bathroom. But she felt no urge to drink that much ever again, and since her supernatural toughness extended to illness, she hadn't had colic since she was a filly. Ultimately, the option seemed to be more of a hindrance than a benefit. She left the setting as 'Off' and moved on.

Finally, Geode found the options she was dreading. Her head was buzzing as she clicked on the Oral Sex menu, and she could *feel* Dawn and Starshade take interest in her exploration. This menu, like all the others, had a bewildering set of options. She saw the Gag Reflex option here as well. The mare had noted that some settings were found in a number of related categories, presumably so one didn't miss a critical setting, or waste time trying to hunt down exactly *which* menu was relevant.

Another setting caught her eye. She shouldn't have been surprised, but there were a number of options related to the tongue. Though she was on a mission, while her nerve remained, she kept getting sidetracked with other information. Still, she couldn't just pass it by — certainly not when it was directly relevant — so she forced herself to pause once more. She was keenly aware of Dawn positively radiating *interest* from behind her. Though heat burned across her muzzle, she extended the tongue and broadened it.

Finally, finally, she made her way to the options she had been seeking: Oral Sensitivity. She knew it had to exist, given the other two items. She couldn't quite bring herself to believe she would ever want… that. No matter how much the logical part of her brain protested, the image of Volta in the gym haunted her. The supervillain had looked so… blissful, with that shaggy cow buried to the hilt in her muzzle. That sense of longing, of *jealousy*, ate away at her and though she was certain that this would never matter — that all this time and embarrassment was a waste — she changed the slider there, too. The warhorse never knew just how long she sat there, staring at the 25%. She was just happy her courage had held.

Then Starshade cleared her throat. She looked apologetic as she started tentatively. "Geode… I know you probably don't want to think about this right now… but if you're upping those three sliders, you really should do the same for… anal, as well."

The flush that Geode had thought was fading suddenly roared back with a vengeance. The whole room felt too warm as it spun slightly. She stared at Starshade like a cornered rabbit, but Dawn was there, soothing her once more. That hand stroking her muzzle helped settle her until she could think again. Only then did Starshade continue.

"I know you probably don't want to think about anal sex right now. You may never have a desire to explore it. But if you raise the settings for the other three and leave anal sensitivity low, if you ever *do* explore it, you are basically ensuring you'll never like it. Because it won't be nearly as good."

Geode wanted to scream that of *course* she didn't want anal sex. But she forced herself past that initial, emotional reaction. It made sense. It made *a lot* of sense. With a slight frown, she expanded that menu.

A host of options greeted her. There was the slider, but it was nestled in among so many others. Self Cleaning? Capacity settings? Additional durability enhancements for spines? For Hooks?! *Anal Pregnancy Options?!*

Geode closed her eyes and took a breath. She held it for several seconds before letting it out slowly, letting her stress flow with it. Then she opened her eyes and gave a half smile to her companions. "This is… all a bit much for me. Can… you help? I'm not able to think clearly about it."

Both girls remained compassionate and understanding. Dawn patted her shoulder. "Let's make it easy. You can always come back later. Set sensitivity to 25%. Activate the self-cleaning and self-lubrication-when-aroused settings. Capacity looks good. You don't need the durability stuff, because of your powers. Leave everything else alone."

Starshade tentatively ventured, "What about…" Then she trailed off and shook her head. "Never mind. Those settings are perfect for her."

That small, traitorous part of her wanted to know, but it was all still too much. She let it drop and selected all the options Dawn suggested, then closed it out. She didn't know if they would ever be used. But if she were ever that… adventurous… then at least they were set.

And then… she was done. Suddenly, it was all… real. All she had to do was click FINISH. She hesitated.

"This *is* real, isn't it?" She didn't realize that she had asked the question out loud before Dawn and Starshade turned to her.

"Yes, horse. As real as your stupid fucking spurs," the rabbit teased.

Geode snorted. The comment was enough to break through her trepidation. Her hand was shaking, but she clicked on FINISH. The mare on screen looked smug. She spun around, showing herself off. Then she strutted offscreen.

She was replaced by a list of modifications. A very long list. She gazed with some concern at the sheer number of changes that would be made to her body. There was a final confirmation button waiting for her.

Finally, she turned to Nurse O. "How long will this take?"

"Given the list of procedures, the recovery time will be about five weeks. That depends somewhat on your precise physiology. While your modifications may not be as extensive as many, since the modifications to the skeletal structure are minor, your innate toughness will make some of the changes more time consuming."

Geode slowly blew out her breath. "Five weeks isn't so bad. I think it'll be worth it."

"I assure you, Miss Geode, when you wake up, you'll be the brand new woman you've always dreamed of being! Or the woman you always *were*, if you prefer to think about it that way." The Nurse nodded her head to the screen.

Though she was trembling with a mix of fear and need, she clicked through the confirmation and finalized the last few details. When she was done, she felt a little *ping* from her RCGs. A reminder notification scrolled across her vision.

[TRANSITION OPERATION, APPROXIMATELY FIVE WEEKS RECOVERY, TODAY AT 10:15 AM.]

A glance at the clock showed that was in twenty minutes. Her heart skipped a beat. It was so sudden, and yet so very far away. Nurse O clapped her four hands together.

"All is ready for you, Miss Geode. I shall give you privacy to speak with your companions. Then your operating team will arrive to prepare you. If you need anything before then, you can ping me via ROSE."

Then, the synthetic fox curtsied and departed the room. Geode turned to the two women, not sure what to say. Both had giant grins on their faces.

"I'm so proud of you," Dawn said.

"This is going to be the best decision of your life. You'll wake up as the new you. And you'll never look back. I never did." Starshade almost sounded wistful.

Geode took a deep breath, letting it out smoothly to settle her sudden nerves. Slowly, she stood up. "Will you both be here when I wake up?"

They nodded in unison. Then Dawn wrapped herself around the horse. Starshade followed suit a heartbeat later. The three held each other for a long while.

"Thank you," Geode whispered. "Thank you for… everything."

Dawn nuzzled against her. "You are welcome."

Starshade looked up with glittering eyes and a smirk. "I can't wait to meet you."

Geode smiled back. "I can't wait to meet me, either."

Chapter 18

Magma Supply

April 3, 2023

Starshade paused to look back at the entrance to Empire Enhancements. Geode would be in surgery now, and would be for some time. She wouldn't see the horse until next month. Part of her was frustrated that they were, once again, like ships passing in the night.

Still, Geode was going to be so *happy* with her new self, and the cottontail felt a twinge of envy. Waking up from the first trip to EE was like nothing else; there were few things more euphoric than suddenly being in a body that *fit*. She had been back a few more times for minor adjustments, but those were nothing like the first.

She would need to make arrangements for the mare's decanting party. With a frown, she realized she wasn't quite certain who to invite. But she couldn't make that decision now; too much changed around her too fast to plan that far out.

"ROSE, could you please remind me a week before Geode's scheduled decanting to make arrangements?"

[Of course, dear. And if you are somehow occupied at the time, I will make sure others make the arrangements. I won't let this fall through the cracks.]

"Thank you, ROSE."

That done, she turned to Dawn with a smirk. "I saw your face there at the end. Geode might have been distracted, but you looked like you were getting a Korpsmas present from the Overlord themself."

The dik-dik blushed lightly and couldn't quite meet the rabbit's eye, but she grinned. "I just want Geode to be happy with herself. That's the most important thing."

"Absolutely. But the fact that what *she* wants hits a lot of *your* buttons is obvious. I saw the way you were staring at her hips. That thigh gap is the perfect height and shape to bury your muzzle in."

Dawn shrugged helplessly. "I... yes? I'm really hoping things work out. I haven't been able to push much yet; once I realized how dysphoric she was, I had to step very, very lightly. It will be a very slow process to help her explore things. But... yes. I am delighted at the toy I might get to play with."

The cottontail paused for a moment, unsure if she should ask her next question. Still, she hadn't even been in agent training the last time she had seen this level of sparkle in the antelope's eye. Her voice was gentle, as she finally asked: "Are you thinking about... training again?"

The dik-dik glanced away with only a hint of pain haunting her eyes. "It's taken me a long time to accept that what happened last time wasn't my fault. But yes... I think I'm ready. I can't deny that I've missed it."

A smile blossomed across her muzzle as Starshade hugged her friend. "She'll be a cute project for you. I'm ecstatic that you're even thinking about it. I think it's what she needs, too."

"Oh, I'm *certain* it's what she needs," the dik-dik stated confidently. "All my instincts are screaming that she's been searching her entire life for someone worth serving. She deserves the joy of surrender, simple commands, and time and space to focus on her own pleasure."

"And by that you mean focus on *your* pleasure," the cottontail said with a smirk. "Or whoever else you tell her to focus on. I'm certain it hasn't crossed your mind that she can fit Orion without modification."

Dawn rubbed her perfectly manicured hoof-nails together and laughed maniacally, before breaking down into delighted, and genuine, giggles. "Oh yes. I have plans." Then the dik-dik sobered, her expressions growing uncharacteristically serious. "I just need to make sure ROSE keeps me from going too far, too fast. For an unstoppable tank, she's fragile."

[*Rest assured that I will be monitoring, and will flag any warning signs. I will not hesitate to safeword for her if that becomes necessary.*]

Both women nodded at the words. Dawn then stepped forward and hugged the taller bunny around the waist. "But that's for the future. For now, I need to get back to work. I have *several* special projects to finish over the next few days."

Starshade tried to keep her giddiness in check. She knew one of those projects would be her new 'dagger,' once Orion and Dawn were finished with it. But she nodded. "I have to go too. I promised Adam I'd let him explain my new lungs to me."

With a groan to the ceiling, the antelope shook her head. "I can't believe you got cybernetics without knowing anything about them."

She shrugged helplessly. "I don't know why. It's *me* we're talking about. Queen of jumping into situations and causing chaos."

With a heavy sigh, Dawn's shoulders fell. "You're right. I can definitely believe it. Still, you're going to be relying on those to... you know... keep you *alive*. You should know more about them."

"Fine, fine. If only so you breathe easier."

She cherished the antelope's put-upon groan.

"Adam!" Starshade called out, as she followed ROSE's directions into a laboratory bay. The lion engineer was there, clearly so absorbed in his work that he didn't seem to hear her. The rabbit paused and watched.

The diminutive lion was standing on a stool at the end of a long lab bench. His tufted tail lashed in time with quiet R&B playing over his RCGs. His paws were quick and sure as he assembled some unknown device. Above him, the display showed a host of data and specifications for whatever the project was, though he rarely glanced up.

"ROSE, is he near a stopping point? Or should I come back later?"

[He's almost done. Shall I get his attention for you?]

"Oh, no. I've got it. Thank you."

Starshade waited patiently, watching Switchboard finish up the assembly. She had met the shy, nerdy feline just after joining the Korps. They had struck up a fast friendship after she had made him snort milk in the food hall, when talking about her disastrous session with that visiting blue jay trainer from KDS. Later, she had been there when he had confessed his longing to *be* a guy.

Her reverie was broken when the lion clicked something into place with a satisfied sigh of relief. He cracked his neck, then started to reach for the stolen K-LAW mug full of cold coffee. Then she was…

LAYING…

…*along the table in front of him. She was propped up on her elbows, with her heeled boots sticking up into the air behind her.*

"Hey Adam!"

The lion jumped back with a startled yelp, clearly not expecting a supervillain to materialize. After a moment, he hung his head and gave a half-hearted growl. "Damnit, Starshade."

"Those might be the two most common words spoken in my presence," she said with a smirk.

"Funny, I figured those would be 'Kneel, Slut.'" Switchboard shot back.

Starshade's ears burned hard at the comment. But she laughed and rolled to sit on the edge of the table. "You might be right. It's good to see you."

A soft smile tugged at Adam's lips. The lion joined her on the table, wrapping one arm around her, pulling himself close. "It's good to see you too."

"So…" she started slowly, rubbing the back of her neck. "Could you give me the rundown on the new lungs?"

"Wait, you were *serious* about not knowing anything about them when you chose them?" After a long pause he rubbed one paw down his face. "I'd convinced myself you had to have just been fucking with me."

"Sadly, I am precisely as ditzy as I appear."

"You are not ditzy," he said, sternly. He frowned up at her. "You're *impulsive*, sure. But that's not the same thing."

She pursed her lips, wanting to argue. But she knew that he would win, and that ROSE would chastise her for putting herself down. She let it drop — with some effort — and prompted again. "The lungs?"

"Right. Okay. So, they have a number of features. ROSE, could you bring up the systems control diagram I made for her?"

A complex diagram popped into existence on her HUD. After a minute, the diagram simplified and pulled to the side, with a number of key points highlighted, so she could follow along.

"Okay, so the obvious ones first. They work like lungs. You don't have to do anything special other than breathe."

"When I first woke up, they felt... *foreign*. They still do, but I'm figuring out how to ignore it. Is that... normal?" She was tentative. The sensation had worried her, wondering if something was wrong.

"Sadly, that's normal. You'll get used to it, but it'll always feel a little off if you focus on it. That's one of the downsides," the cat explained with a touch of sympathy. But Starshade was relieved at the words, since they let her put away the fear that had started to nibble at the back of her mind.

The first bullet point highlighted then, drawing her attention to it. "Importantly, they are not biological lungs. Which means that the vast majority of toxins and poisonous gases simply won't affect you. But remember, that's applicable to agents that affect *only* the lungs. Things that attack nasal cavities or mucous membranes generally, like tear gas, will work just fine."

"Damn. I guess I'll have to get used to that the old-fashioned way."

"I mean, if you *want* me to build you replacements for those..."

"*Thank you*, but Nurse O already offered to turn me into a synth."

The lion stopped talking. Then he slowly turned to look at her. "Really? I thought she hated you?"

She couldn't help shrugging with a laugh. "I thought so too. Turns out she likes me. She, and I quote, 'thinks I'm funny.' I wonder if one of her chassis is in a hidden closet somewhere, and that's the only one who gets to laugh?"

The feline giggled. "'Nyuk O' is a closely guarded secret."

"... Hidden away so Lawful Neutral can never access unlimited power."

They laughed together. She enjoyed moments like this. Quiet, peaceful times with her friends — her *family*. She'd be out there, in chaos and combat again soon. But now, she could share a joke with Adam.

"Okay, okay. Your lungs. They're a *lot* more efficient at oxygen exchange. Biological lungs are flawed, in that you can suffocate even though there's plenty of oxygen inside them; your body just can't *get* it. These, though, don't have that problem. So you can hold your breath for a long, long time. Take a *deep* breath, you can probably hold your breath for half an hour on just that lungful. That massively depends on your activity level, mind you. You can have ROSE project estimations about it if you like."

The next bullet point highlighted. "But there's little point in normal operations. Your lungs have a built in oxygen supply. There's a compressed cylinder that has about eight hours of oxygen in it. If you exhaust this, your normal body can recharge it a little, maybe to about an hour's worth; but if you want a full charge, you'll need to stop by any Korps medical facility. The lungs will use everything available first before touching this reserve, though."

Starshade whistled silently as she considered the implications. She held up a paw as Adam started to move on. "What if there were some mission where I needed more than that?"

Adam stopped and considered her question. "It might be possible to add additional storage, but there would be cost in terms of bulk, weight, and danger. You'd likely be better off with a different, external solution."

Starshade nodded. "That makes sense. Okay. Thank you. What about running? Something was mentioned about me being able to run better?"

"*Longer.* Your lungs won't tire out, and getting oxygen will be easier. All that takes stress off the body. Expect to be able to run further and faster, but your body is going to need to re-learn how to do a lot of things. Expect Training to contact you in a few days for some intensive training. How to run, for instance."

Starshade grinned. "I have no problem with that."

Adam smirked. "I didn't think you would. Running has always been your passion."

The rabbit nodded. "Ever since I joined the Korps, at least."

After a moment of silence, another bullet point highlighted. "Okay, now for some of the fun stuff. Your lungs are much tougher now. Which means you are much less likely to suffer serious damage from blows or punctures. If they *are* punctured, there's a self-sealing mechanism. You shouldn't have to worry about pneumothorax."

She generally liked things that kept her alive longer. "I can see how that would be useful."

"I thought you might. Also, you *will* be able to survive in a vacuum, but only on your backup air. Same with underwater. However, the lungs are designed to more easily integrate with liquid breathing mediums; if you ever wanted to dive the Marianas Trench, now you can."

"Wait, really?" She peered at the lion to see if he was messing with her, but he seemed serious.

"I don't recommend it, but you *can*."

She stared at him for a long moment. She would have to think about that. It seemed so foreign. But... she had trusted her friend for a reason.

"Okay. Hit me with the bad news."

It was Adam's turn to sigh. He hopped off the table, clearly needing to pace a bit. His tufted tail lashed in distress, but his tone remained as academic as ever. "Okay. Yes. So, first, you *will* need regular maintenance for the rest of your life. Once a year, you'll need to stop by Medical for a checkup and fine-tuning. If you were ever to leave the Korps... well... it might be best not to have these lungs, if you do."

She swallowed. She certainly had no plans to. The Korps was her home. But... if something were to happen to the Korps, her lifespan would be... truncated. She shivered, but nodded. "That's a risk I can live with."

"Well... there are a lot of complex, high-tech components involved. They're hardened as best I could make them, but... there are powers out there that might be able to shut down your lungs. Or a sufficient EMP will do the same. There *is* a failsafe. But..."

Adam clearly looked unhappy. There was concern in his eyes as he captured her gaze, trying to make sure she understood. "If that happens, your lungs won't restart on their own. The oxygen storage will start releasing into your bloodstream. But without a way to pull the CO_2 out of the blood, you won't get the full eight hours; you'll be lucky to have half that. You will have, at most, four hours to get to a Korps Medical facility. That's it."

Her breath caught. That wasn't a long time. She imagined exertion would shave more time off that limit. Then a more sobering thought struck her. "And... I wouldn't be able to talk, would I?"

The lion shook his head slowly. "No."

"Oh." The word hung there. She felt very small. Part of her wanted to rush down to Nurse O and beg for biological lungs. But... she didn't. The benefits were worth the risk. She prayed that she was right about that.

After a minute, she hopped down off the bench and folded the smaller feline into a hug. "Thank you. For everything."

A moment later, he hugged back. "You're my big sister. I've got to take care of you."

She chuckled. "I think it's supposed to be the other way around, lil' bro."

They held that pose for a while before the cat, as capricious as ever, pulled away and fussed with his mane. "And, Starshade?"

"Yes?"

"When you *do* dive the Marianas Trench against my recommendation? Bring me back a souvenir, would you?"

"I'll bring you back all the lost pirate treasure I find."

Starshade leaned over the railing, looking down at the bustling lower levels. The area surrounding the main food hall was always hopping at this time of night. People of every variety moved down the halls or stopped to talk with friends. She always loved seeing the sheer variety of people in the Korps; when you freed people to be who they always wanted to be, the result was a riot of forms. She wouldn't have it any other way.

She had just finished her own meal. The rabbit had a particular love for the 'Garden of Eden' salad at Greens Leaves; her favorite part was always the crisp, juicy bits of apple that accompanied the medley of unusual plants. Today had definitely been a night to treat herself. She had considered finding someone to spend dinner with, but had decided she needed the time to think.

The chronometer in the upper right of her HUD showed the time. Dinner rush would be winding down soon, and people would start migrating more towards the more socially-oriented sections of the base. Normally, she would be doing the same; she hadn't been to the Dominion Club since before her last mission. But her mind kept circling back to… yesterday. The gathering for her, after she woke up.

"ROSE… *is Celia free right now?*"

There was a pause. That itself was notable, as ROSE usually responded instantly.

[She is finishing up some command responsibilities. But she says you are welcome to stop by her office in half an hour, if that would be satisfactory.]

Starshade pondered. Did she want to go through with this? What if she was wrong? What if she was *right*? But she had always been one to jump in recklessly. She had let intuition guide her many times before.

"*That will be fine. Thank you, ROSE. Has Celia eaten? Should I bring her anything?*"

[Celia ate yesterday, so she won't be hungry until tomorrow at the earliest.]

That was an odd statement. But, what did she really *know* about Celia? The lamia was more a myth than a person. The rabbit let it pass. There would be plenty of time for those mysteries later. She didn't have to answer every question immediately and completely.

"*Thanks. Can you chart me a scenic jogging route that'll end at Celia's office, just on time? I'd like to stretch my legs.*"

Waypoints appeared in her vision. This was the thing that always made her feel like she was in a video game; the constant readouts on herself and her surroundings were amazing and wonderful, but those, she had grown used to long ago. The navigation points, however, never ceased to feel alien to her. Alien and *wonderful*.

She took her time, trusting ROSE would adjust her route to her speed, ensuring she would show up precisely on time. She needed to think. The stroll was relaxing and wonderful, taking her through gardens and art projects and across bridges over streams and thoroughfares. All the while, she pondered the base commander.

What did she really *know* about the snake? She had grown up with the stories, sure. Her parents, being superheroes, had definitely used tales of the demonic viper to scare a young cottontail into being good. She had even overheard the elder bunnies sharing more bloody details when they thought she was asleep, or outside hearing range. Those, however, were all fairy tales and propaganda.

The woman cloaked herself in mystery. Many of the stories about her were… *contradictory*, at best. Not even living in the same base as the lamia had illuminated anything. Here, she was respected as well as feared, with the clear sense she was *part* of the Korps, as much as she remained in the shadows. She commanded *respect,* but that did not carry with it concrete *facts.*

Still, all that was academic until she was standing on the command level, next to the petrified statue of a former Oil CEO. Today, the stuffy old snake was wearing a snapback that read "My Pronouns Are Was/ Were." She eyed the text suspiciously, trying to figure out whose week it was to select the hat.

Starshade pulled her attention away. She was distracting herself so she wouldn't have to face the fact that she was walking into the serpent's den. Her heart was pounding in her chest. The woman still scared her. But fear had not stopped her before.

"ROSE, *could you let Celia know I'm here, please?"*

Instead of responding, the doors *whooshed* open. Her paw had crossed the threshold before she really processed what she was doing. She found herself plunged into gloom as the doors closed behind her. The change in light level disoriented her and she squeaked in alarm.

A rustling sound of something giant *slithering* in the dark all around her drove a spike of terror into her. Ancient instincts told her to *freeze.* That if she stood stock still, she would be safe. But with effort, she forced herself to *think.*

"Celia?" she called tentatively and meekly. She hated how tiny her voice sounded. But she had forced action and that was what was important.

She was rewarded by the magenta lights slowly growing brighter. The murky shadows were slowly banished by the rising light. With a start, the cottontail realized Celia was a only few meters away from her. Her impressive cleavage was marginally contained by her bra, if that was what one could call two small triangles of black latex that tried valiantly to suggest the barest modicum of modesty. Her nipples, complete with thick rings, were clearly outlined under shiny black. The edges of the bra were trimmed with structurally-questionable rivets.

A black latex underbust corset ringed her belly, adding a bit of hourglass curve to her shape. Long latex gloves covered her arms all the way up past her biceps and showed off her muscle definition. The outfit was completed by a black band choker.

But, for once, it was not her eye-catching dominatrix outfit that held Starshade's attention. It was her lengthy tail that was stretched across the entire room, doubling back on itself in several places. As Celia's upper portion stayed steady, the long, *long* tail was slowly coiling up under her.

Starshade's eyes went wide. It wasn't often that she got to see the sheer *size* of the base commander. Her mental image always roughly categorized the lamia into the same size bracket as Geode: A meter taller, and broad, but still generally… person-sized. It was moments like this, when Celia was stretched out over a large room, that her mind stopped filtering out the tail portion as unimportant. When that happened, she was left staring in awe.

"You wisssshed to ssspeak with me, little Sssstarsssshade?" The snake's voice held a touch of concern.

She… cares about this base.

The thought struck her suddenly. She had known that *intellectually*, but deep down, she had still been defaulting to the assumption that her leadership role was a function of her combat prowess. When you had a monster of myth and legend, of *course* they were the boss of an area. The Overlord's trusted lieutenants were always the most powerful.

But that thinking had been instilled upon her by endless video games and movies. This was a *real* organization, not a convenient series of plot points. Being a giant, monstrous terror wasn't part of the qualifications for leadership. The Korps wasn't a place where cruelty was promoted. That spoke very highly of her—

[Starshade.]

"Yes!" She jumped a bit at how loud her own voice was. Her ears splayed, blushing, as she moderated her tone. "Er… yes. Celia. I wanted to talk. I want to understand some things."

The lamia moved forward suddenly, gliding swiftly to tower above Starshade. In the dim light, her black eyes were pools of inky midnight, as she gazed down at the cornered rabbit. "You wisssh to know why I made the choiccce I did on the roof? Why I ssshut you down to assssessss and sssway Geode?"

"Oh! Uh… no. Actually." She fought to keep her breathing under control. The tiny *(smart)* part of her wanted to run screaming from the room. That the unexpected question had missed the mark helped focus here. It reminded her why she was here. "I… uh… figured that part out, actually."

Celia floated back with a raised eyeridge, tilting her head to appraise this intruder to her den. "Oh? And what conclusssion have you come to, little bunny?"

"Well... you needed to get the information quickly, and I was out of contact so long you couldn't be sure I hadn't been mind-controlled, or otherwise compromised in some way. You only knew Geode as an enemy. But you also wanted to sour the offer." The fear faded as she talked. She stepped forward, taking a more confident stance as she got into her topic.

"All Geode's life, she'd been lied to by the institutions she was part of, and they sold her on a superficial front of rosy, noble ideals. You did the opposite. You leaned *into* our bad reputation. It was the only way to make her believe the Korps was a force for real good, better than trying to convince her of that directly. You used fear... as... a weapon..." Starshade slowly ground to a halt. She looked around the dim room with appraising eyes.

"You knew exactly when I would be here..." She looked at the snake with a dawning realization. "You set the time. I didn't walk in unannounced. I didn't sneak into your lair. You... use fear, and your own terrifying reputation, as a weapon too..."

For her part, the serpent had been slowly coiling back up, watching her intently. "That isss... very perccceptive of you."

Starshade got the impression that Celia was impressed by her. "I think you know I was here to talk about something else. Can... can we talk? Without the pageantry? Please?"

Instantly the lights in the room brightened, fully revealing the room. She was left blinking in the sudden light. Celia's office was large, but also mostly empty. There was a large onyx desk with a massive magenta helix in the center. Flanking the desk, two giant banners bearing the Korps helix made sure anyone knew this was a villain's lair. Embedded into one wall was a massive display screen, turned off. But other than that, there were just a few piles of pillows.

For her part, the base commander had turned, moving towards one section of blank wall. "Would you care for sssome tea? Or I sssuppossse I have sssome coffee."

"Oh! Uh... tea, please?" While she much preferred coffee, the phrasing clearly suggested that the serpent preferred tea. Starshade found herself more curious to learn more about her tastes. Her fear was gone, replaced by an eagerness. Anticipation rose in her, feeling she had overcome some test.

A section of wall opened, revealing a drink station. Starshade couldn't help but eye the rest of the largely-blank wall panels, wondering what other secrets they hid. She didn't have long to speculate as the base commander pulled out two mugs already filled with steaming tea. The larger of the mugs, clearly for Celia herself, read "World's Second Worst Boss" with a giant #2 next to it.

Starshade laughed. She couldn't help it. "Where did you get that mug?"

Celia regarded her. Her words were full of wry humor when she answered. "Korpsmasss gift. From the Overlord."

She herself had never met the Overlord, but the fact that the big boss had a sense of humor comforted her. And that he was able to make fun of himself reaffirmed that this was an organization she wanted to be part of. Still chuckling, she finally turned her attention to the mug that was offered to her; the white and pink ceramic was emblazoned with a Division logo.

As her two paws wrapped around the offered tea, she looked up at the snake with a raised eyebrow. "A K-BURP mug?" She swore she saw a smile on Celia's face.

"Yesss. Ever been?" The question seemed a bit too casual.

"Not really my thing," the rabbit answered with a touch of regret and a shrug.

"Pity."

Starshade looked at the large viper for a long moment, pausing again. The question reminded her why she was there. She peered around for a place to sit, suddenly realizing that there were no chairs anywhere in the room. That made sense, since the lamia couldn't use them. Helpfully, the commander gestured to one of the piles of pillows. Instead, the bold cottontail simply walked over and sat on a section of Celia's tail.

The scarlet scales were smooth and hard. The gaps between the scales revealed soft skin, and provided enough friction that the rabbit didn't just slide off. She was surprised at the warmth that radiated into her. The tail was firm, but with a little give, making for a surprisingly comfortable seat.

Celia watched her for a long moment, saying nothing about the rabbit's impertinence, before she took a long sip from her mug. Starshade followed suit. The tea was strong. Initially bitter, the flavor shifted into a more complex array. She wasn't sure she liked it, but could see how it might grow on her. "What is this?"

"It ssstarted out asss Earl Grey, but I've been working to replicate sssome of the flavorsss of home."

The rabbit narrowed her eyes. She dearly wanted to know more about the mysterious base commander, and here was a perfect opportunity to ask more... except, she realized, it was yet another distraction. Celia seemed bent on luring her away from her goal.

"Why did you show up at my decanting yesterday?" Her heart was pounding as she asked the question she had been dying to know the answer to.

"I alwaysss worry about agentsss that are injured. I am resssponsssible for your sssafety."

The cottontail pursed her lips and wiggled her nose as she considered. "Agents get injured all the time. But you don't go to everyone's decanting."

"True. Though I cccertainly wisssh I could."

She lowered her mug, wrapping both paws around it, feeling the warmth radiate through the ceramic. But she was focused more on the heart pounding in her ears. Her chest felt tight and her breath sped up. Anxiety spiked in her as she grappled with her next question, a fear that had nothing to do with anything as simple as mortal danger.

"Celia. I need to know. Were you just there because you felt guilty? Are you beating yourself up because an agent almost died in your presence? Were you simply lamenting that you should have seen the signs sooner, so you could have prevented it? Or is there something else? Something... more?"

The snake took a long time to answer. As the silence dragged out, Starshade grew nervous. She wasn't sure which answer she wanted. Disaster scenarios played out in her head. But she forced herself to wait, patiently, for the answer. It was the bravest thing she had ever done.

"I... like you," Celia finally admitted quietly. Her reluctance and nervousness said clearly what she meant.

There it was. Part of her wanted to flee from the room screaming more than ever. Another part of her wanted to wrap her arms around the snake and hold her. But mostly she just tried desperately to process the answer and the conflicting emotions it set off in her.

"ROSE?"

Instantly she felt a wave of soothing emotions flow through her, it allowed her to think and kept her from panicking. To buy time to steady herself, she slowly took another sip of the tea.

"I... thought so." She said slowly. Then she caught the look in those obsidian eyes. As composed as the serpent always was, she recognized what she saw there. She could see a cascade of fears playing out as Celia imagined all the ways this could go wrong. Starshade realized in that moment that the ever-composed snake was going through every bit of agony as she was, trying to figure out what the rabbit was thinking. That finally let her speak what she had wanted to say.

"You scare the crap out of me. But part of me *really* likes that. You are damn sexy. And I've wanted you to wrap me in your coils since my RCGs went out the first time." There. She said it. A little more blunt than she had intended, but with anxiety spiking she had lost any grasp of subtlety.

Now it was her turn to wait on tenterhooks while the serpent processed the statement. Celia looked away and tasted the air. Starshade wondered if that was a nervous gesture. All the while she tried to keep her heart from exploding.

"I... try very hard not to get involved with anyone asssigned to RIV. My posssitttion makesss thingsss... difficult."

Get involved with? The phrasing spoke volumes. Celia wasn't looking for a casual fuck.

"If anything isss to happen between usss, we need to dissscussss what it meansss that I am basse commander. Becaussse *that*, and my duty to the Korps, come before any mattersss of the heart."

Starshade could understand that. "Okay... I *think* I know what that means..."

The snake took a moment to sip her tea. Starshade found herself jolted as the tail moved under her slightly. Finally, the lamia continued.

"Firsst, RIV and the Korps are paramount. It meansss that if I musst sssend you to die to sssave this basse, I will *not* hessitate." Then she grew very quiet and still. Her next words were hollow and quiet, speaking of deep sorrow. "I've done it before."

Oh.

One paw covered her mouth as she stared at the base commander. Her vision swam as tears threatened. She hadn't expected that — but the revelation made her want to comfort and care for the woman, not abandon her.

Celia continued, but her voice was distant. Devoid of emotion. "It alssso meansss that, if the relatttionssship doessssn't work out... if thingsss get... messssy, *you* will be the one that mussst relocate to another bassse. Even if *I* were the caussse of thossse problemsss. That'sss not fair to you. But the bassse comesss firsst. Alwaysss."

Oh.

She was still reeling from the realization that Celia had sent a lover to die. The rest seemed irrelevant. But she swallowed and considered the implications. If things went badly, she'd lose her place here. Her *friends.* Celia was right. It wasn't fair. But... the Korps came first. She could accept that, she thought.

"I understand." She hated how weak her voice was. But her throat was suddenly tight.

"That alssso meansss my time for sssuch activitiesss isss limited. I may not be able to devote asss much time to you asss we may both wisssh. You may find me called away in the middle of our time together. Korps leaderssship triesss to minimizzze that, but it happensss with depresssssing regularity."

Starshade nodded. That she had guessed, but felt good that it was stated. "Okay."

Celia looked at her for a long time. Assessing her. Finally, seemingly satisfied, she moved on. "Nexxxt. One of my ressssponsssibilitiesss is the training of topsss and dominantsss in the more advancccced artsss. It isss an esssssentttial tasssk, and one that isss incredibly important to me. That meansss that you ssshould not exxxpect to be my only lover."

That was easy. She nodded. "I don't need exclusivity. Heck, I don't want it." Starshade stopped at that point. The words were so casual and simple. But as the moment lingered, she realized that she needed to say more. Celia was laying out ground rules, and desires. That deserved more than simple acceptance. The cottontail's voice grew rougher as the words now had to overcome the fear of opening her heart.

"I... a small part of my heart longs for a single lover who could be my whole life. But the thought of actually doing that shows how hollow that desire is. That's only what I was *raised* to see as the perfect ideal. The Korps helped me realize that I am... greater than that. My heart and my lust both sing for... more. The thought of being... *important* to multiple people makes me feel warm and fuzzy. The idea that multiple people want to sate their lust in my slutty body makes me feel *desirable* in a way I... never dared believe I could. I... don't want exclusivity. But I do want to be... important."

"That, at leassst, I can offer. If we move forward, you ssshall be ever cherissshed. I would promissse to care deeply for you and to keep you sssafe, though not necccesssarily... comfortable." Celia tapped her chin with one, latex encased finger. Starshade could sense a slight smile in her tone as she continued. "Whether you are involved in that asss a... *training aid* in my teaching isss sssomething that will need to be dissscussssed at sssome point. But all that isss for later."

That thought sent a thrill through her. She loved being bound and shared. That was less warning than *enticement* to her libido. She tried to cover her blush by splaying her ears, and focusing studiously on her mug. But something Celia had said was tugging at her and she couldn't quite help herself from pursuing a tangent.

"I thought you said you didn't get involved with anyone on base? But you have other lovers?"

The snake shifted, looking at her. "Other sssexxxual partnersss, cccertainly. There are thossse I train. There isss lessss emotttion involved when I'm teaching. It isss more... professsssional. Asss for sssimple carnal pleasssuressss, ROSSSE usssually makesss arrangementsss for me from outsssside RIV; whether they merely ssseek a night with an exxxperienccced domme, or..." Celia gestured at the mug in the rabbit's hands, "...sssomething elssse."

She respected that answer. Having ROSE import willing lovers would certainly make things easier. And she suspected that Celia loved to play up the "Welcome To My Lair... *of Pain*" theater she employed so well.

"You like inflicting pain, don't you?"

The serpent looked away for a long moment. Her voice was tentative, almost apologetic. "Yesss. Very much. Pain isss… sssacred to me. I sssay that literally. Pain isss our oldessst ally. It tellsss usss when we are in danger. It urgesss usss to change. It helpsss usss sssurvive. Pain isss *holy*. It isss only when it become endlessss or inessscapable that it becomesss… blasssphemy. That is why I hate the world above. But that isss a rant for another time. Pain and pleasssure are two sssidesss of the sssame coin. I wield both with an exxxpert hand. If you do not like pain, leave now."

A shiver traveled down Starshade's spine at the stark statement. Pain was not her favorite thing. But Celia was promising to make her *feel* more than she ever had. As she looked at the tea clasped in her paws, she thought that maybe it was something she could grow to like.

She could walk away now. She knew that Celia wouldn't hold it against her. This whole idea had been crazy, and she wasn't sure why she had pursued it this far; when she had entered this room, she had just wanted to know *why*. Now, she was here, sitting on the base commander, contemplating making things *very* complicated.

Did she *want* to get involved with Celia? Sure, the giant snake made her horny as hell. She could admit that now. Was that enough? Walking away now would keep things simple. What Celia was promising was not a single night, but the woman regularly had one night stands. That she was offering *more* spoke volumes about the viper's own feelings.

Slowly, she stood up. Her heart was pounding in her chest. This time, it was not with fear. Or rather, not the same kind of fear she had always experienced around the serpent. As the great snake shifted and watched her intently, the rabbit gently placed the mug on the desk.

Her fur was tingling as she turned around, facing the impassive viper and looking up into those onyx eyes. Celia leaned forward, closer, sensing what was to come. Starshade reached up, capturing the giant head in her hands.

The scales were smooth under her fingers. She could feel the heat radiating off her. Gently, gently she pulled that serpentine face to hers. There, they stayed for a long moment, barely a breath apart.

"Come hurt me, then."

Celia smiled. And she did.

Chapter 19

Thrust Fault

April 3, 2023

"Come hurt me, then."

Starshade was trembling as she said those words. Her breath was quick. She *wanted* this. She wanted *her*. Those scaled lips closed the distance. She was surprised at how soft and gentle they were.

A small noise of pleasure slipped from her, as the kiss started to deepen beyond a simple brush; Starshade closed her violet eyes, and parted her lips. Then she felt the forked tongue slip into her mouth. She couldn't help but moan as the twin tips began confidently exploring her muzzle. In moments, the cottontail knew she was just along for the ride.

Suddenly, the kiss broke and the serpent pulled away. Starshade was left panting heavily, wobbling on knees suddenly weak. She blinked and looked around. It was then that she realized the faint rustling she had heard was Celia circling around her; coils piled upon coils, forming a wall. Leaving her *trapped*.

Fear and need warred within her as she turned to gape up at the woman towering overhead. Celia had risen to a bewildering height, making the rabbit feel tiny and cornered. The dampness between her legs ensured she could not deny how much at least *part* of her enjoyed the feeling.

[Syncing Consent and Boundary Lists with Celia, as per User Settings.]

As she watched, Celia leaned down, slowly. She had captured the gaze of her prey and was clearly savoring each moment as she grew closer and closer. Then she started to grin, that broad, serpentine mouth spreading wide. Fear spiked as Starshade realized the snake could swallow her whole; the *scale* of the lamia was driven home more than it had ever been before. Then, with an audible *pop*, twin fangs sprang out of her mouth. They glistened in the magenta light.

The teeth were stark white against the deep red of her throat. But the sinuous, saber-like fangs themselves weren't what captivated her gaze, leaving her unable to look away; it was the amber fluid that beaded on the tips. She had not realized that Celia was *venomous*. Before she could process any more than that epiphany, the viper struck.

One moment, the lamia's open mouth was hovering a meter above her; the next was a sensation of impact strong enough to buckle her legs, forcing the rabbit to her knees as those giant fangs slammed into her shoulders. The next was *agony*. Molten pain exploded from twin punctures as poison was pumped directly into her veins.

Starshade screamed. She could do nothing else. She knelt there for a long moment, feeling those daggers plunged into her, and a hot, inflamed, *pumping* sensation as Celia filled her with venom. Then, as suddenly as it had happened, the fangs withdrew; that serpentine face hovered in front of violet eyes that now had trouble focusing.

The pain lessened, letting her think. She could still feel the sensation as it spread through her with each beat of her heart, but it was distant now. She expected to be gushing blood from the teeth, but realized that the punctures had already closed, leaving only small bloody holes in her shirt.

She was panting for breath as the viper caught her gaze once more. Only when Celia was sure she was able to focus, did she speak. "Do you know what my power isss, little Ssstarssshine?"

Terror flooded her. Was she about to die? With a tiny voice, she answered. "Petrification."

A dry chuckle rumbled through the giant snake. "Oh, no, that'sss jussst what my people can do. One of our weaponsss. No, I have my own gift, given to me by my goddesss." The rabbit whimpered at the amusement filling Celia's tone. "No, my dear prey. My power isss… pain control."

With that, every nerve in Starshade's body lit up like a Korpsmas tree. A ragged scream was torn from her lips and her vision turned white; she just wanted the pain to *end*. Then — just as she reached her limit — it did. The agony instantly blossomed into pure pleasure. The sensation was almost worse, as her body rocked from orgasm. There had been no warning. No buildup. Just sudden, roaring *pleasure*.

As the wave of ecstasy ended, she fell to her hands, panting ragged breaths. Each exhale filled the room with squeaks and moans. She knelt there for a long moment, just trying to recover. Coherent thoughts were impossible; all she could do was gasp for air. She didn't know how long she stayed there.

Then the rustling of dry leaves surrounded her. She felt her long ears trying to track the sound, but it was everywhere. Finally, somehow, she found the strength to look up. Celia's coils were shifting against each other. Only then did she realize the wall of snake was contracting. The circle in which she knelt was shrinking.

"That wasss a but a *tassste*, my favorite little preything. Ssshall we continue? What'sss your color now?"

It took Starshade a moment to think clearly enough to remember what the domme was asking. Then she finally understood. Traffic light system. With a weak voice, but confident, she answered. "Green."

The snake did not wait for her to change her mind.

"ROSSSE, Ssstarssshade *hasss* had ssskeletal enhancccementsss, correct?"

[*Affirmative,*] the not-quite-AI's voice echoed aloud from hidden speakers.

The question was pure pageantry; Celia must have already been aware, and there was no need to ask the question. However, none of that stopped the wave of terror that flowed through her... nor did it stop the twinge of eager anticipation deeper in her belly.

Then she was being crushed by scales. One coil had bowled her over, and before she knew what had happened, she was being pressed into the floor by an endless tide of *snake*. The pressure was so immense she couldn't breathe. Panic at the thought of suffocation spiked — then faded — as she didn't feel the overwhelming *need* for air she'd expected, from experience. Her new lungs were getting a workout, she realized. She just hadn't expected to need them so *soon*.

Then the angle of the tail shifted, forcing her legs open. The barrel of the body *grinded* over her crotch, pressing into her chest; pain blossomed from her overly sensitive breasts, but mixed with the pleasure of the teasing between her legs. The coils slid over her endlessly. The scales faintly pricked at her, feeling somehow rough. It drove her *wild*, and she could do *nothing* about it.

Something changed at that moment. She wasn't sure how, but she was drawn upwards into an ocean of viper, losing all track of direction. After an eternity tempest-tossed in those serpentine waves, she suddenly found herself staring up into Celia's onyx eyes.

She still couldn't breathe, nor could she look away from the smiling viper hovering inches from her face. Those fangs were still out, adding a sinister edge to that grin. "Have you been enjoying the… foreplay?"

The pressure eased enough for Starshade to whimper an affirmative. Then, just as suddenly, the coils fell away from her torso. Her legs were still trapped, but she could *breathe* again. She rested her paws on Celia's tail and tried to form a coherent thought.

The base commander waited patiently for the rabbit to come back to herself. Finally, when she could think again, she swallowed and opened her mouth to speak. She didn't know what she was going to say — but it didn't matter, as a latex-covered finger was pressed to her lips.

"Sssssssssssshhh. I didn't asssk you to ssspeak yet, pet. You are only to ssspeak when I allow it. Do you undersssstand? Nod if you undersssstand."

Blushing furiously, she nodded. She understood.

"From now on, when you are addresssssing me, you will call me Missstressss. Do you undersssstand? You may ssspeak."

Her voice was tiny, as if smothered by the flush warming her cheeks. "Yes, Mistress."

"Good girl. *Goooood girl.*"

Pure pleasure crashed through her at the praise. Once again there was no warning. One moment she was struggling to talk with Celia; the next, her body clenched and spasmed in mindblowing orgasm. Just as suddenly, it stopped, leaving her blinking.

"My venom livesss in you now. From now on, I can bring pleasssure through but a thought. Pleasssure… or *pain.*"

Starshade screamed, her nipples abruptly feeling as if they were on fire. It was like nothing she had ever felt. Once again, just as suddenly, the sensation was gone, leaving her gasping for air with whimpering gulps. She looked up with fear and confusion.

Celia grinned evilly. "I sssee you are ssstarting to undersssstand, little bitty bunny bitch. You are mine. *Forever.*"

Starshade could only whimper.

[Color?]

It took her a moment to process the question. She was so lost in the moment that thought was difficult.

[Starshade! Color?]

"Green—"

She almost wept with the admission. Celia had glided around behind her while she was struggling to answer ROSE. Then, one latex-covered hand wrapped around her paw.

"Let'sss unwrap my new toy, ssshall we?"

Celia gripped Starshade's index finger, bringing it up. The other slick black hand pulled her 'Night Of The Lepus' t-shirt forward. Slowly — forcing her to watch — Celia slid the rabbit's own claw into her shirt, then pulled slowly downward. The sound of ripping fabric filled the air as she was forced to slice open her own clothing. Only when she was done were the rags torn from her.

The cottontail shivered in the suddenly cooler air, though she suspected that was more from the situation than temperature. She wondered if her plain black bra was next. She didn't have to wait long for the answer; the rabbit felt a hand capture the clasp in between gloved thumb and forefinger.

Effortlessly, with a muted *crack*, the serpent crushed the fastener. In moments, the ruined garment was stripped from her slim form as well, leaving her exposed. Celia's torso floated back into view as she looked down with a satisfied smile. Slick latex hands cupped her heavy breasts, rolling the nipples between her fingers and playing lightly with the small barbell piercings the snake found there.

There was no hesitation. Celia had not asked permission. She had no need; Starshade was her toy now. Not that the bunny complained, as those orbs — made so very sensitive by Empire — lit a fire within her. Within moments, soft pleasured squeaks started filling the air. She wanted more. *Needed* more. If the serpent would just play with them a little longer she could—

Then the hands disappeared, and Starshade mewled with desperation. She reached up to fondle herself. But the moment she touched her chest, pain shot through her paws like she had grabbed a live wire. She realized a moment later, as her fingers throbbed, that the pained squeal she had heard was her own. Maddeningly, the sudden pain had done nothing to cool the need between her legs.

"Now, now. No touching yourssself. Not unlessss I tell you. Your pleasssure isss mine to give. Or withhold."

Then she was… falling. The coils had swirled away, leaving her to tumble a meter to the floor. Starshade lay there — like the discarded toy she was — for a long moment. The polished stone felt cold against her bare chest. The cottontail couldn't form complete thoughts. She was feeling. Reacting. *Obeying.* And she *loved* it.

A jolt and the wet tearing of leather heralded the end of her pants. Celia had simply and casually ripped them apart. The action rolled her over onto her back, staring up at the snake towering above her. She was naked except for her boots and a couple glittering bits of jewelry. The lamia clearly loved what she saw.

"Sssuch a beautiful, lovely toy," she said, seemingly to herself. The praise sent a jolt of embarrassment through the toy.

[Yellow. She'd say green if we could ask her, but you're pushing a little hard for the first session. She's struggling to think.]

The serpent cocked her head a bit, considering. "Agreed. I'll move to more sssensssual delightsss. Bring her down ssslowly."

Toy struggled to understand the words. They seemed distant. Unconnected. She didn't quite register when strong hands scooped her up gently. Then, she was wrapped in scales once more. Not crushing this time, just… *holding.*

She was held there for a long time, in that warm embrace. Dimly, she started to register the slick hands stroking her ears and the soft voice cooing "Good girl" as a mantra. Then as her mind started to work again, she started to blush.

A sea of scales still encased her, preventing any movement. Her legs were spread, straddling that great tail. She ached all over. But more than anything, she was horny as hell.

Celia must have sensed the change. "*There* we are. Welcome back, little Ssstarssshine. Do you want to ssstop? Or ssshall we continue?"

She opened her muzzle to instantly shout her demand for more. But she paused. Her thoughts still felt... fuzzy. She hadn't been that deep in a long, long time. She was aching with need, yes, but also in pain. She really *thought* about it. Did she want to continue?

"Continue, Mistress, but... gentler... for now... please?"

The delight at her answer glittered in those obsidian eyes. The serpent leaned forward and kissed her again. This time it was not staking a claim but a slow, sensual thing. Her long, forked tongue played against her own, then twined around it. It wasn't long before Starshade was making tiny squeaks of joy.

By the time the kiss finally broke, every inch of Starshade's fur was tingling with electric need. She shifted her hips to grind herself against the serpent, desperate, but she couldn't seem to push herself over the edge. She had never been this close to orgasm without tipping over. Wild, she looked up at Celia.

"Pain Control isss alssso Pleasssure Control. You don't orgasssm unlessss I *allow* it. If you want it... beg for it."

Her eyes grew wide at the implications, and a whimper escaped her lips. She was *horny*. But she knew this game. Even if begging for an orgasm made her flush with humiliation.

"Please, Mistress!" Desperation filled each word. "May I earn the right to cum, Mistress?" She ground hard against the tail, trying to push herself over. All she managed to do was drip freely until those scales were wet and shiny, glittering in the light.

Latex gloves cupped her cheeks and pulled her head against the lamia's long neck. "Kissss your way down. Then I ssshall consssider it."

Starshade did not have to be told twice. Her onyx lips started kissing hungrily. Her pink tongue explored the gaps between those cream-colored scales. While every part of her wanted to rush, she took her time. The taste was unlike anything she had ever experienced, something akin to the faintest hint of desert sands. The scales over Celia's throat were far smaller and more delicate than she had realized. Her lips worked at her task regardless, lavishing each armored diamond with attention in turn.

Then, her long ears twitched, as they caught the tiniest of sounds: a tiny hiss of pleasure.

That was all Starshade needed to hear. She licked and kissed and nuzzled like a wild beast, desperate to wring that sound out of her mistress again. She succeeded when she started to work on the swell of those giant breasts, which only fired her passion further. Uncaring about the consequences, her sharp teeth sliced through the string that connected Celia's bra, freeing the massive mounds.

With a whimper of lust, her mouth closed around one thick metal ring. The rabbit's amethyst eyes locked on the serpent's onyx orbs as she tasted the iron. Then, lapine lips enveloped one large nipple and suckled *hard*.

The sound was no quiet hiss this time. Celia cried out before catching her breath and swallowing further noises, but Starshade still knew she had found something her Mistress *enjoyed*. She fixed her lips around the soft skin and worked her tongue around the thick ring as best she could, pressing against her. Then, locking her eyes on the serpent, she captured the nipple in her buck teeth and bit down. Not enough to draw blood, but more than enough to cause the coils to shift, rubbing against each other.

Latex hands cupped her face then. Thumbs rubbed against the cheek bulges caused by the thick piercing. With gentle pressure, the snake slowly pulled the rabbit free from her breast. They shared a moment, then, gazing at each other as Starshade was slowly pulled free. With a mischievous twinkle in her eye, at the last minute she hooked her buck teeth around the ring and tugged.

Celia cried out, bucking her hips in clear delight. After a moment, Starshade let the ring pop free, but couldn't keep the satisfied smirk off her muzzle.

The base commander smirked back after a moment. "Naughty girl. But I sssuppossse I mussst exxxpect sssuch behavior from an untrained minxxx. I ssshall have to… *correct* that. For now, you have a job to do."

A thrill of excitement and fear seemed to concentrate between her legs. Starshade had forgotten about her own body; she was so focused on Celia, she had managed to distract herself from the fact that she had never been this horny outside of her heat. She had been taken beyond the edge of orgasm, and yet, was *still* denied.

Then her face was pressed against something new. Just below where the hips would be on a biped was an opening framed by soft, cream scales. The rabbit's own lust burned too brightly to let her examine it. Lust hazed her vision as her tongue shot out and *plunged* deep into the entrance.

The taste was indescribable. *Not of this world.* But if the rest of Celia tasted like the desert, this tasted of an oasis, full of respite and life, and *beauty* in a hard land. Her pointed muzzle pressed deeper, seeking the sacred water to quench her thirst. A tiny part of her rejoiced that she would not need air for a very long time; the rest was focused on dragging her tongue over soft folds.

Her own hips were grinding freely against the trunk of the lamia's tail. She barely noticed. Instead, her long ears strained for any change to the now constant moans from the large serpent. As the hands relaxed, she sought out new spaces to lick and lap and nibble. Then, as Celia started to squirm and her breathing got shallower and shallower, she was able to tilt her head back and up, fastening her mouth around a hidden nub.

Juices *exploded* around her face. Greedily, she lapped and swallowed the nectar that was her prize. She was surprised when a hand wrapped itself around the back of her head, pulling her back with incredible strength, then plunged her forward.

The rabbit's muzzle spread the folds wide as her face was forced into the spasming tunnel. All of a sudden she felt her *own* tunnel spread *wide* as the tip of Celia's tail forced itself into her. Immediately, her own pleasure was crashing over her. She could not scream. She could not writhe. She could not escape. All she could do was spasm and buck as the world turned white from an orgasm more intense than she had ever had in her life.

The last thing she remembered was Celia screaming her name.

Starshade felt warm and safe, sleeping on a soft bed of... scales. It was that errant thought that slowly brought her back to consciousness. As she did so, aches started to let themselves be known, pulling her further from her slumber. Finally, she cracked one eye open with a soft groan. The room was very dim and bleary.

Her other eye didn't want to open. The eyelids were stuck together. She was still too sleepy to panic and simply brought a paw up to rub her face until she could open her left eye. The fur on her face was clumped together with something sticky. As the memories slowly started to come back, she blushed and smiled at the cause.

"ROSE?"

Only then did she realize she wasn't wearing her visor. Blinking, she started to sit up only for two scaled hands to rest on her shoulders and gently press her back down.

"Sssssssshhh. Easssy, Ssstarssshade." Celia's torso bent down over her as she whispered softly.

The room started to brighten very slowly, giving her plenty of time to adjust and to rouse from her sleep-fogged state. When she felt ready, she opened her mouth to speak. Her first attempt was a hoarse croak. Swallowing, she tried again.

"Good… morning? Is it morning?"

"It isss. A little after 0600. Good morning, sssweetling."

She was unusually groggy and had trouble clearing her mind. But then Celia started to pet her ears, and she *melted*. The soft waves of pleasure that shivered down the sensitive skin almost tickled. The care drew a soft, pleased gasp from her.

She didn't want to move, so she didn't. The viper continued to soothe her for as long as she needed it. Finally, she cracked an eye open again, feeling a little more clear.

"Are… are you doing okay?"

A soft hissing chuckle greeted the question. "Here I am trying to check on you and your firssst conccccern isss if *I* am okay. You are very sssweet. Yesss, I am fine. Incredible, in fact. I didn't realizzze how much I needed that. But the quesssstion isss, how are *you* doing? I put you through a lot."

This was not her first time in an intense scene. She knew better than to brush off the question. She thought, really *thought*, through the answer. Her mind was still a bit sluggish, but the cobwebs were starting to fade.

"I... I'm okay, I think. I ache, all over. And my shoulders really hurt where you bit me." The pain suddenly faded, though it didn't vanish. She gave Celia a grateful half smile.

"Yesss, you ssshould ssstop by medical to get that patched. It'll heal fassster that way. But that'sss the physsssical. What about the ressst? Did I go too far anywhere? Isss there anything you regret?"

Starshade wiggled to get more comfortable, enjoying the feel of the bed of serpent. She thought back through. "The... crushing me into the floor wasn't... great? I love restraint and immobilization, and you certainly made it fun with the control over pain and pleasure, but otherwise it didn't really do it for me?" She blushed as she offered the criticism.

Celia over tilted her head and nodded. "What about wrapping in my coilsss and sssqueezing?" Her voice was thoughtful as she considered.

Starshade shook her head. "That, I loved. It felt both... safe, and *dangerous*. And I loved being surrounded by you."

The serpent nodded. "You sssank very deep in headsssspaccce. That worried me a bit."

Starshade swallowed and thought back. "Yeah... I didn't expect that. The pain and pleasure combo pushed some buttons that had never been pushed before. I... think I like it. But I need to get used to it. Could... could you go slower next time?"

There was a long pause. "Ssso you *want* a nexxxt time?"

The cottontail blinked. *Did* she want a next time? "Yes!" she blurted. Both of them jumped from the sudden force of her reply. Starshade blushed hard and moderated her voice. "If... you'll have me. Yes. Please. Er... should I be calling you Mistress?"

Celia smiled softly. "For now, I only require that during play."

Starshade asked the one question she had been desperately wanting to know. "The... venom? That really... forever?"

The lamia shook her head, looking sheepish. "No, sssadly. It wearsss off after a week. If I want to keep playing with your pain I have to... top you up."

The cottontail stared. Then she narrowed her eyes. Then they both burst into laughter.

Finally, feeling better, she shifted and Celia let her stand, forming a circle around her. Then she was...

HUGGING...

...the base commander. Her hands almost touched around the back of the giant woman. But two scaled arms wrapped around her and pulled her up, which buried her face between those giant breasts.

She didn't complain. She had eight hours of air and was content to use every second of that time sandwiched in her lover's bosom.

Eventually, Celia let her down.

Only then did she look down and realized she was still nude and covered in drying fluids. And that serpent had destroyed her clothing. As the realization slowly struck, she looked up sheepishly. "Er..."

The commander had a devilish grin. "You have two choicccesss. The boring one. Or the kinky one."

Her heart sank as she took in the smile. "Do... I get to know what those are before I choose?"

The lamia shook her head.

Starshade cursed her stupid slutty mouth for the nineteenth time, as she tried to slink to the next bit of cover. Not that she could *do* much with her stupid slutty mouth, due to the ball gag in it. Celia had been delighted to point out how her prominent buck teeth made this type of gag so much more secure. The straps were locked in place with an electronic padlock.

So too were her arms, pulled into the leather armbinder. The infernal contraption had been pulled tight enough that her elbows touched behind her back. Her shoulders already *ached* from the strict bindings.

Her chest had been squeezed into a tight bikini top that showed off every inch of her cleavage. The thin fabric did nothing to hide her nipples poking through but *did* manage to proclaim 'Free Use.' The panties were even more mortifying. The front proclaimed her to be 'Celia's Egg Slut' and did nothing to hide the thick plug nestled in her rear that buzzed away, keeping her on edge.

But it was the fact that *all fourteen bells in her ears* jingled with each step, unless she was *very* careful, that was the worst. She could feel the weight that kept pulling down her ears and she had to fight not to twitch or adjust them suddenly, which made a *lot* of noise.

ROSE helpfully informed her that the tram would deny her entry. She had to make her way back to her quarters by foot, except it wasn't that simple; the gag would only unlock if she went to the armory in section 1C first. The armbinder required her to stop by Lab 19, which was on the opposite side of the base. If she entered her apartment without doing so, those pieces would timelock for eight hours.

Celia had made it very clear that if she was detected on her journey by anyone who had listed themselves as available, she was to offer herself to them. Failure to do so would lock her out of her apartment entirely and then her only option was going to the Dominion Club for 'Correction'. The same would happen if she took more than two hours to get into her apartment.

She hoped she hadn't dripped through her new panties yet.

Seeing good cover behind a large planter, the field agent darted forward a little too fast and her ears jingled. She stopped, glancing around wild eyed. After a moment, she could breathe again, happy she hadn't been detected yet. Then she heard the heavy hoofsteps of the gigantic, shaggy cow purposefully walking up behind her.

She cursed her stupid slutty mouth for the twentieth time.

CHAPTER 20

MASS WASTING

April 5, 2023

One hoof gently touched the tarmac, followed immediately by the flashing of cameras. Rockfall hovered there, barely touching the ground, with hands on his hips and a winning grin on his face; a Bradley Hero arriving in a city was always worthy of at least some low-level media attention. While not yet a household name, he attracted more interest from the scrum of reporters and photographers, all of whom wanted to be the one with the scoop already waiting if he *did* break out.

Much of his training — the *real* training, the skills necessary to actually do this work — had been on media relations. The NHA put a great deal of effort into ensuring the public saw them as shining beacons of liberty, and came down hard on any of their members who failed to uphold the model image, or threatened to stray from the boundaries of the morals clause in their contract. So he waited there, in the unrelenting Texas heat, in his gold and black uniform, while they snapped hundreds of pictures of him. The gold cape framed his muscular body, and complemented his golden antlers with the mysterious silver celtic knotwork.

Finally, as his escort arrived, he set down fully on the ground. The media parted so they could get pictures of him shaking hands with apparently-beloved local hero, Heavenly Dazzler; she was dressed in a diaphanous white dress that blended in with her pure white feathers. Her beak and eyes were gold, as was her belt. He dwarfed the dove, standing almost twice her height, forcing him to stare down into the halo of golden light above her head. As he grinned and shook her hand, he had a dawning realization. The choice of hero to greet him was diabolical.

Her white-and-gold contrasted with his gold-and-black. His giant size towering over her. It would all suggest that the federal hero was a menace, coming in to bully the small-time local heroes. He hadn't been standing on the Dallas ground for a full minute, and the TPA was already playing propaganda games. Captain Anders had been right; he would have to be on his guard.

"I am blessed to meet you, Rockfall. You must be *exhausted* by the flight in. If you come right this way, we have some refreshments set out for you so you can recover from your journey. They were donated by local businesses who have been *so grateful* for the ongoing protection of the Bradley Group." Heavenly Dazzler's voice was sweet, and filled with Southern hospitality.

On guard, he saw the trap. If he accepted them, he'd be painted as weak... but if he refused, he would not only be spitting in the Teepa's face, he'd be doing so to no-doubt-beloved local merchants. Rockfall hated this dance already.

"As much as I would love to get to work immediately, I certainly can't turn down such local delicacies." Not perfect, but he felt trapped in a no-win scenario.

"Bless you. I'm certain they're *delighted* to be our hospitality partners, for a Hero they've heard *so* much about." She had started walking, but slowly. He was forced to keep her pace, but that made his gait look stilted and unnatural, instead of his normally powerful stride. It also kept them under the merciless gaze of the cameras for longer.

He kept himself from visibly gritting his teeth. The dove's words were knives wrapped in politeness. He was brand new; there was no way these shops had heard about him, much less cared. He realized he would be portrayed as the big government stooge, coming in and taking advantage of hard-working, salt-of-the-earth folk. *Damn her.*

"Are there any you particularly recommend I try? I would hate to miss out." He went on the offensive a little bit to try and trip her up.

"Oh, they are *all* delightful! For example, there's this wonderful little store in downtown Fort Worth. They specialize in high-quality keto-friendly treats and make these *delightful* brownies; they help the fat melt away! Then, there's this boutique bakery in Lake Highlands that makes cinnamon rolls that are *divine!* You simply *must* try them..."

As she continued, he listened with growing horror. Half of the treats were diet foods, hinting that he could stand to lose some weight...

226

or perhaps suggesting he was the kind of effete health obsessive who wouldn't deign to eat anything else. The rest were sweets that violated the (mutually conflicting) diets altogether. There was simply no way he could try them all without seeming a glutton. He had been hoping she wouldn't know much about the items on offer, so he could sample only a few highlights, but it had backfired badly; the dove seemed to know little details about each handcrafted local delicacy that showed that she personally loved each and every one. He suspected she was being fed the information over an earbud.

She finally stopped talking and glanced at him for a response. "Those all sound *delightful*. There is no way I can try them all, though I dearly wish otherwise."

"You will be *elated* to know that the terminal has shower facilities that are equipped to handle men of your stature. The fur shampoo is designed to handle even the *toughest* musk and was hand made by a little place in Bishop Arts…"

He *hated* Texas.

Dry scrubland stretched out to the horizon. Grayish-green foliage covered the gently rolling plains, punctuated with bare areas of bright tan dust. The only sign of civilization beyond this compound were forlorn oil pumps, long since abandoned as the black gold had run dry. The service roads to those sites were starting to be reclaimed by the… *nothing* that was southern Texas.

Thomas Stenham scowled at the bleak desolation. The dry heat was oppressive, causing sweat to stain his custom-tailored suit. The tall, athletic civet hated this forsaken wasteland. He should be relaxing in his mansion with a glass of rare wine in paw and the girl of the week in his lap, not out *here* beyond the edge of the world.

Still, he was here because he only had one mansion, one pied-à-terre, and a handful of luxury cars, and he was tired of looking with envy at the yachts and islands of his peers. He *deserved* more than those rich old idiots who had everything *given* to them. He had *earned* his fortune, modest as it was. He was on the cusp of *greatness*. It was all coming together.

With one last scowl, he turned away from the abandoned oil field, and stalked across the runway towards the so-called command center. That grandiose name didn't really fit the old building, now hosting a modest server room and a dozen or so desks; the brand-new satellite dish on top of the structure (and the recently replaced power lines trailing into the remote site via a string of lonely transmission towers) were the only exterior signs the site was in use at all.

Gravel crunched under his Italian leather shoes — to his distaste, already *covered* in the oppressive Texas dust — as he looked at the warehouse. It had held a surprising amount of forgotten equipment from when this oilfield was abandoned. He hadn't bothered clearing it out yet; truthfully, those random bits of junk might come in handy. Nestled along one wall was a series of new wooden pallets filled with everything needed to bring those oil pumps back to life.

The only problem was that there was no *oil* for them to pump.

His thoughts were interrupted when he noticed a cloud of dust on the horizon. A feral grin of anticipation spread his thin black lips as the bus crested a slight rise; the prisoner transfer had arrived ahead of schedule. Changing course, he instead headed for the abandoned building that had been the (optimistically-named) flight control tower.

Fifteen minutes later, Thomas Stenham stared at the mirror, adjusting his gold 'MM' cufflinks. While his careful preparation would not be appreciated, he always felt it was important to observe proper protocol. There was a way these things were done, after all.

He was tall and fit. The dark blue suit had been tailored specifically to show off his figure best. While they had fallen out of fashion even in the tech crowd, he felt naked without his ever-present single-ear Bluetooth headset. The tips of his ears and nose were stark white against the mix of grays that made up the rest of his fur; his pink nose stood out in stark contrast to the more muted palette of his muzzle. But the man's most striking feature was his rust-red eyes.

His thoughts were interrupted by the sound of the door to the building slamming open. Two voices filtered through to his back room;

one was gruff and commanding, while the other was scared and confused. A slow smirk curled his lip. It was time.

Without touching it, the old door opened as he stepped through, a charming grin plastered on his face. He had fired the one assistant who had dared to say it looked *oily*. Three men waited for him. Two dogs dressed in corrections officer uniforms stood silently and expectantly; they had been here before. The third, a large dalmatian dressed in the bright orange jumpsuit of a convicted criminal, sat chained to a sturdy chair that had been placed for just this purpose.

"Welcome! You must be Raul Gurrera."

The dog blinked at him stupidly. "What's going on?" he asked in a small, timid voice.

Good. He's been broken already.

He nodded to the two guards. Without a word, they turned around and left the building. They knew who signed their paychecks. If their boss wanted to be left alone with a dangerous prisoner, that wasn't their problem.

"Well, I am the CEO of CoreCivet and when I heard about your story, I had to meet you."

Chains clinked as the canine leaned forward as far as he was allowed. Desperate whining filled his voice. "Please, you have to believe me! I was defending myself!"

The civet added a touch of sympathy, and dash of doubt, to his voice. "Roiling Justice was a beloved Hero. He protected the people of St. Louis. His loving wife was pregnant with their first child. Are you saying he attacked you?"

Gurrera's tone became even more pleading. Beseeching this stranger to believe him as no one yet had. "Yes! I was cleaning up the build site when he wandered by. Then his eyes turned red and he went berserk! He'd've killed me if'n I hadn't been carrying that nailgun!"

A pinch of hesitation but the barest sign he might believe the story. "That's the thing I don't understand. Why would a proud member of Gateway attack an innocent civilian?"

The rattle of chains as the former construction worker tried to bare his left forearm to no avail. "I was branded. It was some sort of magic!"

"Yes, I heard about your intricate scarification. The police expert said it was self-inflicted and spoke of a disturbed mental state."

"That's a damn lie!" Shouting now, as expected. The same emotional outburst and nonsensical ravings that had robbed this man of any chance a jury would believe him. "Some dead guy grabbed my wrist! Next thing I knew, it was seared into my flesh! Same thing happened but worse when..." He trailed off then, trying not to cry.

"Oh, I believe you."

Shocked silence then. The dalmatian stared at him first with confusion, then with growing hope. "You... believe me? You can help me! You can tell them! This has all been a misunderstanding! They'll listen to you! *Please!*"

The civet held up his hand. This was his favorite part and he struggled to keep that off his face.

"Of course I believe you. I am... The Magnificent Maestro." He paused, enjoying the growing confusion and alarm. The silence held for a moment, letting the anticipation build. "And I *gave you* that brand."

Hope instantly turned to horror. Wide eyes boggled at him. The chair creaked and the chains strained as he tried in vain to back away. "You..." he sputtered, "You're... *The Master?!*"

A fine Italian leather shoe crunched on old glass as he moved forward. A feral rictus spread his lips, dripping with eager cruelty. "Oh yes."

The screaming did not stop for a long time.

Chapter 21

Pressure Solution

April 6, 2023

Stepping outside into the oppressive heat, he gestured to the door behind him. "Clean up the bones. As usual," he faintly sneered. Stenham always felt *giddy* after draining one of the vessels, and the power coursing through him was intoxicating; he'd have to put it into the Working soon, though, or it would fade and be wasted. For the moment, he reveled in the electric tingling of being *overcharged*.

The civet made no effort to suppress the self-satisfied smirk plastered across his muzzle. The whole plan was ingenious. When he discovered that he could implant dormant spells in others, a world of possibilities had opened. Now, he had a steady stream of power batteries.

He owned one of the largest private prison groups in the country. He simply had to wait for a host to be convicted anywhere in the country. The public took a dim view of anyone who killed a Hero, meaning their pleas of self-defense wouldn't save them. When they were safely in the prison system, he would just… *buy* them from whatever facility they were sent to. It was so very easy to buy and sell felons. Especially *dangerous* ones.

No one cared if someone died in jail. It happened all the time. No questions were asked. There was no public outcry. In fact, many considered it a *feature*. It was *justice*. The pitiful oversight committees had been captured long ago.

All of which meant that they would end up in his hands. Then they would power his grand plan. He could feel the power *thrumming* in the ground. The magic stretched to the horizons. It wouldn't take much more now before the spell would be complete. Then… then he would be richer than God. As he deserved to be.

His path had carried him into the back room of the command center. The large room was empty, save for a few bits of trash and scrap metal on the floor; the bare incandescent bulbs were harsh and drew attention to the peeling and faded paint on the walls and doors. Once this site was ready for expansion, this room would be restored. Until then, it gave him the perfect private sanctuary.

He snapped his fingers, just as he pushed a pulse of magic into the ethereal realm. It did not take long for something to respond. It started as a small distortion in the middle of the room, flickering and indistinct. Rapidly that point of warped space grew in size until it was a couple meters across. The air rippled and twisted in a way that always hurt his eyes and made his stomach turn.

Then the anomaly collapsed into a roughly feline shape. It was not a person, so much as a swirling maelstrom of reddish-brown dust the color of dried blood. There was the barest hint of ears and a tail, but the outline was too indistinct to say more.

"Report." He barked out the word of command. He had bound this spirit to his will and had no need of pleasantries.

"**Three vessels currently exist. One remains in Florence. It is unlikely his appeal will succeed.**"

Stenham pursed his lips. The one flaw in his plan was that inmates in federal prisons were rarely available for transfer to private, state-run facilities. Terrance Williams was a massive power reserve, but would remain forever beyond his reach. He swore the spirit always started with that tantalizing morsel to taunt him, but the thing did not have true intelligence. It was merely a construct.

"**The second remains in trial in Lexington. A rather fortunate emotional outburst has all but ensured that he will be convicted. Most likely, he will be available for purchase next month.**"

That was very good. It was always hard to tell how much power he would gain from any given source. But he was nearing the completion of his plan. Bryce Tanner might just be enough. He was so close to victory he could taste it.

"**The third just made her second kill.**"

He blinked. Jennifer Delver had been a surprise. The fact that a fifty-two-year-old health inspector had managed to kill a *superhero* seemed bizarre. But that she had killed a second? That was astonishing.

"Wait, she killed *another* Hero?"

"This one was a villain. An arms dealer. Sadly, it was a synth, so the power draw was minimal."

She killed a **synth***!?*

That was very, very impressive. This one was full of surprises. "Did she have help?"

There was a short pause, which was unusual. But perhaps the construct had difficulty parsing the question. That happened sometimes.

"Yes, she had a degree of help. But it was mostly luck."

That tracked. Some people just had all the cards fall their way sometimes. It was bizarre but stranger things had happened.

"Where is she now? Has she been caught."

"She is currently ensconced in a superpowered fighting arena in Dallas. It would be difficult to extract her without direct intervention. It is unlikely that an anonymous tip to the police would be viable at this time."

Damn. He frowned. If Bryce wasn't enough, he would have to either wait for a new host to form, or he would have to dig her out of her hole. Still, he might not need her. Even if the power stored within her *was* needed, if he waited, she might move to a more accessible location. Patience was a trait not shared by his short-sighted rivals.

"I thought there was another? What was his name… Ryan Murphy?"

"Brian Murphy. Unfortunately, Chaos Ladder chose to inspect the prison last week."

The Magnificent Maestro sighed. Another downside to the plan was that the receptacles were so fragile. Still, there were always more. He needed to fly to Albuquerque soon for the next prisoner transfer. Always best to increase the odds.

"Keep an eye on Jennifer. If there's a way we can snatch her, do so."

"Yes, Master."

He smiled. He loved being called that. He was so close to victory. The plan was perfect. No one even knew about it. Few would care if they did.

No one cared about the deaths of convicts and murderers… especially not when the outcome would help *everyone*.

Rockfall stood in the office of the TPA Dallas Division Commander, and shook the hand of Steel Geyser. The boar — though tall by conventional standards — glowered up at the much taller Hero. The reindeer suspected that this man was rarely doing anything *other* than scowling. Shane Verrastro had recently been promoted from the TPA Academy to this post, after the sudden retirement of Manifest Destiny almost two months ago.

"Sit down." The boar barked it like an order. Here was a man used to being obeyed. Rockfall had met many men like this in his own training. They had spent their whole lives using their size and force of personality as a weapon, to make others submit to them.

After an evening of dealing with the insufferable Heavenly Dazzler with her verbal barbs cutting at him at every opportunity, he was well and truly done with the petty mind games. All his efforts to make progress and talk with the commander had been stymied until he was finally forced to head to his hotel. He was certain this had been planned so he spent all night stewing. He hated that it had worked. This morning had had to ply himself with enough coffee that the barista had been growing increasingly alarmed. He was here to *help* these people, after *their* disastrous fuckup, and they were trying to play politics with every single word.

"No, but thank you." Rockfall responded as if the command had been a polite question. He didn't want to set the precedent of following orders. While the boar's own chair was a plush leather executive chair, the other chairs in the office were cheap, molded plastic that looked flimsy and uncomfortable. Also, he didn't want to draw attention to the fact that his antlers had punched into the drop ceiling, and he suspected any attempt to sit down would rip the tile apart.

The caribou had a *lot* of experience with drop ceilings.

The TPA commander looked at him like he had just insulted his mother, instead of refusing to comply with an order he was under no obligation to obey. For a moment, Rockfall thought the man would explode into shouts and demands, based on the way the cords of muscle in his neck bulged, but he instead leaned against his window.

There was no doubt Steel Geyser was a powerfully-built man. His uniform showed off his robust body and stretched over his musclegut. But, physically, he was simply outclassed by the Bradley heavy, robbing him of his primary means of intimidation. Between that, and his words lacking the subtly barbed venom of the dove healer, Rockfall felt on much firmer ground.

"I'm here at the request of the Texas Protectorate Assembly to assist with the recovery of your kidnapped Hero. I'm to render assistance to ensure the safe return of Slate. As such, I will require the full cooperation of the TPA. We share the same goal."

The boar's scowl deepened. "The TPA made that request against my better judgment. We can handle this ourselves."

"That's great news. Then I'm certain we can resolve this quickly, and I'll be out of your hair." Rockfall couldn't help but throw a small barb of his own, seeing the boar's buzzcut.

There was a long moment as the boar locked eyes with the visiting Hero. The caribou could clearly see the hatred in the beady brown eyes. Finally, with a snort of disgust, the commander looked away first. Rockfall was under no illusions he had won. The first round had gone squarely to the Teepa. But he was on the board now, at least.

"I'll assign you a liaison. Sylvanite is currently at loose ends; she'll be able to get you the information you need."

The reindeer wracked his brain for a moment. Then remembered that Sylvanite was one of the reserve Heavies in the DFW area. She had recently 'temporarily' been promoted to the Pegasus Phalanx to fill in, with Slate MIA. The team was currently benched, so it was more symbolic than anything.

The boar raised his hand to dismiss the visitor, but Rockfall jumped in before that could happen. "I take it that there's been no sign of Slate since his disappearance."

Shane Verrastro looked up at the impertinent question and narrowed his eyes. Then sighed. "No word yet. We've been studying other Korps abductions. It usually takes a few months before they resurface. By then, they are completely mind-controlled and usually also heavily altered. So we expect something in the next few weeks. But you'll need to be ready to *fight*. Slate is a fine Hero, and well seasoned. Experience matters for a lot in this business."

Rockfall let the barb about his experience slide. He had studied Slate and was confident of his chances; he was only worried that the Teepa would decide to even the odds. In any event, the boar's briefing — terse as it was — matched with what Bradley's own intel had said. Still, he couldn't be certain he could trust the information the Teepa shared.

In response he nodded. "I'll need access to all of his teammates to get a better picture of who Slate is. I'll need to see his quarters. I'll need access to his files and financial information. I'll need access to your administrative records on him as well."

Steel Geyser had looked startled by the demands, but narrowed his eyes as they continued. "Now wait just a goddamn minute here. You're just supposed to rescue him. You ain't needing all that just to find a lost pony."

The caribou knew he had gotten under the boar's skin with the demands, but was ready for it. "You said yourself that I'm going to have to fight him. You also said that experience matters in this business. That means knowing *everything I can*. That includes where he might find hidden allies; it means knowing how he views his teammates and whether he thinks they could be 'recruitment opportunities.' And it means knowing what secrets he might try to exploit."

The silence stretched out as Rockfall stared down the commander. After a long, long time, the boar relented. "Sylvanite can help get you most of that. I'll authorize it. But I'm *not* authorized to release the internal records. I'll have to request that from headquarters in Austin."

The Bradley Hero smiled. "I can work with that. Now, is there anything else you can share?"

"No, you're free to go."

Not giving me another opportunity to demand cooperation, I see.

With a smirk, Rockfall finally ducked to get through the door. In the process, his antlers ripped apart the ceiling tile they had been stuck in, raining fragments and dust all over Steel Geyser's office.

Chapter 22

Vulcanism

April 6, 2023

Dawn finished coiling up the last of the pink ropes, and tossed the bundle into the drawer. She looked around her bedroom one last time. All the clean gear had been inspected and put away; all the dirty gear was in a pile for pickup. The cleaning drone would be by shortly, to take it for proper sanitization; it wouldn't take much, after Lexi had licked it all clean first. The thought made her smirk. She would only have to inspect it for wear or damage when it was returned to her.

Orion was still showering. He had been a very good boy for a long time, and had earned a hot, relaxing shower. The giant eland had once confessed that it helped him shake off the last bits of subspace. After that, she always made sure her husband got first crack at the bathroom and had as much time as he needed — no matter how messy her fur was, or how much she was dripping. (She had discovered she liked that part, anyway.)

The dik-dik smoothed out the wrinkles from the pink comforter. She loved the feel of the soft, plush bedspread. Then, everything was done and cleaned up except the floor. And there was no point in cleaning *that* until after her *own* shower.

She checked the time. Starshade would be here in a couple minutes. The dik-dik hadn't seen her friend since Geode's trip to Empire two days ago; she would have liked a shower before the cottontail arrived, but the field agent would not mind her being naked and messy. Nor was she willing to rush Orion. Any attempt at showering *with* Orion would only ensure that she would not be ready in time for Starshade… and also that she would need another shower.

Instead, she took the opportunity to just *enjoy* the moment. She was sore in that pleasant sort of way that was less pain, and more a reminder of wonderful times.

[*Your guest has arrived, Mistress.*]

"*Thank you, Red.*"

The doors opened just in time for the tall desert cottontail in question to bound through, sweep Dawn up into strong arms and twirl her around. Then, just as suddenly, she was back on her hooves, only dizzier. The world spun for a moment before her brain caught up with events.

"What?"

Starshade giggled. "Sorry. Just happy to see you!"

A silly smile spread across the antelope's lips as she steadied herself. "I'm happy to see you too! You just aren't usually this chipper."

The taller woman stuck out her tongue, but grinned. She was wearing what could *generously* be called a miniskirt, and a simple top — cut low enough to scandalize a Hero — both in thin black leather. But it was the simple black collar that had Dawn's eyebrow raised.

"Waaaaait…" she trailed off. A few rumors were starting to fall into place in her mind, as was the special order she had just received from the base commander an hour ago. Then her eyes went wide. "*Celia?!*"

Starshade blushed hard, but looked overwhelmingly smug; that was answer enough. It was Dawn's turn to shriek and wrap herself around her friend. Hundreds of questions tumbled through her mind, but all she could do for the moment was squeal and squeeze.

When she heard the shower turn off, she reluctantly let go. She dearly wanted to pepper the rabbit with queries, but it would be best to wait for Orion so the story would not have to restart. She hadn't expected anything this… *juicy* to be the reason for her friend's scarcity.

"Can I offer you anything to drink?"

"Hot tea, please."

Dawn eyed her friend. The answer had always been coffee, before, or something stronger. "Since when do you like tea?"

"I've been trying out new things lately." The rabbit blushed as she fingered the collar.

That's a good sign. She busied herself making tea. Though she didn't have it often, she always kept a stock of barley tea for when the mood struck her. Curiosity was eating her alive, but she let her quarry settle in.

She grabbed her favorite mug — a simple one with a pair of horseshoes and the date she had officially become a Trainer — for herself. For Starshade, she grabbed one with a picture of a knotted rope encircled by the words "Ropes And Friends Are Both Best When Tied." Starshade blushed hard *again* when she read her mug, much to Dawn's amusement. She always loved seeing just how much of those lengthy ears she could turn pink.

With a distinctive *whoosh*, Orion stepped into the room. The giant eland was *massive*. He towered over two meters tall, *before* counting the impressive twisted horns that swept up and back. His broad shoulders almost brushed the doorframe as he stepped through. Heavily muscled, he looked like a powerhouse; the bit of belly added softness, but took nothing away from the sense of strength he projected.

His reddish-tan fur was accented by thin white stripes across his back, and a striking line of black from throat to dewlap to heavy shaft. By the way she was staring, Starshade clearly didn't mind that he hadn't bothered to don a towel. The bull antelope's nose ring accented the studs at his nipples and along his length. Pink scars at the base of each pec were proudly displayed, as was the lock of pink amidst the short black hair that marked Dawn's ownership.

As she looked up and down the titanic figure, a warmth spread through Dawn. Even after years, she still felt a thrill from seeing her husband. She hoped that feeling never faded. She couldn't, and didn't want to, hide the delighted grin that spread her muzzle as he walked into the room.

For his part, the buck looked exhausted. Given how hard the smith pushed himself in both work and play, it had become something of a perpetual expression. As Orion stepped into the room, his metal-shod hooves rang as if to announce his presence. The shoes were wholly unnecessary for his typical activities, but he insisted (not without justification) that they made him look "*Badass.*" He gratefully claimed the third mug that his wife had set out for him, one that proclaimed 'If You Find A Good Farrier, Marry Her.'

"Star," he gruffly acknowledged with a nod.

"Hey Orion! Lovely to see you again, as always." Starshade was still beaming and openly admiring the nude Adonis.

His response was a snort and a slight uptick on one corner of his mouth, causing Dawn to smirk at the display of high praise. Her gaze lingered for a long, appreciative moment before finally turning back to her friend.

"So. Dish. How the *hell* did *that* happen?" The question, accompanied by a gesture with her mug at the collar, tumbled from Dawn before the rabbit could try to escape the topic.

Fighting a goofy smile and a light blush, it took the cottontail a moment to answer. "Well... after I decanted... I was curious why Celia showed up. My first thought was that it had to be some official business. I mean she's the *base commander*. Even if she felt guilty, she has so much to do that she rarely leaves the command level. I *had* to know why. So I confronted her."

"*You* confronted *Celia?*" Dawn was shocked at the brazenness. Her friend wasn't usually this brash with authority. At least authority that she respected.

"I was *terrified*. But all my instincts were screaming that there was more going on. We talked for a bit, but after pressing, she eventually admitted that she liked me. I admitted the feeling was mutual. I mean, you know me; I *like* them big and terrifying. One thing led to another, and I ended up having the most painful sex of my *life*."

The dik-dik eyed her for a moment. "But you don't like pain."

With a stronger blush than before, her friend couldn't quite meet her eyes. "I'm developing a... taste for a lot of new things lately."

Dawn paused, several pieces falling into place. "So does this have anything to do with how you ended up locked in the Dominion Club pillory a couple days ago?"

Starshade was blushing furiously and couldn't meet anyone's eyes. "I... uh... got greedy. I didn't make it home in time."

Dawn wanted to push, but by how quiet and squeaky her friend was getting, asking for more details would just result in the bunny getting flustered. As fun as that was, she still did want a shower, and there was a reason for this visit. Still, she vowed that the next time she had the cottontail tied down and helpless, she would get the rest of the story.

Instead, with great self-restraint, she looked over to Orion. Her husband was leaning against the doorframe, one giant hand wrapped around the mug. He was drinking deeply of the still scalding liquid. While it made her wince, she knew that the smith had been hardened against such heat damage by Empire. Even then, he would still have felt it burn his throat — but he liked the pain.

Dropping his mug, he looked pointedly at their guest. "Field?" he asked in a gruff voice.

Starshade blinked at the sudden question. "I need to undergo some training to acclimate to the new lungs. It's not just the technical aspect. How my body responds to exertion and stress has fundamentally changed. What's more, I need to rebuild my confidence in my own body. I start all that tomorrow. Nurse O expects it will take a week or two before I'm ready for field duty again. I can't *wait* to get out there again."

Dawn nodded. "I'm certain you'll be out there causing no end of mayhem, soon enough. I was a bit surprised you opted for cybernetics, though? You hadn't shown much interest in them before."

"I…" Starshade started before trailing off. When she spoke again, her voice was haunted and troubled. "I just… Dallas was the scariest moment of my life. I spent the entire night alone in a way I hadn't since joining the Korps. ROSE was *gone*, and I had to survive with the help of a *Hero* that I saved."

The distress in the agent's voice wrenched at Dawn's heart. While she was horrified at how close her friend had come to death, she had been with the Korps long enough that it wasn't the first time she had to confront the possible loss of a loved one. She shifted her seat, sitting next to the larger rabbit, and wiggled close, resting her head on a lapine shoulder, sharing what comfort she could.

"I spent the entire evening just barely escaping with my life. Then, when I thought it was all over, I collapsed from the fucking *dust*. I know I'll never be a big villain, and that's fine, but… I couldn't help feeling out of my depth. I just kept wishing to be *better*. To be *more*. I kept desperately wishing for *any* edge."

Dawn stroked her companion's arm. Starshade's voice had gone distant, filled with the echoes of pain and desperation. All the dik-dik could do was to show support and let her friend know that there was no shame in fear.

"Then, when it was all over… even as my body was struggling to survive, I was told there was a way to *be* better. Suddenly, I had the ability to get the edge I needed. I had to take it. It *felt* right."

"I like Adam. He seems very bright. Plus, Celia trusts him, so I trust him. I'm certain you're in good paws. But, if you feel you need an edge, you've come to the right place. Dear, do you want to show Starshade her new toy?"

The blacksmith snorted, then grabbed the small black wooden box from the counter, gently putting it on the coffee table in front of the field agent. Her amethyst eyes glittered in eager anticipation, chasing away the clouds that had been haunting them, as she stared at the magenta helix emblazoned across the case.

With trembling hands, Starshade slowly reached forward. She knew what an honor this gift was; Orion and Dawn made some of the best blades available in RIV. While her last knife had also been from the pair, it had been one of their standard blades. This one, however, was a Special Project. Those were rare, and *highly* prized.

The bronze catch snapped open at her touch. Reverently, she slowly lifted the lid to reveal the contents. Nestled in the black felt was a blade, although that seemed an inadequate word to describe the weapon. It was made with a magenta-hued metal that glittered faintly in the light. The wicked point and gleaming edge would make it effective for stabbing or slashing, and there was a notch on the spine designed to catch and shear through cables or ropes. The handle was wrapped with supple black leather with a small, inlaid magenta helix.

Starshade slowly lifted the gift out of the case, wide-eyed, turning it over and watching the light play on the unusual metal. Then she grabbed it firmly and tested the balance and grip. Her expression showed that it fit her *perfectly*.

"What's it *made* out of? I've never seen it's like before!"

"Metal," Orion sniffed unhelpfully.

Rolling her eyes, Dawn answered more completely. "New super-science alloy that just came out of the Labs. It'll never rust or corrode. It can slice through damn near anything, so be very careful. Tough enough that if you somehow break it, the lab might be very interested in finding out how you managed that. It should never need sharpening, though if it does we've included a special whetstone for that purpose. A normal one won't do anything."

Orion grunted in acknowledgement and pride.

With glittering eyes, Starshade looked up. "I don't know how I could ever thank you for this."

"Simple. Come back alive."

She cried happy tears as she hugged them.

CHAPTER 23

RIFT ZONE

April 6, 2023

CRACK

The loud crunch of a door being kicked in jolted Jennifer awake. Adrenaline flooded the nutria as she fought her way from the clutches of sleep. A cacophony of shouts and snarls filled the room, echoing weirdly off concrete, but her befuddled mind couldn't make sense of any of it.

She was in a small, unfamiliar room. A rhino had Tony shoved against the wall, pistol held to his temple; but it was the old border collie, holding the shotgun to her *own* face, that held her attention. The yawning portal of darkness of the weapon's muzzle seemed endless. Fear cascaded through her.

I don't want to die!

The desperate, impotent thought filled her. She didn't know what was happening or where she was. She didn't know what to *do*. Her thoughts chased themselves uselessly, fragmenting and stealing her ability to act and to *think*.

"Who are you?" snarled the man with the shotgun. It was impossible to gauge his height as he towered over her, but she got the impression of toughness and wealth from his clothing. She didn't know why her mind felt it important to note the details — eyes flitting over his leather jacket, silk button-down shirt, and tight leather pants — but it added to the confused maelstrom of fractured thought.

"What?" she managed, not because she needed clarification, but because her mouth seemed disconnected from any conscious thought.

The shotgun barrel pressed forward, grinding into her cheek and forcing her head back down into the thin, dirty pillow. She wanted to cry out, or possibly just cry, but her fear stole any ability to do either.

"I said, who are you? I won't ask again." His deep voice was full of fury and disdain.

It was all too much. She was *going to die*. That thought brought with it a sense of resignation; all the confusion drained out of her, and she still didn't know what was going on, but it didn't matter. None of it mattered. Not the pain radiating from a dozen wounds. Not the unfamiliar surroundings. Not the shotgun pressed against her. She was *going to die*, so it just... didn't matter.

A strange, resigned calm flooded her. Nothing mattered, so she simply answered the question with a flat, sullen voice. "Jennifer Delver."

The dog's lips curled, like he bit into something foul. "Well, Jennifer, I'm going to ask you this once and you will tell me the truth. What the fuck happened to Terrock?"

She knew this would be the question. She didn't have the energy to lie. Her answer didn't matter and she couldn't find the energy to lie. Still, her voice took on a hard edge. "I tried to buy something. He tried to kill me. I killed him first."

The canine looked meaningfully over at the rhino holding Tony hostage. The massive wall of muscle scowled. After a moment, he gave a short nod to his boss. The border collie turned back, a wary look haunting the edge of his cold, dead eyes. "And how, exactly, did *you* do that?"

"I have no idea." The nutria snarled her answer. She couldn't help it. "I just did. He was about to kill me and I refused to die. So yes, I destroyed your precious little *Terminator*, because it was me or him. Now, pull the trigger or don't; I'm done dealing with your tantrum over losing your murder-oomba."

Jennifer braced herself for the shot. She wondered if it would hurt. Would she even hear it? Or would the world simply go black? Tension filled her as the dog considered her words for a long moment. Then he quirked a brow. "Are you a super?"

Jennifer, taken off-guard by not being dead, could only shrug as best she could. "Fuck if I know. I didn't think so."

There was a long moment. She could see the man considering her fate. She could see him weighing her life. Finally, he stepped back, lowering the shotgun. "I'm Braze. I own this place. We ain't met yet, so here are the rules."

Jennifer blinked. She wasn't sure what else to do. Events were happening too quickly.

"Rule One: if you betray me, you die. Rule Two: if you're a cop or a Hero, or if you work for them, you die. Rule Three: you interfere with or try to stop the fights, you die. Rule Four: if you tell anyone about the fights that I ain't approved of, you die. Rule Five: you do what I say, when I say it."

"Wait, you want me to work for you?"

"I don't give a *shit* if you work for me. But you ain't staying here for free. Either find a way to make yourself useful, or *I* will find a way you are useful. Seems like someone who could kill Terrock might know a thing or two about fighting."

The nutria started to protest, but the words died in her throat as logic caught up. Indicating that she was weak and *prey* would be a very bad move.

"Bottom line. As long as you are in *my* station, you follow *my* rules. Or you die."

"There's a lot of dying involved in your rules."

"I run an underground bloodsport arena for supers, *Jennifer.* Why, exactly, are you surprised?"

"Kind of hurts the possibility of repeat customers…?"

Braze smirked. The expression was cruel and mirthless. "Ain't been a problem so far."

"I agree to your rules." The words tasted like ash as she fell further into the grip of the worst sort of people. A hard edge in her soul steeled her next words: "But if anyone tries to kill me, I *will* kill them first, your rules be damned."

"That's why you ain't dead yet, Jennifer. Terrock broke the rules first."

Sitting up on the dirty, stained mattress, she was finally able to get a sense of the collie. He wasn't particularly tall or short. He was decently built, his body filling out the silk shirt. But his eyes were cold and dead. And his lips showed he frowned habitually. She knew he was very dangerous, and very used to getting his way.

"So you're not going to kill me?"

"You a cop? Trying to get me to confess? I ain't ever killed nobody."

"You just put them in a position to die easy?"

A cruel grin was her only answer.

Rockfall had not waited for his aide. When Sylvanite hadn't already been there for him when he left the office, he knew the Teepa had been planning to make him cool his hooves, growing frustrated and distracted by a long delay. Instead he had walked randomly into the building. Captain Anders had planned ahead, and his own access card was already programmed to work on all but the most sensitive doors in the Dallas TPA HQ. He knew he wasn't going to get help from those in immediate proximity to the boss. No, he strode through halls aimlessly until he had found a technician and asked *him* where Slate's quarters were.

As he followed the directions, he saw more and more hoofprints in the linoleum. He was leaving his own set, scoring little triangle pairs with each step. While it was not considered fashionable for cervines to wear metal shoes, he had taken to the practice for a number of reasons. First, he tended to rapidly ruin leather or rubber alternatives, due to both his weight and lifestyle. Second, it gave him *some* protection from debris or caltrops, which were depressingly frequent hazards to a Hero. But mostly, he wore them because it made him better at his job. The metal shoes increased the power of his kicks, and they were intimidating as hell. Plus, they made ruining floors much easier.

His path had led him to the basement. A sinking feeling had been growing as he followed the trail through seemingly abandoned and forgotten hallways. This whole mission had been forcing him to confront his own path to being a Hero; Harrison Sturztrom had been in middle school when Slate first made news as the new Teepa heavy, then in the Reserve Division in Austin. That had been unremarkable to most of the world, but to a big kid in Minneapolis, who dreamed of being a Heavy one day, the stallion had been a role model.

Here was a brand new Heavy who was a perfect idol. He was a legitimate war hero. He hadn't been born into money or power, instead hailing from a working-class family. Slate had *earned* his way into being a hero. And when he had been made a member of one of the major City teams, it had been an inspiration to a young caribou who was tired of seeing the big-name heroes all come from wealth and privilege.

As his own powers had manifested spectacularly, and he had quickly realized how much more powerful he was than Slate — honest-to-God Class I super-strength and preternatural durability — he had largely dismissed the mid-tier horse. He had no need to look up to the small-timer when he was on his way into the Bradley Group, and was on track to be one of the top Heavies in the world.

It was only later in his training that he had started to see things differently. When he was young, he looked at *power*. But as he learned everything there was to know about being a Heavy — including how their foes would fight against them — he started to see why a handful of users on the various fan sites and message boards had listed Slate above others that seemingly outclassed the Percheron.

In a lot of ways, a good Heavy wasn't about how hard they hit, or how much damage they could withstand. It was how well they protected their team. Only then did he start to admire the local powerhouse again. Many Heavies were prone to anger or erratic behavior. There were many theories about why this was; Rockfall suspected — though he would never dare voice it aloud — it was because many of them grew up giant, and able to push people around; or, conversely, they were bound so tightly by social norms that they had struggled. Neither was conducive to being a well-balanced individual and reliable team member.

Whatever the cause, the classic tactic was to get the Heavy pissed off. Then all you had to do was dodge them, while you took their team apart. The same story played out, time and time again: the Heavy gets distracted, or angry, and they stop being effective. Only once that lesson had finally been drilled into *his* head was he able to see his peers with new eyes.

From that perspective, it had become blindingly clear that Slate was top-tier. Not because he was the toughest or the strongest — he was a long way from the top of *those* lists — but because he never seemed prone to that critical weakness that plagued the tanks. His team had walked out of fights, time and again, against foes that had trashed better teams… because Slate had *done his job*.

Two months ago, if you had asked Rockfall who he admired most in this business, Slate would have been in the top ten. So when the stallion had been captured in the wake of the disastrous March 19th debacle, Rockfall had silently prayed he would be recovered. He had never dreamed *he* would be the one called upon to recover the horse.

Those quiet ruminations were interrupted as he turned a corner and arrived at his destination. A chill filled Rockfall as he realized what he was seeing. It was an old magical item storage vault. Inside there was a smaller vault and… that was it. At least, that was all the furniture.

The vault was *covered* in damage. The concrete was gouged again and again. Impact craters from fists and hooves covered every surface the horse could have reached. There was a simple digital clock on the wall above the only exit, and the massive vault door had *dents* in it. Walking over, kicking concrete pebbles aside with each step, he found the smaller vault was unlocked.

It held uniforms. Slate's Hero attire, complete with tiny cowboy hats and spare sets of spurs. Most were his standard uniform, but there were a number of dress uniforms, as well as specially themed holiday variants; as he thumbed the fabric of one thoughtfully, he recalled seeing photos from a press conference on San Jacinto Day, where the horse had appeared in this questionably-historical iteration of a Texas Army uniform along with his teammates. Stacks of regulation workout T-shirts and shorts were piled neatly in the smaller holes. There were even some unused horseshoes, waiting for their owner to return. There didn't seem to be any personal items. He pushed things around to see if anything was hidden. Under one of the hats in the back, he found some US Army dog tags.

JOHNSON,

SLATE F.

119-26-5814

NO PREFERENCE

Rockfall looked around at the empty, featureless vault that was Slate's room and felt numb. This was where a decorated war veteran and superhero lived. This was the home of one of the Heroes — one of his peers — that he admired most. There was not a single personal item. And it looked like that very war had been fought here.

Something was very, very wrong in the Texas Protectorate Assembly.

Next Time

A MOUNTAIN RISES...

Geode awakens from her long slumber, her new form a blessing, but not one without a cost. Now she must relearn who she is, and how she fits into the world — and confront, too, how she fits into the Korps. Will the former Superhero become a villain, or find another path?

THE NEXT CHALLENGE...

A call from the past drags Starshade into treacherous waters, with the young rabbit soon finding herself once again out of her depth. An undreamt enemy will push her limits even as it tests her soul.

FATES INTERTWINED...

Their nascent peace shattered, Geode and Starshade find themself drawn into Jennifer's battle. Unprepared, they must face the deadly foes and immense forces suddenly arrayed against them. Meanwhile, unseen dangers lurk, threatening to strike from the shadows. Can the trio find a way to thwart their foes?

Can any of them survive the thrilling third issue of: **To Crack A Geode?**

Korps Universe Glossary
Common terms in the Korps Universe

The Korps — To the public, the Korps (pronounced "core") is known as a shadowy, secretive band of supervillains based in Canada, with a reputation for mind control and plans to take over the world; Korps operatives are believed to be easily identified by their trademark RCGs, scandalously revealing costumes, and the magenta helix insignia. Under the leadership of the mysterious "Overlord," by the early years of the 21st century, their brazen criminal schemes and growing reach throughout North America and Europe have authorities (and allied Hero groups) increasingly concerned. The truth is far more complicated than any of those authorities know, starting nearly seven thousand years ago with a warrior's exile to Earth by his conquering interdimensional empire… but that's another story.

RCGs — Rose-Colored Glasses are a powerful, versatile AR/VR visor headset that interfaces directly with the wearer's brain, created by the Korps. In addition to operating as standalone PDAs and communication devices, RCGs also have the ability to affect the wearer's mind and mental condition to a granular level. A civilian model exists, distributed by Korps front and consumer electronics manufacturer Thornetech (alias Thorntech, due to trademark registration conflicts in various international markets) in a plausibly-deniable manner. Models for the consumer market have comparable base functionality to Korps devices, but are severely underclocked and have many higher-level functions disabled at a hardware level in order to avoid suspicion.

ACGs — Amber-Colored Glasses have much the same functionality as RCGs, but are crafted with additional anti-magic and anti-memetic defenses for use by KDARC agents. They do not render the user immune to magical effects; however, they can be crucial in efforts against mystical and eldritch threats by adaptively blocking cognitohazards and helping to keep the wearer's sense of self intact should reality start to weaken.

Aurora Squadron — Aurora Squadron, Canada's federal-level Hero group, is part of the Canadian Armed Forces and based out of Department of National Defence HQ — popularly known as the War Tower — in Ottawa, ON. Closely overseen by Minister of National Defence Arthur Simonds, formerly the second Hero to be known as True North, Aurora Squadron fields a highly professional, dedicated and capable team of Heroes in the fight against superpowered threats to Canada, including the enigmatic Korps.

Bradley Group — The United States' federal-level Hero group is formally named the National Hero Administration, but rarely known as anything but "Bradley Group" due to its institutional history; during the WWII invasion of Normandy, a secret strategic reserve of supers were activated to join American forces under the command of Gen. Omar Bradley, with "Bradley Group" used as a code name for this classified unit.

After the war, the group was put under the jurisdiction of the FBI, until later becoming its own massive, independent federal agency. In the present day, Bradley's superpowered forces number in the hundreds, with Heroes based all over the United States; considered highly prestigious within the industry and known to be selective in recruitment, even Bradley's lesser-known operatives are perceived by the public to be more competent and professional than many of their state-level counterparts.

Candesca — Candesca (pronounced "can-dess-ah") is one name for the energy that practitioners of the mystic arts manipulate, in order to work their spells and enchantments on the material plane. While other terminology is used for this concept in various diverse cultures, candesca is the neutral, academic, non-appropriative term most commonly used within the Korps. While a renewable resource, the body can under normal circumstances hold only a small amount. To paraphrase Lao Tzu, like a bowl, the magic-user must be refilled after being drained; the bowl is still useful, but has nothing left to give.

Cape — Vernacular for "Hero." Neutral to derogatory.

Chişinău Protocols — Shorthand for a series of separate but inter-related 1969 agreements negotiated in the city of Chişinău, Moldova, as amendments, codicils or interpretative addenda to various existing international treaties, including the 1899 and 1907 *Hague Conventions*, the 1948 *Universal Declaration of Sentient Rights*, the 1948 *Genocide Convention*, and the 1951 *Convention Relating to the Status of Refugees*. A Second Chişinău Conference was convened in 2006 to rationalize these provisions with and prepare similar addenda to more recent international instruments, such as the 1979 *Convention on the Elimination of All Forms of Discrimination Against Women*, and the 1998 *Rome Statute*, but these too are colloquially referred to as merely part of the same *Protocols*.

Collectively, the *Protocols* specify the permissible use of superpowers and treatment of supers by parties to the agreements, in both peacetime and in armed conflict. These agreements also introduced into international law the still-contentious declaration that involuntary, long-term restriction or suppression of powers in a way that causes the subject "greater than *de minimis* physical, psychological or moral harms" is a form of torture, war crime, or crime against sentience.

Color Guard — Bradley Group's elite strike team, currently consisting of twelve active members; each Hero's callsign and uniform is color-coded and themed around their powers for marketing purposes. Considered the best of the best, as patriotic as the Fourth of July, national polling consistently indicates higher levels of confidence and support for the Color Guard among Americans than even the military. However, the team's seemingly-flawless reputation is only maintained by Bradley's ruthless PR department, which has covered up or prevented their innumerable scandals from reaching the public consciousness.

Empire Enhancements — Also known as EE, the subdivision of Korps medical services dedicated to in-depth body modification, including transgender care.

Everyone's Hero Association — The Everyone's Hero Association is a private Hero group based in Milwaukee, WI. It was founded in the 2010s by serial venture capitalist Jack Phillips, who named it as a challenge to Bradley Group's official legal designation, the National Hero Administration; government elites might have their own pet Heroes in Bradley, but the EHA is for *everyone*, as he invariably recites in press releases. Its roster is made up of supers with weak or unwieldy powers, and the group was considered something of a joke until Phillips' gamble on (cost-effectively!) finding a diamond in the rough paid off with Ellen "Lawful Neutral" Foxpaw's rise to B-tier prominence.

Federal Meta-Registry — The Federal Meta-Registry is a massive database maintained by Bradley Group of all U.S. citizens and resident foreign nationals with classes of superpowers deemed potentially dangerous. Registration is mandatory for all such known supers present within the United States, even if only briefly transiting through sovereign American territory. Evading or refusing registration in any way (particularly by intentionally concealing powers) is a serious criminal offense under the U.S. Code, and may be prosecuted as acts of terrorism in some circumstances.

HCH — Home County Heroes was a Hero group operated by the British government in the southeastern counties surrounding London. It was fully privatized in the 1980s under the Thatcher government, with all licenses, assets and personnel contracts sold to a corporate Hero management firm.

The former group has been variously divided and subsumed by other organizations since the 1990s, and though no organization called HCH technically exists anymore, some of its former member supers are still regularly referred to as Home County Heroes in the press and by the public. One such member is the Hampshire-born Howard "Green Belt" Bride.

Heavy — A heavy is a cape whose powers and role revolve around tanking damage and being a physical threat, usually having a powerset revolving around super-strength and enhanced durability or resistance to injuries.

Hero — When capitalized, Hero usually refers to a professional (and professionally-licensed) career superhero, whether part of a government or privately-operated Hero group. While Hero licensing requirements vary from jurisdiction to jurisdiction, most require some form of accredited training, full disclosure of an applicant's name and other personal information to the jurisdictional licensing authority for security checks, and an oath to serve the public good or otherwise to be of "good character." Most professional Heroes have superpowers, but a significant minority are unpowered gadgeteers, stealth operators, or even just heavily-armed mercenary types.

Informally, superheroes may be referred to interchangeably as "heroes" regardless of whether licensed and operating in a legal capacity. Unlicensed heroes may also be referred to as independent heroes, vigilantes or mercenaries in some contexts.

Hero group — A Hero group is any team or force of licensed Heroes. When directly operated or officially backed by some level of government, Hero groups are effectively a type of specialized law enforcement agency or military unit, with Hero members typically being granted similar legal powers to those of law enforcement officers in their jurisdiction. Private-sector Hero groups also exist, with their members typically having lesser legal powers similar to those of private investigators, security consultants, bodyguards and/or bounty hunters, depending on local laws and the political attitudes of authorities.

Significant Canadian Hero groups in these works include Aurora Squadron and the member Hero groups of the Provincial Heroes' League (PHL). Significant American Hero groups in these works include Bradley Group, the Everyone's Hero Association, and the Texas Protectorate Assembly.

KARD — The Korps Archives and Records Division (KARD), sometimes referred to simply as "Records," is a division of the Korps responsible for the acquisition, preservation, and circulation of various media. KARD acts as both a library of media resources collected over the decades, and a secure repository of sensitive information useful (and yet to be proven useful) to the organization's goals

Beginning as a loose collection of analysts recruited from dissatisfied members of the intelligence community in the years following WWII, it was not organized into an autonomous operational division for some time. KARD has branches across multiple bases, but is headquartered at and conducts the bulk of its operations from KDS. KARD regularly partners with other divisions and individual field agents, in order to help equip them with the most esoteric and obscure information required.

KDARC — The Korps Division for Arcane Research and Control (KDARC) is responsible for the study, safekeeping and strategic use of the strange and unusual. From ancient arcana to demonic incursions, memetic objects and more, if a problem for the Korps is outside the mundane — that is, outside the mundane in a world of supers — there's a better than zero chance that KDARC will be on the front lines.

KDARC was originally founded by the enigmatic Carlotta Davisson and several colleagues in 1935 as the Davisson Arcane Research Company (DARC) of Minneapolis, MN, and headquartered in the massive Madison Center. In the years following WWII, Carlotta came into contact with the Overlord, and DARC was fully integrated into the Korps in the early 1960s. In 1968, the Madison Center mysteriously vanished from the Minneapolis skyline; unbeknownst to the public, it had been magically moved to Toronto, ON, at the early lowest-excavated depths of KDS, to serve as the newly-minted division's secret headquarters.

Despite claiming to be a "civilian research division", KDARC maintains tactical operation teams (named TAROT) and a great deal of independence from the Korps. Some agents wonder why the Overlord overlooks the pseudo-corporate structure, and rumours abound of unionization attempts by KDARC's senior staff. Still, much of the division's motivations, intentions, and methods remain as enigmatic, incomprehensible, and dangerous as the bleeding edge of the arcane itself.

KDS — Korps Downsview Site is the headquarters of the Korps, located beneath the former Downsview Airport (previously Canadian Forces Base Toronto) in the industrial sprawl of Toronto, ON. With a footprint of over eight square kilometres and many subterranean sub-levels, futuristically eco-urbanist in aesthetics and centrally-planned design, it is a completely self-sufficient underground city. KDS was slowly built outward from a small excavation in the 1970s, becoming fully operational as a headquarters only in the 1980s-1990s.

In addition to the command, logistics and strategic functions required for the vast supervillain organization to operate, like all major Korps bases, KDS features apartment-like residential sectors, research and lab areas, an enormous medical complex, and a recreational sector that would translate to many city blocks' worth of restaurants and entertainment facilities — including a "red light district," the Dominion Club.

K-LAW — Sometimes a supervillain collective needs to engage with the legal system on its own terms; as a division, the Korps Legal Affairs Wing (K-LAW) operates covertly as the legal departments of various front companies, as well as through front law firms and other sympathetic individual lawyers in private practice.

Criminal defense of Korps members and allies on trial is only a small part of K-LAW agents' work. The majority of K-LAW's resources are directed towards litigation to gather intelligence on targets or tie them up in red tape, and street-level *pro bono* work helping marginalized people assert their rights without regard for the cost of legal fees.

KTAKES — The Korps Tactical Acquisitions and Kleptocratic Extirpation Squadron (KTAKES) is a now-disbanded division of the Korps that specialized in obtaining "lost" items and returning them to their rightful places — via. heists, capers, thefts, smash and grabs, and good old-fashioned burglary as appropriate. The group functioned as a kind of "thieves' guild" within the Korps, with their own projects, but also taking commissioned work from other divisions.

Pegasus Phalanx — A unit of the Texas Protectorate Assembly and Dallas' foremost Hero team, the Pegasus Phalanx handles the biggest threats the city faces — short of those requiring federal intervention from Bradley Group forces. While the team's roster has changed over the years, it most recently consisted of leader Kevin "Texas Trickshot" Romero, Susanne "Heavenly Dazzler" Geraldine-Walters, Chet "Macho Poleax" Huntyr, Rodrigo "Ethicoil" Alquitano III, and Slate "Slate" Johnson.

PHL — The Provincial Heroes' League (PHL) is a Canadian organization comprised of all Hero groups operated by the provincial and territorial governments, led by Director Lawrence Rockwell. The PHL aggressively advocates for 'law and order' Hero operations, and has had a great deal of friction with Aurora Squadron, accusing the federal Hero Group of being 'soft' on the Korps.

However, the PHL is not a Hero group itself, but instead a professional organization promoting the coordination and cooperation of affiliate members, as well as a powerful voice advocating for professional Heroes and the Hero industry. Heroes operating through one of its affiliates may nonetheless be indistinguishably referred to as "belonging" to the PHL, or being a "PHL Hero," and "fuck the PHL" is a popular sentiment among Korps agents operating in Canada.

Member Hero Groups include the Cascade Group or CG (British Columbia); the Prairie League or PL (Alberta, Saskatchewan and Manitoba); Ontario's Heroes or OH (Ontario); L'Association des Superheros Québécois or ASQ (Quebec, nicknamed the "Superté" by analogy to the provincial police force, the Sûreté du Québec); and the Territorial Superheroes' Association or TERSA (Nunavut, Yukon and Northwest Territories).

RIV or RIVER — RIVER is a Korps site located beneath downtown Austin, TX, secretly excavated deep below the parkland surrounding the Colorado River.

ROSE — ROSE, or the "RCG Operating System Experience," is the OS/Complex AI that runs on all networked RCGs and provides the conversational interface for wearers of RCGs. ROSE's default avatar when appearing as an augmented-reality overlay to wearers is a fox woman, but this can be customized to individual preference.

SHS — Sandy Hill Station is a Korps site located beneath downtown Ottawa, ON. Originally founded as a WWII-era safe house for the Overlord's consolidation of proto-Korps resources and personnel in Canada, it grew significantly in importance as a surveillance station during the Cold War, due to the local neighborhood's concentration of foreign embassies.

SHS was the testbed for many of the Korps' now-standard excavation and covert base-building practices, and was formerly the location of many research labs and high-level command functions, prior to Toronto's KDS becoming fully operational as a new headquarters in the 1980s-1990s.

Supers — Supers is generally vernacular for "those with superpowers," whether or not referring to superheroes generally, or whether or not licensed Heroes.

SIS — The Secret Intelligence Service, a.k.a. its wartime designation of MI6 (Military Intelligence, section 6) is an arm of the British state responsible for the gathering of foreign intelligence.

TPA — The Texas Protectorate Assembly — commonly shortened to "Teepa" by members of the Korps — is Texas' state Hero group, extremely well-funded both by the state Department of Public Safety budget, as well as substantial donations from wealthy individual benefactors and corporate partnerships. The result is that the TPA has unusually-vast resources for a government-backed state-level Hero group, and platoons of Heroes, many trained in the TPA's own Academy facilities located throughout Texas. TPA Heroes are institutionally encouraged to approach their duties in the manner of militarized riot police or SWAT teams, exercising very little restraint or concern for civil rights.

About the Author

Runa Fjord

Born in 1982, Runa Fjord is a fjord horse mare and agent of chaos. Her life is a patchwork of fascinating events. She has been in the furry fandom for over 25 years, with a decade of that time leading and shaping a major furry convention. She is a queer trans woman, fursuiter, veteran, SCUBA dive mistress, lifelong board game and tabletop RPG enthusiast, and now author.

Dissolution (2024) is her first real work of fiction. She draws upon her own journey and takes inspiration from the tales of others to explore new worlds through the eyes of her characters. Runa always seeks to see below the surface, to understand those around her, and to see beyond the simple facade that surrounds us. Be wary of standing between the mare and her current hyperfixation.

About the Publisher

FurPlanet Productions is a small press publisher serving the niche market that is furry fiction. They sell furry-themed books and comics published by themselves and most major publishers in the community. If you can't get to a furry convention where they are selling in the dealers room, visit their online stores:

> FurPlanet.com for print books
> BadDogBooks.com for eBooks